The
Christmas
Murder
Game

Alexandra Benedict

Poisoned Pen
PRESS

For Guy and Verity, my home

Published by Poisoned Pen Press, an imprint of Sourcebooks
P.O. Box 4410, Naperville, Illinois 60567-4410
(630) 961-3900
sourcebooks.com

Originally published as *The Christmas Murder Game* in 2021 in Great Britain by Zaffre,
an imprint of Bonnier Books UK. This edition issued based on the hardcover edition
published 2021 in Great Britain by Zaffre, an imprint of Bonnier Books UK

Library of Congress Cataloging-in-Publication Data

Names: Benedict, Alexandra, author.
Title: The Christmas murder game / Alexandra Benedict.
Description: Naperville, Illinois : Poisoned Pen Press, [2022]
Identifiers: LCCN 2022006663 (print) | LCCN 2022006664 (ebook) | (trade paperback) | (epub)
Subjects: LCGFT: Detective and mystery fiction. | Christmas fiction. |
  Novels.
Classification: LCC PR6102.E536 C48 2022 (print) | LCC PR6102.E536
  (ebook) | DDC 823/.92--dc23/eng/20220304
LC record available at https://lccn.loc.gov/2022006663
LC ebook record available at https://lccn.loc.gov/2022006664

Printed and bound in the United States of America.
VP 10 9 8 7 6 5 4 3 2 1

I tell my secret? No indeed, not I;
Perhaps some day, who knows?
But not today; it froze, and blows and snows,
And you're too curious: fie!
You want to hear it? well:
Only, my secret's mine, and I won't tell.

From "Winter: My Secret" by Christina Rossetti

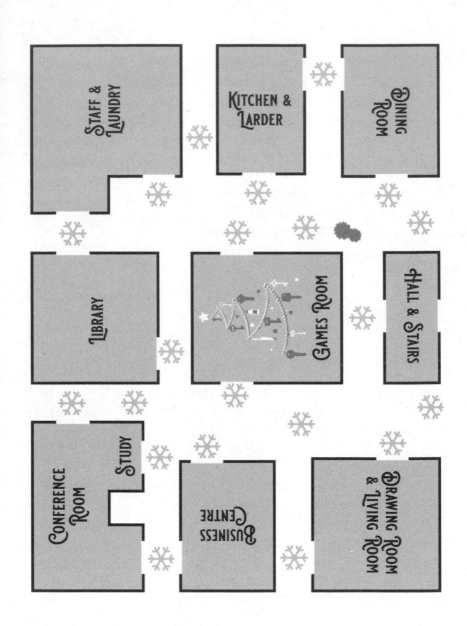

STAFF & LAUNDRY

KITCHEN & LARDER

DINING ROOM

LIBRARY

GAMES ROOM

HALL & STAIRS

CONFERENCE ROOM

STUDY

BUSINESS CENTRE

DRAWING ROOM & LIVING ROOM

· Armitage Family Tree ·

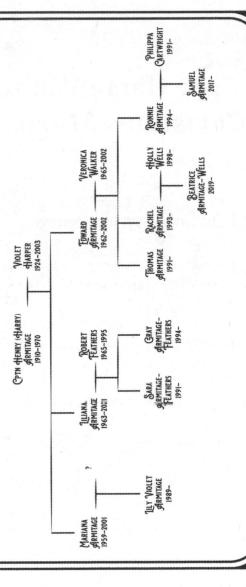

Cptn Henry (Harry) Armitage
1910–1970

Violet Harper
1924–2003

Mariana Armitage
1959–2001

?

Lily Violet Armitage
1989–

Liliana Armitage
1963–2011

Robert Feathers
1965–1995

Sara Armitage-Feathers
1991–

Gray Armitage-Feathers
1994–

Edward Armitage
1962–2002

Veronica Walker
1965–2002

Thomas Armitage
1991–

Rachel Armitage
1993–

Holly Wells
1998–

Ronnie Armitage
1994–

Beatrice Armitage-Wells
2019–

Philippa Cartwright
1991–

Samuel Armitage
2017–

The Game Within *The Christmas Murder Game*

Game 1: The Twelve Days of Anagrams

The clues in the book are revealed on each of the twelve days of Christmas, so I have embedded anagrams of each of the twelve gifts in the relevant section of the book.

First Day of Christmas: find the anagram of "A partridge in a pear tree"

Second Day of Christmas: find the anagram of "Two turtle doves"

Third Day of Christmas: find the anagram of "Three French hens"

Fourth Day of Christmas: find the anagram of "Four colly birds"

Fifth Day of Christmas: find two anagrams of "Five gold rings"

Sixth Day of Christmas: find the anagram of "Six geese a-laying"

Seventh Day of Christmas: find the anagram of "Seven swans a-swimming"

Eighth Day of Christmas: find the anagram of "Eight maids a-milking"

Ninth Day of Christmas: find the anagram of "Nine ladies dancing"

Tenth Day of Christmas: find the anagram of "Ten lords a-leaping"

Eleventh Day of Christmas: find the anagram of "Eleven pipers piping"

Twelfth Day of Christmas: find the anagram of "Twelve drummers drumming"

Each anagram appears as a sequence of full words. For example, one anagram of "My true love sent to me" is "novelette sore tummy," which I will work into a sentence, i.e.: "Alexandra rapidly consumed the novelette. Sore tummy aside, she considered it an interesting addition to the country house mystery." Or similar.

Some anagrams are easier than others to squeeze into a prose corset. Watch out for ones that don't quite fit.

Game 2: Title Deeds

The titles of twelve of my favorite country house mysteries set at Christmas are sown throughout the book. Can you find them all?

Good luck!

Chapter One

December 24th
Christmas Eve

Snow is falling. Because of course it is. Nothing about this is going to be easy.

Lily presses her forehead against the cold window, her duvet wrapped around her. It's four in the morning and she can't sleep. Streetlights shower gold rings onto Catford High Street. Snowflakes dance down from the sky. Two blokes stumble along the middle of the road, arms around each other, shouting, "It's Christmas!" A fox runs away from them, eyes glinting.

At one time, lying awake on Christmas Eve would have been down to excitement. But Lily doesn't believe in Santa anymore. She hasn't believed in anyone since Mum passed. And today she has to go back to the place where her mum died.

Lily hauls a hoodie over her head and gets out of bed. She fights her way between the rails of costumes and into her tiny living room. Well, that's what the previous tenant had called it. Lily doesn't really *live* anywhere. This is her workroom. It's stuffed with starched cotton and velvet; thread, trims, and ribbons; boxes of beads, bone, and steel. Her sewing machine waits by the window. A paper dress pattern lies in pieces on the floor, like the silhouette of a body at a crime scene.

It's not much of a home, but at least she doesn't have to house-share. She needs solid walls between her and other people. And the lack of space is a good reason not to bring anyone back, even if she is lonely. That's what Lily tells herself anyway.

Avoiding the piles of material, she steps from one glimpse of exposed carpet to another over to the kitchen in the corner of the room. If you can call a camping stove, toaster, and microwave a kitchen. She puts the kettle on, and a tea bag in her mug, then drags her suitcase out from under a box of tulle. What should she take for Christmas at a country house she hates? The high street doesn't cater for that. Good thing she makes clothes for a living.

Wash bag filled, corsets and dresses folded inside the case, Lily sits on the sole armchair to drink her tea. Only now does she let herself think about the journey ahead. Of the relatives she'll have to see. Of Endgame House itself.

Just the thought of the place makes her heart hammer like her sewing machine at full blast, so she takes out her latest commission and starts embroidering by hand. With every flick of the needle, each satin stitch in place, Lily calms. Her heart is back to slow pedal speed. Maybe she should stay in her flat till Christmas is over. Not go anywhere at all. Get back in bed with a box of chocolates and pull the duvet over the holiday. That would save a lot of driving and, more importantly, it would keep the pain where she's placed it behind walls and locked doors in her mind.

But if she doesn't go, she'll let down Aunt Liliana. Again.

Lily reaches into her handbag and takes out the envelope. She strokes it. Traces the looping letters made in her aunt's handwriting. When she eases the letter out of the envelope, the paper is as soft and smooth as Aunt Liliana's rose-powdered skin. It still smells of the base notes in her Calvin Klein perfume—Truth.

Dearest Lily,

I hope you never have to read this letter, because if it now lies in your hands, then I am dead. I've entrusted your old friend Isabelle Stirling with the task of making sure you get this if I die before the Christmas Game begins. I fear that I shall. I hope I'm utterly, shamefully askew on the subject. But I don't think I am.

So, this is my insurance policy, delivered by my lawyer. I know you don't want to come to Endgame, or play a silly divertissement. I know that you have absolutely no interest in inheriting the house, even though I dearly wish it to be yours. But I have another reason for asking you to take part in the game. It is time that you learned the truth, and the game is the way I will reveal it.

If that's not enough of a reason, then let me give you one part of the puzzle. Your mother was wrongfully killed. There. I've said it. I know you will have so many questions, and the answers will come. They will be there, in every clue: the beginning and end of all that has haunted our family for so many years. The coldest of cases. Each clue, bar one, is a message to you. Heed them. Dead women's words cannot be ignored, diminished, or apologized away.

I haven't had the guts to come forward and say what happened to Mariana—your mum, my beautiful, brilliant big sister—because I've also done wrong. Maybe you will have more courage. Maybe you will have the fortitude to sing out. I hope so. You have always been loved. I know you don't like to talk about your mum, but she loved you so much, and she didn't leave you. She never would. I'm so sorry I couldn't prove it at the time.

Please go to Endgame and play this Christmas. You'll be well looked after. I've hired a housekeeper, but other than that, it'll be you, your cousins, and their partners, if they have them. It won't be a merry gathering, but it's essential that you're there.

It's my last wish. How awful is that? The deceased asking a favor of her favorite. That's awful, too. Don't tell Sara and Gray. If I weren't dead, I'd be ashamed of myself.

Your mother and I taught you so much, as did your grand-mother. Search the past for memories that can help you solve the clues and what happened to Mariana Rose. You'll need to remember everything, I'm afraid. And I am afraid. For me, and for you. Don't trust ANY of your relatives, for their sake as much as yours. Knowledge can lead to death. You'll also have to keep that secret I suspect you've got hidden. I want to give you freedom, Lily. To help you escape your own walls. It's time to take those doodles and transpose them onto the real world. Cast those corsets of F. Major clues are hidden among the minor. You'll need to remember how good you are at this. No more hiding.

Adopting you was the best thing I ever did. I hope this game is the next best.

Your ever-loving aunt, and adoptive mother,
Liliana Armitage-Feathers

Lily's heart feels like its stitches have been unpicked. She has to go. And soon. If it's snowing in London, you can bet there'll be drifts by dinnertime in Yorkshire.

Chapter Two

Sure enough, it's deep snow by the time she gets to the Dales. Not the pictur-esque kind of snow—not soft flakes landing on the tongue like peppermint feathers—this is great gobbets of white hurtling toward the windshield. Lily speeds up the wipers to double time but it's still like driving into a vortex. She can't see where she's going. And that doesn't just apply to the snowstorm.

The light's fading already. Two thirty, and the sky is the cold dark blue of flames tickling a Christmas pudding. The Yorkshire lanes don't help—artery narrow, hedgerows encroaching on the road like bad cho-lesterol. And then there are the trees, whispering and shushing above her, heads together, plotting.

Last time Lily was on this road, she was going the other way. Aged twelve, driven from Endgame House for what she thought was the last time. If Lily believed in ghosts, it'd be different; she'd have stalked its halls forever, trying to find her mother's specter. But she doesn't believe in ghosts, or much else.

As she drives round a corner, a deer rushes out. Slamming on the brakes, time treacles as she tries to stop the car from spinning into the bank. Greenery whirls around her. She hears a screech but can't tell if it's from her, the wheels, or the deer. If this is it, the end, maybe it'd be easier to lift her hands from the wheel and close her eyes.

No.

She grips the wheel and steers away from the open arms of a tree. She has responsibilities now, and part of that involves returning to Endgame House.

When the car steams to a stop, there's no sign of the deer. *Please don't be dead*, she says in her head as she climbs out. Heart pounding, she bends to check under the chassis. Nothing.

And no heart-wrenching remnants on the wheels. She breathes out and, at the same time, hears a harrumph, an exhale from the bushes. A deer is among the trees to the side of the car. Her fawn stands next to her, its ears cupped.

The deer stares at Lily, and she gazes back. Snow settles on both of their heads. The deer blinks, then walks away, her fawn following. Their breath condenses into ghosts. She watches till both animals disappear, safe, into the trees.

As Lily gets back into the car, she spots the snowflakes on her sleeves. Cog-like, silver in the half-light, they turn the black arms of her coat into steampunk chain mail. She has an image of making a corset-dress of armored snowflakes for her first collection, of standing on a runway with an army of models wearing Lily Armitage couture.

Then, like a chamois on a windscreen, she swipes the thought away. She's learned to not stick her neck out, in business or otherwise. She'll keep to the historical replicas she's known for. Don't stand out. Don't speak up. Stay in the shadows, and then you can't be seen.

Driving away, the car coughs and sputters like it's got something in its throat. She pats the steering wheel. "We can do this," she says. She hopes the car is more convinced than she is. "Not far now." And it shouldn't be. The villages, with their single, clinged-to pubs, are getting further apart. Why are country houses plonked in the middle of nowhere? Probably because the resident lords owned the whole area and wanted to avoid the plebs. She imagines the onetime owners of Endgame House standing by the front door, looking out over their land from the top of the hill, tenant farmers far off below—worker bees kept at a distance so the queen needn't be bothered by their buzzing.

Lily prefers London, or any of the other cities she's lived in. There's always something to listen to, even if it's the sirens that sound as regularly as the chapel bell at Endgame House. And you're never cut off from people, at least not in the same way. She can choose to isolate herself in the city, hunker down with a sewing pattern, not see anyone for days. Here, snow doesn't give you a choice but to stay put. She used to love the snow days at Endgame House, running around the maze—even more difficult to navigate in a whiteout—hearing the silence a snowstorm brings. Now, the thought of being shut in with her family makes her throat constrict.

Which is why, when Aunt Liliana had first sent the invitation to Endgame House, Lily had turned it down. She had no interest in playing one last Christmas Game to see who would win the title deeds.

But then, a month ago, Liliana had died and, two days later, her letter arrived. Everything changed. Feelings she thought she'd stuffed down deep enough to never resurface had emerged, like last year's gnarled and forgotten orange from the bottom of a stocking. Coming back to where it all started would only make it worse.

Even the GPS doesn't want to direct her to the house. With hardly any signal here, it keeps glitching, refusing to refresh while she continues to drive. As a result, she only sees the burgundy sign for ENDGAME HOUSE HOTEL as she drives past. Her heart beats faster. This is the first time she'll have seen it as a hotel. When she lived at Endgame House, it was a conference center, run by Uncle Edward with help from Aunt Liliana and Mum. Edward had long had a dream of turning it into a fancy hotel, but his dream had only recently come to pass when he died. Moral of the story: don't have dreams, and never let them come true.

It's another five minutes before she finds a place to turn round, and every one of those minutes involves wondering whether she should go back to London. And now's the time to make the decision. She's at the gates to Endgame that bar the road into the estate. As the gates part, the family crest, sculptured in bronze, splits down the middle. *You don't have to stay,* she tells herself as she drives through. *You can leave at any time.* In the rearview mirror, the gates clamp closed behind her.

The car groans and digs deep, as does she, as they start up the hill. She'd forgotten how steep it was, but then she'd never had to drive up it in a fifteen-year-old Mini whose suspension had gotten lower with every one of those years.

The forest that encircles the estate presses in, as if trying to stare through the car windows. She used to play among the trees with Tom and Ronnie, two of her cousins. Playful images of wading in the stream disappear as the muddy incline relents its gradient and is clothed in gravel. The forest stands back, as if afraid to go any further.

She drives onto the circular gravel driveway. Every sound of the stones moving under the tires brings up a new memory: bringing a huge Christmas tree home on the roof of her mum's car; her cousins arriving for a summer of fun; the silent ambulance taking her mum's body away.

The car gives a throaty sigh of relief as she pulls up. Lily, though, holds her breath. Her shoulders lift as if they could hide behind her ears. Her hands form fists. She can't bring herself to look at the house, not yet, but she feels its presence all the same. Endgame House looms just out of her peripheral vision, as it has every day since she left all those years ago.

It takes every bit of strength she has not to turn the car round. Instead, Lily takes her aunt's letter from her pocket and reads through it again.

She then closes her eyes and conjures the last time she saw Liliana. It was a few weeks before she died. They were in the Orchard Tea Rooms, walking distance from the house Liliana had lived in ever since moving from Endgame when Lily's mum died. She had accepted a fellowship at her alma mater, Clare College; adopted Lily; and taken her, with Sara and Gray, Liliana's biological children, to live in Grantchester. They were having lunch to celebrate Aunt Liliana's retirement from her position as chair of English at Cambridge. At least that's why Lily had thought they were there.

Liliana had piled a scone with so much butter, jam, cream, and fruit that it was a patisserie Buckaroo, toppling before she got it to her mouth. She laughed so much, she spilled cider on her tweed skirt. She brushed it off and said, loudly, "That's why you should make corsets out of tweed, darling; it resists the most pernicious of stains."

"There aren't many historical frocks made of tweed, Aunt Lil."

"You should be moving on from all that, Lily," her aunt said. "Rehashing the work of others is hardly artistic. It's not like you're putting a new spin on things. Don't you think it's time you did something with your life?"

"I'm fine as I am," Lily said. Her lips knitted together.

"No one says they're 'fine' and means it. 'Fine' means anything but." Aunt Liliana then sighed and grabbed Lily's hand. Her face suddenly serious, she whispered, "You will come this Christmas, won't you?"

"I can't," Lily replied. "You know that."

Liliana fixed her eyes on Lily's and said, "If not for me, then for your mother."

She was invoking Mum, blackmailing Lily into attending. Anger unspooled in Lily. She whipped back her hand. She wanted to shout, say exactly what she thought. Instead, she gripped the table and looked down at the place mat. "That's not fair, Liliana," Lily said. "It's only a game."

"This isn't entertainment, Lily; it's life or death."

"I thought it was about inheriting the house."

"On the surface level, it is. But it's more than that."

"Then tell me," Lily said, leaning forward. "Let me in, for once."

Aunt Liliana laughed. There was a splinter of ice running through the sound. "Says you, the snow queen herself. You have your locked doors, Lily, and I have mine. And I shall open mine, in my own way. At Christmas." Aunt Liliana looked around the tearoom. Bunting fluttered from wooden beams as the door opened, letting in the autumn wind. "Winter is on its way. It's time both you and I faced up to things. Time you stepped out of your locked room and found your way home."

"I don't have anything to face," Lily said, quietly. "And I don't have a home."

"Everyone has a home," Aunt Liliana replied. "It doesn't have to be a place; home could be a person. Or a cat." Aunt Liliana stroked her leg as if her cat, Winston ("after Smith, not Churchill"), was hunkered down on her lap. "Sometimes it takes a very long time to find our home." She looked out of the window, a flash of pain on her face, then turned back to Lily. Her eyes were the same dark blue shot through with skeins of green as Lily's. Liliana, though, had a corona of amber around her pupils, which now seemed to blaze: a lump of coal surrounded by fire. They always did that when she was about to say something cruel or insightful. "But if you don't have a home, why are you drawing the maze on your place mat?"

Lily looked down. Her right forefinger was tracing the way through Endgame House's famous hedged labyrinth.

"You got stuck in that maze when you found your mum dead at the center," Liliana said. "If you don't enter it again, you'll never get out."

Anger ran through Lily. She closed her eyes and imagined that rage as thread, wrapped round a bobbin and fed through a needle. She would use it later. For now, she took two ten-pound notes from her wallet, let them float like autumn leaves onto the table, and left.

Liliana had phoned many times in the days that followed, but Lily hadn't answered or replied to her messages. She hadn't known what to say. So she didn't. She kept silent.

And then it was too late.

After she'd first read the letter, she sat with it on her lap for what must have been an hour. Her heart hurt and she kept whispering "I'm sorry, I'm sorry," over and over.

Lily now folds the letter and places it carefully back in its envelope, trying to tuck the memory away with it. She takes a deep breath and taps the steering wheel—the car's done its job. Now she has to do hers.

Out of the safety of her little car, she walks across the gravel, head down so she can't see the house. She concentrates instead on the way the snow battles with the stones—the early skirmishers fall and melt, but the next phalanx of snowflakes settles, and the next. Row after row of snow soldiers stand on each other's white shoulders until all is conquered.

At the center of the drive, she stops at the sundial and swipes the snow from its top. The message on its cracked face reads: THERE IS NOT TIME ENOUGH. Cheery. Especially in bleak midwinter, when the day scarpers before it's started. Mum taught her to tell the time in this very spot. Lily traces her fingers over the raised numerals, her touch covering that of her mum's from years ago.

The low sun leaves a long shadow, telling her it's just turned three. The letter told her to arrive at teatime—3:30 p.m. Teatime here, in the gorgeous north, the wilds of Yorkshire, means dinnertime in the south. Only at a posh place like Endgame House would teatime mean anything other than supper.

She can't put it off any longer. She'll have to look at the house eventually; it might as well be now. Lily takes a deep breath. Raises her head.

Endgame House is even darker than she remembers. A hulking, seventeenth-century gray manor house made from marble and limestone that once, she was many times told as a child, seemed to glow at dawn and dusk. Now it absorbs all the light around it and keeps its secrets close. Curtains are drawn on the many windows. Ready or not, here she comes.

Chapter Three

A curtain flinches at one of the windows. The silhouette of a head appears, then retreats behind the velvet.

Lily yanks her bobble hat down over her ears. She'd forgotten how the Yorkshire wind wants to get to know you; it probes at sleeves and collars, trying to winkle out your secrets. Well, it's not getting hers. Pulling her coat tighter, she walks up to the front door. It's a shinier black than she remembers. She touches it. The paint is slightly tacky. Someone's been tarting up the house. Good luck with that. A lick of paint, a hiss of polish, and a kiss of air freshener won't hide its sins.

She raps the door knocker three times. They'll have to deal with her being early. The knocks ring out across the gravel. For a moment she listens for the footsteps of Aunt Liliana, and then she remembers with a sickening lurch: Liliana is dead.

Other footsteps, though, echo behind the huge door. You'd think a forbidding door at a house like this would open with a skin-itching creak and behind it you'd find a tall, morose butler whose face would be at home in a grave. Instead, the door glides open, bright light spills onto the steps, and a woman with long red hair and a grin that seems to take over her whole face steps out. Lily can't help smiling back. The more Lily looks at her, the more familiar she seems.

The woman bounds forward, and Lily is wrapped up in her hug. "Lily!" she says, also sounding familiar. It makes Lily feel hugged on the inside, too, a warmed-up, brandy-rich *glühwein* of a voice. The Yorkshire twang makes Lily feel suddenly homesick. And yet she doesn't have one.

The woman stands back, holding Lily by the shoulders. She looks her up and down. Her eyes fill. "You look like them both," she says, her voice splintering like snapped cinnamon bark.

And then Lily knows. Her heart crumples like wrapping paper. "Isabelle," she says.

They stand and take each other in. Isabelle has changed completely. She is now taller than Lily, her willowy limbs, red hair, and solidity make Lily think of the copper beeches in autumn that stand sentry at the entrance to the Endgame woods. She's the kind of stunning that makes you forget to breathe.

The last time they had stood on these steps together must be twenty-one years ago, maybe more. They were the other way round then, Lily welcoming Isabelle into the house to play. Isabelle would accompany her mum, Martha, who was the Armitages' lawyer and a friend of Liliana, when she visited Endgame House. Lily can't remember a time when she hadn't known Isabelle. They went to the same nursery and then the same school in the nearest village, ten miles away. During school holidays, Martha would drop Isabelle off at Endgame before commuting into Richmond, and they'd spend all day playing. Their favorite games were Murder in the Dark, Wink Murder, Cluedo…anything to do with death. (Apart from their other game: kissing. That had everything to do with life.) She was eleven when she stopped playing those games, along with her mum's piano and the flute, and—her favorite—singing. Mum died and there was no point in playing. Death got too close, and she didn't want to be reminded of life.

"Are you coming in, then?" Isabelle asks, in a reversal of what Lily used to say to her. "Have tea with me before the rest descend."

"Only if you've got cake," Lily replies.

"More kinds than you can count." Isabelle's eyes twinkle, but Lily can see sadness in there. She must be missing Liliana, too.

Isabelle turns and Lily follows. She sees Isabelle's shoulders rise and drop suddenly, as if she's trying to forcibly relax. Why would she do that? *Don't get involved,* Lily tells herself. This is why she stays away from people. Too complicated. Too many layers to unpick. Liliana once told her that people were like poems, there's what lies on the surface, and then there's the internal rhyme, the apparent contradictions, the nuances and patterns and truths that are there to be read if you put in the effort. But Liliana was a professor of poetry and liked most people. Lily wasn't. And didn't.

"Let me take your coat," Isabelle says.

Lily undoes her buttons and hands the coat over. She immediately feels vulnerable, a satsuma whose skin has been peeled.

"That is an amazing dress," Isabelle says, her eyes traveling down Lily's frock and back up to her face. "Where did you get it?"

Lily feels her cheeks flare. "I made it," she says.

"It's a poinsettia, right?"

Isabelle's appreciative scrutiny as she gazes at the red bodice with its yellow fastenings, and the skirt constructed from dark green crinoline leaves, makes Lily wish she hadn't changed at the last services. The poinsettia gown, like all of the dresses she's made and brought, was supposed to be her armor in the country house, not a way to make her feel more exposed.

"Liliana didn't tell me you'd gone into couture," Isabelle says. "Last I heard, you were copying corsets worn by Elizabeth the First. This must be much more satisfying. Shows the real you."

"I'm still making reproduction corsets," Lily says. "I like having something to copy and bring back to life." Makes it harder to fail, too.

"Sure," Isabelle says. "Of course." She gestures through into the hallway. "After you."

The paneled walls of the hallway are darker than Lily remembers, the grand staircase that rises up seems duller, no longer buffed to a shine by generations of children using it as a slide. Strangely, though, the house isn't smaller. You'd think it would seem that way, when you come back to the place you grew up, but if anything it appears bigger and more forbidding. The staircase sweeps up to the second and third floors, the chandelier on the ceiling high as a dusty moon. Armitage family portraits stare down from the walls. They go back to 1944: a blown-up, blurred photograph of Grandad—Captain Henry "Harry" Armitage—standing on the Endgame terrace when it was taken over during the Second World War to rehabilitate shell-shocked officers. The next photo is of Grandad shaking hands with a distraught-looking Lord Cappell, who had to sell the house in 1955. Then there's Grandad Harry and Grandma Violet's wedding photo, standing outside the Endgame chapel. And a picture of Mum, hugely pregnant, sitting under the willow tree. A protective hand rests on her belly.

The largest of the pictures is an actual painting. Lily can remember sitting for it, a few months before everything changed at Endgame. Uncle Robert and Grandad Harry had died by the time it was painted, but otherwise, they're all there. Lily, eleven, acned and gangly, sits between Tom and Ronnie on the bottom step of the staircase. Sara scowls on the next stair, her arm around Gray as if holding him back. Next to him, Rachel looks off beyond the painter's sight, already dreaming of leaving. Behind the cousins, Uncle Edward lounges over two steps, with Aunt Veronica draped over him. Mum and Aunt Liliana hold hands on the step above them and, at the top of the staircase, tiny Grandma Violet beams down, wearing a gold velour jumpsuit, arms outstretched like a Christmas star.

Lily looks away to stop the feelings from surfacing. She turns to the Christmas tree next to the staircase that reaches up to the minstrel gallery on the floor above. Unlit, it looks like a huge looming stranger in the shadows.

"I should have turned that on already," Isabelle says, crouching down and plugging in the lights. Now beaded with hundreds of orange lights, the tree looks full of hidden creatures, watching without blinking. "Liliana specified the decorations." Isabelle gently lifts one of the ornaments from a branch and places it in Lily's hand.

A turtledove sits in Lily's palm. Made from marl gray, blue, and yellow felt, and embroidered with lazy daisies to look like feathers, it's one of the Twelve Days of Christmas decorations that she'd crafted with Mum.

"They're all on there," Isabelle says. Her voice is soft as a dove's breath. "With some typical Liliana bling." She points to the glitter ball baubles that punctuate the tree.

Lily walks around the tree, looking for all the other decorations she'd had a hand in making. She and Mum had set up a production line: Lily traced the templates onto felt; Mum had then cut out the pieces and embroidered each one by hand; then Lily added sequins and beads before sewing both sides of the pear, the partridge, the drummers, etcetera together. They'd bonded and stitched right up to Christmas Eve the year she died. Now some stuffed birds and revelers are all that's left.

Lily hands the turtledove back to Isabelle. She won't give in to the memories that knock like a bird's beak at the window.

"Must be difficult for you," Isabelle says, "coming back after all this time."

"I've had easier days," Lily replies.

"It's going to get more difficult. But I'm sure you can handle it." Isabelle places the turtledove next to its mate, then turns to Lily. Her gaze is intense and contains layers of meaning. They're standing so close that Lily can feel the heat radiating from Isabelle's skin.

Lily turns away and walks toward the kitchen, sweating on the coldest day of the year. "Shall we have that tea?" she asks.

The kitchen is full of Christmas smells and memories. An image of her mum making pastry for mince pies smacks into Lily's head like a robin into plate glass. She glances into the pantry, the door open, showing rows of jam and mincemeat and marmalade. Lily doesn't know if she's looking at the present or the past. This is the problem with going back to where you grew up. She'll always be preserved at age twelve in this house.

Lily feels Isabelle watching her—summer sun burning her winter skin. "Do you remember when we used to crouch under here while Tom counted to a hundred?" Isabelle asks.

"It was always a very quick hundred," Lily replies. "He caught us every time, didn't matter where we were. But then time seems slower—"

"When you're young," Isabelle says, finishing off one of Aunt Liliana's many sayings.

"Right now, Lily," Liliana would say to her, "you're making slices of memory all the time, which makes time feel as if it's passing more slowly than it does for me. Revel in it." And Lily had, until Mum died. Then she longed for time to speed up and away, for the days to pass as quickly as Mum. That is why she hasn't been back.

Isabelle fills the kettle at the butler's sink. "As you're the first here, I thought we could have a catch-up before all the ceremonial stuff starts."

"Ceremonial?"

"The rules read out, legal scraps, served up with scones, parkin, and tiny sandwiches. With champagne, of course."

"I'd expect nothing less from Aunt Lil."

Isabelle places the kettle on the hot plate of the stove and sits opposite Lily. She smiles and her eyes crease at the edges like the sun's rays in a child's drawing. "Where do we start?"

"In her letter, Liliana said that my mum was m—" Lily's voice cracks down the middle. She can't say that word. Can't even think it.

Isabelle exhales a puff of air. "I was thinking we'd do the small talk first, you know—great loves, careers, that sort of thing—but no. You always did want to get to the heart of things." She pauses, takes Lily's hand. "Your aunt thought that Mariana was killed. Murdered."

There's that word. Echoing against the kitchen's surfaces, reflected in the knives shining in their block. Lily withdraws her hand and places it to her chest, as if that could hold back her heart from beating too fast and stop the indigestion already rising. How do you process that word? Ever? "So, she didn't…" She can't say these words either.

"Kill herself? Not according to your aunt."

The kettle begins to scream, stopper wobbling under pressure from the steam.

Lily gets up, holding out her hand to stop Isabelle from rising. "I'll make the tea." She starts opening cupboards, looking for mugs. "Gives me something to do."

"Right of the sink, second along," Isabelle says. "The caddy is on the counter."

Lily takes down two big mugs and opens the caddy, immediately smelling the familiar Yorkshire Tea tang of tannin and moor. She wonders if Isabelle is right in saying that Lily always got to the heart of things. That feels as far away from who she is now as her little flat in London. "Do you mind if we don't talk about it? About my mum, I mean. I know I brought it up, but…" She doesn't look at Isabelle but she can feel her pity, sticky as treacle.

"Whatever you want," Isabelle says.

Lily feels her eyes itching with backed-up tears, like she's as allergic to thinking of murder as she is to cats. But that doesn't stop her from picking up cats and burying her face in their fur. She doesn't want to get that close to murder.

Lily sticks tea bags into the mugs and, after pouring in water, looks out of the window to the walled kitchen garden. It still has the same bench, but it is now surrounded by climbing roses, hips showing. Two holly bushes stand sentinel, and mistletoe entwines its limbs into a tango with the ivy. "Wherever I look, I see old games of hide-and-seek," she says. "I just had an image of counting down on the bench and coming to look for you all."

"You are the only person I've ever known to actually count to a hundred," Isabelle says. Lily can't see her face, but she can tell Isabelle is smiling. Her voice warms up as if in the sun.

"Those are the rules," Lily says.

"Do you always follow rules?" Isabelle asks.

Lily doesn't answer at first. She squishes the tea bags with a spoon. "Most of the time. Unless they're unfair."

Isabelle gets up and moves over to the huge fridge-freezer in the corner to bring over the milk. "I'm not speaking as a lawyer now, but you should be aware that not everyone will be playing the game as fairly and faithfully as you."

"Well, I'm not here for the game."

Isabelle gives a big grin. Her eyes spark. She raises a mug. "Cheers to that."

They clink mugs that are already chipped. Lily raises hers to her lips. It smells weird—a marine scent, as if a fishing net has been used to catch and contain the leaves.

She puts the mug back on the counter. "Liliana said all the hints about what happened to Mum would be hidden within the clues for everyone."

"If only she could have just spelled things out," Isabelle says.

"Everything was a game to her," Lily replies. "Even death."

"You'll work it out. You were always good at the game."

"I was not!"

"You're forgetting—I was there. You got the clues almost every time; you just stopped coming forward as the others hated that you won."

Lily has a sudden flash of memory—solving the final clue and finding the chest full of presents, only for her cousins to pile in and pull her away. Sara had even made off with her winning gift—a PlayStation 2—saying that Lily wouldn't appreciate it as she would. And Lily had let her. So, yes, she had pretended she didn't know the answers after that. But she always thought she'd kept it hidden. The thought of being seen makes her feel sick. A wave of dizziness sweeps over her. She sits back down at the table and tries to take a deep breath.

"You OK?" Isabelle places a hand on her arm. It feels familiar and right. And strangely intimate.

"I will be." Lily closes her eyes. "It's a lot. Especially after a long drive."

"I shouldn't have bombarded you. But the others will be here soon and I have to get into official lawyer mode. I then must leave after reading out the method of the game. It's part of Liliana's commandments to me."

"So, you're a rule follower, too."

"What can I say, we have a lot in common. We always have," Isabelle says. They look at each other for a moment, eyes connecting. Something illuminates between them like fairy lights. Isabelle leans forward, still touching Lily. Her face becomes serious. Her voice dips, as if on a dimmer switch. "I've got to tell you something. Before the rest arrive."

"What?" Lily asks.

And then the door knocker booms from the hall.

Isabelle sighs. She withdraws her hand, slips her jacket back on, and pulls back her hair into a ponytail. When she next looks at Lily, her eyes have hardened like chestnuts baked in vinegar. Her face has almost changed shape, cheekbones more prominent. And then Lily remembers. This is Isabelle's game face. Lily doesn't think she has a game face, other than the one she chose to make herself a loser. Problem is, when you pretend something for long enough, you begin to believe it.

"If you'll come with me, please, Miss Armitage," Isabelle says. Her voice is now cut glass, with no brandy inside.

The shift fills Lily with unease. "You weren't kidding when you said you had to slip into lawyer mode," she says.

"I have a role to perform," Isabelle says. "As do you." She rings the bell by the kitchen door. Footsteps hurry down the stone back steps that come out into the pantry.

A woman appears, hands full of yellow dusters. She smells of wood polish, beeswax, and Opium, the Yves Saint Laurent kind.

"This is Mrs. Castle," Isabelle says. "The housekeeper. She babysat you when you were little. She'll be looking after you all, and—most importantly—the house, during the game."

"Pleased to meet you, Mrs. Castle." Lily has no memory of her, but then her prosopagnosia—face blindness—is particularly bad from that time.

"Miss Lily," Mrs. Castle says with a stiff nod. She does not look pleased to see Lily in return. Mrs. Castle looks as if she has never been pleased in her life. She's candy-cane thin without any of the sweetness. There are no lines around her lips or eyes, and yet she looks as if she's lived a long time. A long time without smiling.

The door knocker sounds again. More insistent this time.

"Would you please answer the door and take the guests to the drawing room, Mrs. Castle?"

Mrs. Castle nods once, then stalks into the hall. Lily tries to prize a conspiratorial smile out of Isabelle but gets nothing. Not even a hint of what had passed before. The world is shifting under her feet. And now her cousins are arriving. The door knocker goes again. She hopes it's not Sara and Gray. She's avoided them since leaving Liliana's house at eighteen to go to Central Saint Martins. She feels a pang of guilt—Gray didn't deserve to be ghosted. But Sara definitely did, and she never left Gray alone.

Lily stands on the rug in the center of the hall, Endgame House around her, pressing down on her shoulders.

The knocker raps one more time. A voice behind the door calls out, "Anyone home?"

Mrs. Castle strides forward and opens the door.

Sara and Gray are in the doorway. Gray peers round Mrs. Castle and Isabelle and sees Lily looking at him. He turns away.

"Good afternoon," Isabelle says. "And welcome back to Endgame House."

Chapter Four

Striding into the hall, Sara takes off her coat and hands it to Mrs. Castle without even looking at her. Mrs. Castle gathers Gray's coat, hat, and scarf and moves away. She tuts like a pissed-off clock.

Sara stands in the center of the hall, looking up and around. Her eyes linger on the portraits of previous Endgame House owners further up the walls. Probably wondering how much they'd sell for at auction if she wins the game. Gray shuffles in behind her, head bent as if playing his one-time favorite game—counting the tiles on the black-and-white checkered floor.

Sara sees Lily and pulls her face into a smile. "Lily!" she says and moves toward her. Lily can't remember a time when they hugged. She'd definitely remember if it was anything like now—she's being squeezed like a tube of toothpaste at the end of its life. Maybe Sara's changed—thawed out with the years.

Sara steps back and appraises her. "You look well," she says. "A bit more weight suits you."

Maybe not. And so it starts. Lily knows a pithy retort will come to her in the middle of the night, when she's lying awake with heartburn due to rich food and undigested memories. Now, though, all she can say is, "You look amazing, Sara."

It's true, as well. Sara's wearing Stella McCartney, and her skin looks accustomed to being similarly cocooned in the ridiculously expensive.

Sara shrugs. She's used to compliments. Her eyes slide away from Lily like the last items on a sales rack. She moves over to the Christmas tree and fingers a shiny bauble. "I saw this set in Liberty. The whole tree must have cost a fortune. Is it coming out of the estate?"

Isabelle's jaw moves back and forth as if chewing down her first response. "Your mother requested every decoration in the house as part of the final amendment to her will," she says at last. "She also specified all of the food and drink to be provided over the twelve days."

Lily feels like a dumbwaiter has dropped down inside her. "Twelve days? We can't stay here that long." She looks to the door. It would be so easy to walk away.

"Then you can leave right now," Sara says. Her head cocks to one side, a smile tugging at the corners of her Channel-Tunnel mouth. "Can't she, Gray?"

Gray looks from the floor to Sara to Lily with his strange, gauzy gaze. Family legend has it that when Gray opened his eyes for the first time, Robert, Gray's dad and Lily's uncle, had said, "His eyes are the color of a fish caught in Whitby on a cloudy day. We should call him Grey." Liliana, Gray's mum, however, insisted on a variant spelling. What a namesake—fish skin.

"She can do what she likes," he says, then returns his gaze to the shiny floor.

"Yes, she can," Isabelle says. She looks straight at Lily. There's challenge in her eyes.

"I'm staying," says Lily.

Isabelle claps her hands together. "So that's sorted. Would you care to wait for the other guests in the drawing room?"

The drawing room has been turned into a festive tea parlor. Three round tables have been swathed in snow-white cloths with settings for eight people. A display of twisted willow, moss, and lit beeswax candles covers the huge stone mantelpiece. A log fire spits in the hearth. At each place setting sits the Endgame House china, a napkin, and a sprig of snowberries.

"Make yourselves comfortable," Isabelle says, and waits until Sara, Gray, and Lily are sitting at one of the tables. Lily would much rather have sat by herself, saving a place for Ronnie and Tom, but that would be rude. "We'll start at 4:00 p.m.," Isabelle continues, "whether everyone is here or not."

"If they don't arrive in time, do they forfeit their place in the game?" Sara asks.

"They must be on the steps of Endgame House, and have knocked at the door, by 3:45 p.m.," Isabelle replies. "Any later, and they will not be allowed in the house or to take part."

"Let's hope the snow stops them, then," Sara says. She looks around for someone to agree. No one does. "Just telling it how it is. Looks like I'm the only honest one here."

Lily looks down at the tablecloth and sees that there is a faint pattern running through the linen. It's raised, embossed with something. She looks closer. It's the Endgame maze. She'd know its configuration anywhere. She used to run out onto the back lawn and chase Mum around the maze. When it was her turn to hide, she'd tuck herself into the secret hiding spot in the center and wait for her mum to find her. And she always did. Until the day it was Lily who found her mum, dead, slumped against a hedge.

Lily swallows down a wave of nausea. She looks up and sees that Isabelle has left and Mrs. Castle is crossing carefully toward them, holding a silver tray. She lays down a teapot painted with holly and a matching milk jug in front of Lily and her cousins. Lily catches a glimpse of something printed on the bottom of the jug before it's laid down.

"Shall I be Mother?" Sara asks, reaching for the teapot. "Or maybe you should, Lily, seeing as you were named after my mum. And the fact that you were her favorite."

Lily says nothing. Anything she could say to the contrary would be a lie. She'd like to say exactly what Liliana told her about Sara, how she felt about her biological daughter. The truth itches behind Lily's teeth. Instead, she says nothing.

"Or perhaps being Mother is a bit close to the bone," Sara continues. "After all, without you, yours would be still al—" Gray places a warning hand on her arm. She shakes it away, but stops talking midword. Lily knows, though, what she was about to say. She's heard it before. Her mum would still be here if it weren't for Lily. That's the family story, told by all but Liliana: Mariana was happy till she had Lily. And then she'd faded, to the point that she didn't want to be here at all. Motherhood had destroyed her.

If her aunt was right, though, someone else had been the cause of her mother's death. And Lily would have to rip open the seams of her life and start again.

Lily looks up, realizing that the whole room is watching her.

The quiet is broken by a log falling in the grate. Tea pours, the strainer catches the leaves, milk is sploshed. The door knocker resounds from the hall.

"Let's hope it's some decent company at last," Sara says, leaning back in her chair so she can see through the drawing room doorway.

The front door opens. "Let us in then, Isabelle. Bloody freezing out here. Holly's a southerner; she's not used to this kind of weather." It's Rachel. Her voice has hardly changed.

"Of course," Isabelle says.

Lily hears shoes stamped on tiles, coats shucked, and hands rubbed together. She's about to get up and go through to meet them when Rachel walks into the drawing room. She hasn't changed much in appearance— just stretched upwards. Lily feels the familiar longing to get to know Rachel. She had gotten on so well with Rachel's brothers—Tom and Ronnie—but Rachel had always kept her distance from everyone. She had often sat by herself, or gazed into space.

Rachel now looks across her cousins sitting at the table. Her eyebrow twitches. A woman walks in behind her. She has a sweet face, full of dimples and freckles.

"This is Holly," Rachel says, placing her arm round Holly's shoulder. "My wife."

"Pleasure to meet you," Lily says. It feels too formal, but she gets a big grin from Holly.

"You wouldn't need to introduce us if we'd been invited to your wedding," Sara says.

Silence royal-ices the room.

"You couldn't have made it anyway," Gray says, quietly. "You were in New York." Sara lances him with a look, and he gazes back at the floor.

"And I was looking after your mother," Isabelle says to Sara.

"Hoping to inherit, were you?" Sara replies. "You must be livid that you didn't."

"I have never cared about the house. Only the people in it."

"Just because you played here when you were young, and Mum helped you cheat your way through your law degree, doesn't mean you're part of the family. You and your mother, well, you're practically the help."

Everyone freezes in place, like figures on top of a Christmas cake.

Isabelle's jaw works some more. She must have so much to say. Lily wonders if it's anything to do with what Isabelle was about to tell her before they were interrupted.

The door knocker goes again. Mrs. Castle is on it this time, hurrying to the front of the house. Rachel and Holly sit down at one of the other tables. Sara's mouth purses into a drawstring pinch. Lily can feel Sara juddering, her knee nudging the underneath of the table.

Lily busies herself with turning over the saucer to see what's printed on the bottom. It's a tiny version of the maze. She traces the way through the maze with her little finger. Still as familiar to her now as when she was a child. She finds herself doodling it when she's concentrating or on the phone. Liliana was right. The maze has been stamped on her, too.

"Where is she?" Ronnie calls out as he runs into the drawing room, still wearing his coat. He's carrying a big pile of bright presents. His wellies track slush onto the rug. He sees Lily and drops the presents onto the floor. A telltale tinkle suggests that one of the gifts is made of glass and no longer as unbroken as it was.

Lily stands up just in time to get enveloped in a Ronnie hug. Ronnie gives good hugs. He's tall, broad-shouldered, and as solid, yet squishy, as a just-made snowman. He picks her up to squeeze a bit more. "Still wearing that corset, then," he says as he puts her gently back on the floor.

"It's my new Christmas model," Lily says, her hand going to the pulled-in waist. "There's an extra panel and longer laces that let you bloat during the festive period."

"When are you going to make me a truss, then?" Ronnie asks, sticking out his nonexistent belly.

"Any time you like," Lily replies. Her heart feels like its laces are yanked tight at the back, cinched in with love for one of her two favorite cousins. When the other one arrives, Tom, she might just pop. You're not supposed to have favorites, but it can't be avoided, especially if the others have always treated you like an unwelcome stray.

Philippa, Ronnie's wife, pulls Ronnie back toward her. "Give her some space, love."

"It's all right," Lily says.

"Even so," Philippa says. And then doesn't go on to say what.

Ronnie gets whatever message she's conveying, however, and moves over to Rachel, his sister.

"Too long, no see, sis," Ronnie says as they hug. "You're looking brilliant. Love suits you." He high-fives Holly over Rachel's shoulder. He then looks over to Lily and mouths, "Catch up later."

Lily nods. She wonders for a moment if she'll tell him, then remembers Aunt Liliana's warning. No secrets told just yet. Ronnie can't be a worry or a suspect, though, surely? They played together throughout this house. Times with him, his older brother, Tom, and Isabelle were some of her happiest. Without them, her connection to Endgame House would only be one of death, regrets, and mourning.

Mrs. Castle walks slowly into the drawing room, holding a five-tiered cake stand like it was a crown. She places it on Lily's table and hurries back for the other two. Lily has never seen anything like it, and she's had afternoon tea at the Savoy. A wealthy client had insisted on taking her there while they discussed the replica of Queen Victoria's wedding dress that Lily was making. The bottomless champagne, sandwiches, and cakes had only stopped appearing when Lily, more than a bit drunk, cried, "No more!"

Now, the bottom tier is full of teeny sandwiches, cut into star shapes. Looks like smoked salmon in one; egg and pepper in another; cut beef, cheese and tomato, and coronation chicken in the others. Above that, round quiches that could fit in her palm. They are marbled with blue, so maybe they're responsible for the Stilton smell. Next layer is one of scones the size of her fist, knuckle-dusted with cranberries; then come slices of cake, from parkin to carrot to Christmas; with the top tier saved for mince pies and snowflake-shaped *pfeffernusse*. The combined smell of spice and meat and fish and Christmas makes Lily gag.

Sara sniffs at the display, as if she could do better. She probably thinks she could, just because she was an au pair for a ski season in the Alps, cooking for posh twats in salopettes.

"Pretty impressive, Mrs. Castle," Ronnie says, reaching for a quiche. Philippa taps his hand and it withdraws. He sits on both hands and gives Lily a rueful look.

Mrs. Castle bestows him with the nearest expression to a smile yet as she brings round a tray of champagne flutes. The glasses sparkle under the chandeliers, and they're empty—what are they going to be like when full of bubbles? She carries over a silver stand filled with ice and three bottles of vintage Bollinger. This is some swanky gathering.

"We'll open the bottles when Tom gets here," Isabelle says from her place behind a walnut desk. She's sifting through papers, wearing her reading glasses. The glasses suit her angular face, framing it, softening it.

"*If* he gets here," Sara says.

"He will," Ronnie replies. "Tom wouldn't miss a drama for anything. Neither would I. It's the only reason I'm here—that and seeing Lily again."

Philippa elbows Ronnie in the side. He rubs it as if quite used to it. Maybe Lily should make him a corset just to withstand Philippa's nudges.

"Tom's probably stopped to get everyone extra presents," Rachel says. "He'll be here soon. He'd hate to keep people waiting."

"Well, he's got four more minutes," Sara says, looking at her watch, "and then he doesn't get to play. All the more chances for the rest of us."

"Three minutes, twenty seconds," says Isabelle, pointing to the clock on the wall. "Liliana states clearly in her rules that all timings should be taken from the drawing room's grandmother clock." She takes her phone out of her pocket. "He'll have to be quick; he's not even on the grounds yet."

"How do you know?" Sara asks.

Isabelle turns her phone round so they can all see. On the screen is a grainy CCTV image. Lily can just about make out the wrought-iron gates at the front of the house.

"You've got access to security footage?" Philippa asks. There's a touch of concern in her voice.

Isabelle nods.

"Not sure how I feel about that," Rachel says.

"I know exactly how I feel about it," Sara replies. "I don't like it. And I don't see how it's appropriate."

"It's all in Liliana's will. I'll explain all of this when I read out the rules," Isabelle replies.

There's movement on the screen. The gates are swinging back. A car with a Christmas tree strapped to the roof waits to be let in; a hand waves from its window. You can't tell it's Tom from the screen but it's enough to make Lily feel a surge of joy.

"There he is!" Ronnie says. "You can rely on Tom."

Sara makes a sound halfway between a tut and a harrumph. A *turumph*. Rachel doesn't look any happier, neither does Philippa nor, in fact, does Isabelle. Ronnie and Lily will just have to give Tom a really big welcome.

The sound of gravel shifting comes from the driveway.

"One minute," says Isabelle, watching the second hand sweep across the face of the grandmother clock as if applying Ponds cream.

A car door slams. Ronnie runs to the window and opens it. "Come on, Tom!" he shouts.

He's answered by one of Tom's big laughs.

"Thirty seconds," Isabelle says.

Lily's nails bite into her palms.

"And he's coming up past the sundial," Ronnie calls out, commentator style. "His hair's grown long so it's flowing in the wind, snow sticking to it like confetti. He's got fine form this year, his trainer's been working him hard and he's been avoiding the sugar lumps, and he's coming up to the final straight now—"

"Ten seconds," says Isabelle, her voice taut as a violin string. Lily can hear Tom's quick steps crunch through the snow. "Nine, eight—"

"Just a few more steps to go," Ronnie continues.

"Seven, six—"

"Neck and neck with time itself, Tom Armitage extends his arms and takes a final leap, his hand grasping the door knocker and—"

Rap, rap, rap.

"Would you let in our final guest, please, Mrs. Castle?" Isabelle says.

"I'll do it!" Ronnie says, running out of the room.

Holly stage whispers, "I like him." Rachel smiles. Lily realizes how rarely she's seen Rachel happy. As a child, Rachel had sat and watched almost as much as Lily, taking everything in but never engaging. Lily had tried to make friends once, going over to Rachel and offering the perfume she had made by soaking rose petals, lavender, and rosemary in distilled water. Rachel had shaken her head and looked away, and that was it. Maybe, now, things could be different.

Ronnie walks back in, his arm around Tom. "Look what I found on the doorstep," he says.

Tom waves at them. "Sorry to keep you all waiting," he says. He holds up a bag of presents. "Lost track of time. Got wrapped up in these."

Lily smiles and Ronnie groans. Tom is infamous in the family for his puns.

"You very nearly lost your place," Sara says. She stares at him with scorn, as if she can't believe anyone would be so stupid as to turn down the chance of cash.

"But he didn't, so everything's all right," Ronnie replies, clapping Tom so hard on the back that he staggers forward.

"Timing is everything," Tom says, catching hold of the grandmother clock to stop himself from falling. It teeters, but holds steady.

"Seeing as we're all here," Isabelle says. "Let's open the champagne, shall we? And, once I've read you the rules, the Christmas Game can begin."

Chapter Five

Champagne popped, poured, and fizzing in the flutes, Isabelle stands by the fireplace. She takes a deep breath. "First I'll read Liliana Violet Armitage-Feather's last message to you all. It was lodged in the safe at the offices of Stirling Lawyers, to be read today, by me, in the event of her death." Her hand is shaking slightly, making the paper flutter as if shivering at its words being exposed.

"*Dear Armitage family and guests,*" Isabelle reads, a ventriloquist for Lily's aunt. "*Well, I'm dead, then. Which is a shame, as I was anticipating a wonderful Christmas with you all and looking forward even more to watching you try to solve my clues and secure Endgame's future. That would have been a delight, especially as so many of you are so bad at it.*"

"She couldn't help herself," Sara hisses under her breath. "Had to get in a last dig."

"Sssh," Rachel says from the next table.

"She was my mother, I think that gives me the right to talk about her any way I like," Sara says, loudly.

"Come on, Sara, love, we want to hear from your mother, not from you," Tom says from the third table. His voice is as Yorkshire as parkin and just as welcome.

Sara is about to snap at him when Gray puts his hand on her arm. She leans back in her chair; it creaks as if talking back on her behalf.

"*Never mind,*" Isabelle continues reading, her voice wavering as much as the paper. "*Dead is dead. I've left Isabelle here in charge until an heir is declared at the end of the game. You should know, though, that this time, my Christmas Game will be different. Before, each clue led to another clue somewhere in the house or grounds, until someone eventually found the stash of presents for all of you. The winner would then get an extra gift. And that much is true—the extra gift, in this case, is the house. The rest of you, however, will get nothing. And this time, there are strict rules to follow for everyone in this house. Deviate from them and you will be removed from the game. I believe the saying is, 'Them's the breaks.'*"

Tom snorts at this point. Sara sends him a curt "Ssshh."

"*Oh, and sorry to have to part you from your children, if you have them, but there's precedent for that in this family. And I thought it best we kept this to the adults. Kids are so good at games, and I'm no Willy Wonka—handing over the house to a child does not seem wise. So, play nicely, big kids. Be as kind to each other as you can bear. And don't give up. Dig in. No matter what happens, there's always a chance, even when there doesn't seem to be. Flatcaps and vowels don't make you Yorkshire folk—persisting does. Do me proud in a major way. And do try and have a merry Christmas. Raise a glass of Bolly to me, won't you?*"

Isabelle folds up the paper and throws it into the fire behind her.

Gray gasps. "Those were her last words," he whispers. He watches as the flames eat up the paper.

"Sorry, Gray," Isabelle says, and seems to be genuine, "those were my orders, too." She nods at Mrs. Castle across the room, and the housekeeper comes forward with a sheaf of yellowed paper. She hands out a thick page to everyone seated.

Lily sneezes, unable to hold it back anymore. Sara pulls a face and pointedly inches away. Lily looks down at her piece of paper. It's a list of six rules. Isabelle reads them out loud while the players read along.

RULES OF THE LAST CHRISTMAS GAME

by Liliana Armitage-Feathers

RULE 1: The possible heirs—Sara, Gray, Rachel, Ronnie, Tom, and Lily—must stay in the house from Christmas Eve till the Twelfth Day of Christmas. If they leave the grounds at all before 3:00 p.m. on 5th January, they forfeit their claim. Cameras are set up around the fenced perimeter of the house and will be under scrutiny by Stirling Lawyers.

RULE 2: You must solve the clues by yourself. Your partner, if you have one, can help you, but anyone else from outside the family is banned from assisting, with disqualification the result. Same goes for the internet. Your phones/tablets/ smart watches, etc., will be taken away, the Wi-Fi stopped. If you are found using any other gadget to look up answers, you'll be disqualified. Basically, don't be an utter dick. It's the library, any papers in the house, or the knowledge in your own heads, kids. I know how some of you will hate that and, to be honest, it gives me great pleasure to leave you at the mercy of books.

RULE 3: One riddle will be received on each of the Twelve Days of Christmas. If anyone searches for, or finds, a clue for another day, they will be disqualified.

RULE 4: Each riddle leads to a key, hidden somewhere in the house and gardens. Players may pool the keys they find or keep them to themselves. What will it be? Help your fellow humans and relatives at Christmas, or not? Just how selfish can you be, huh? We'll see.

RULE 5: On 5th January, twelve clues will have been given

and, if you're lucky, twelve keys found. One of the twelve possible keys will open the door to a secret room in the house. A major clue will be given during the whole of the Christmas Game as to the location of the secret room. So keep looking at what you've been given.

RULE 6: Inside the secret room, players will have to find the deeds to Endgame House. Isabelle will make an appearance on 5th January and, at the stroke of 4:00 p.m., sign the house over to the winner. If no one has found the deeds, or everyone is disqualified, then the house, my money, and all other assets will go to Isabelle Stirling, to dispense as she wishes. I suggest a cat charity, Isabelle, preferably for blind cats in honor of my dear Winston whom you have so kindly agreed to adopt. But it's up to you. I'm dead, after all.

Isabelle places down her copy of the rules. Silence hangs over the room like dead mistletoe.

"That's Mother for you," Sara says. "Publicly declaring a preference for pets over her own children's rightful inheritance."

"Legally speaking," Isabelle says, gently, "it's not rightfully yours at all."

"What do you mean?" says Sara, leaning forward, voice sharp as ice.

"The house passed from Grandma Violet to Mariana, her eldest child. As Mariana then died before Lily came of age at twenty-one, the house went to Edward, and then to Liliana when Edward died in the accident. With that generation now all dead, the legal heir up until the change in will was, in fact, Lily."

Lily's heart is drummer-boy loud. She'd had no idea.

"And, should she have heirs," Isabelle continues, "it would pass to them."

Lily feels eyes land on her like fruit flies on perspiring bananas. If she could disappear under the table, she would, but moving in this corset is hard enough as it is without limbo dancing under the tablecloth.

"Did you know this?" Sara asks Lily. "Is that why you're here for the first time in forever, to lodge a legal complaint?"

Lily shakes her head. "Not at all."

"No point in the rest of us making a complaint against the estate, then," Tom says, looking pointedly at Sara. They'd never gotten on, even as children. She used to call him stupid and he could never stand that. Something bigger must have happened for them to fall out like this, but Tom's never told Lily. There's a lot she missed by staying away from Endgame.

"Not unless you want to waste your time, energy, and money," Isabelle replies. She takes another folder out of her briefcase and comes over to stand next to Lily. "I'm afraid I've got to ask you to sign this document, Lily. It means giving up any prior claim to the house and agreeing that Liliana's new will shall stand."

Lily has so many questions and the only person who could answer them is dead. Liliana's games extend far beyond the riddles she set for Christmas.

"Do you want me to look it over, Lily?" Ronnie asks. Before he was a chef, Ronnie was, briefly, a lawyer at a top London union. Not that you'd have known it when he was out of his wig. Lily's always thought of him as a muppet, in the very best way. His arms flail like Kermit's, though his party skills have a touch of Animal running through them.

"I don't want the house," Lily says. "I'll sign whatever you want. That's why I'm here, not to inherit a place where people I love died."

"Yeah, right," Sara says. Her eyes roll like Boxing Day dice.

"You haven't lost your saracasm, then," Tom says to Sara. "Saracasm" was the word Liliana had made up for Sara's tendency to scorn.

"Are you saying you believe her?" Sara asks.

"I do," Tom says, simply. Lily feels a swell of relief and support. "No reason not to. She doesn't have to sign anything, but she is. You're projecting your own greed, Sara."

"Don't give me your psycho-crap, Tom," Sara says. "We're not your 'clients.'" Sara places finger quote marks round the word as if Tom were a gigolo, not a psychoanalyst.

"So soon?" Tom replies. "No niceties, no small talk, no 'How you doing, Tom, haven't seen you in years?'"

Lily feels the tension balloon in the room. She stands up, holds out her hand. "Give me the papers, please, Isabelle. I'll sign and then we can move on."

Isabelle hands her the sheaf of papers and a pen. Lily places them on the maze-embossed tablecloth and signs away her rights. She doesn't want this house. And Liliana knew that. She'd asked Lily here to tell her about Mariana's death, after all, not to get the deeds to Endgame.

"You're mad, Lily," Ronnie says. "I've always liked that about you." He plucks a pepper biscuit from the cake stand and sits back down. "Can we eat now? I'm starving."

Chapter Six

When afternoon tea has been reduced to tiers of crumbs, Isabelle stands. "Time for me to go," she says. "And for you to hand over your phones, Kindles, tablets, laptops, smart watches—anything that has internet access."

"Is this necessary?" Rachel asks, hesitating before placing her phone in Isabelle's briefcase. Her voice lowers, "It's not as if Aunt Liliana is here."

"Then why whisper? Worried her ghost will hear?" Sara says. Her saracasm is stronger than even Lily remembers.

"You'd better hope not," Tom says.

"What do you mean?" Sara snaps.

Tom smirks. "Do you think your mum would be proud of you? Not going to her funeral but making sure you're in the running for her house?"

"At least I'm not a hypocrite like the rest of you," Sara replies.

The atmosphere chills as if placed in an ice bucket.

"The rules of the game will be adhered to," Isabelle says. "While I've been close to your family for all of my life, I'm still acting according to Liliana's will and wishes. As such, I hand the running of the game and the house over to Mrs. Castle. I'll be back on the fifth of January to crown the winner."

Lily feels an undertow of panic. "So that's it till then?" she asks. "We won't see you at all?"

"Liliana made it plain where she wanted me," Isabelle says. "And that is out of your way. I intend to keep to the letter of her instructions."

"There's eight of us. That's a lot of work for Mrs. Castle," Tom says. "I presume we can help out?"

"Nothing in the rules says you can't. As Ronnie is a chef, he may want to cook a few—"

"Damn right!" Ronnie says.

"There are supplies and ingredients in the pantry, ready-made platters in the freezers, wine in the cellar, ice in the freezer and icehouse," Isabelle continues. "With more storms forecasted over the next week, you may get snowed in. Should the very worst happen, we've ensured there's enough food and drink to last a month, even with your impressive appetites."

Lily shivers at the thought of being trapped here: snow outside, Sara's cold sniping inside.

Isabelle must have seen Lily's concern as she's looking at her when she says, "But don't worry. That's really unlikely. You'll be fine." She pauses, scans the room. "Any other questions before I go?"

"I presume when one of us wins and inherits," Sara says, "we do what we like with the place?"

"Absolutely," Isabelle says. Lily detects, though, the curl of her lip as Isabelle lowers her head to pack up her briefcase.

"Even sell it?" Gray asks.

"I don't see why the winner can't sell it," Lily says.

"You would say that," Sara says. "You were always shit at the Christmas Game."

"She wasn't," Tom says, quickly. "She won a few, then dropped back when you all made fun of her." Tom smiles over at Lily and she feels a wave of gratitude. Another person who saw her.

Lily had often known the answers to the Christmas Game. Probably because she loved learning from Mum, Grandma Violet, and Aunt Liliana. But standing out made her a target, so she backed off, feigned ignorance. Sometimes she thinks she was born with a laced-up corset for a mouth.

"You always did have rose-tinted spectacles when it came to Lily,"

Sara says to Tom. "Sweet, really." Her sneer says she thinks it anything but sweet. "If Lily knew the answers, why wouldn't she say?"

She has a point.

"Time for me to leave you to your Christmas bickering," Isabelle says.

"Are you allowed to speak to us like that?" Sara says. Her chin dips into her neck.

Isabelle smiles, and a flicker of the woman who met Lily at the door re-emerges. "I represent Liliana and her memory; I don't have to be more polite to you than necessary," she says, closing the belt on her bag. Lily suddenly thinks of making a business-wear corset shaped like a briefcase and giving it to Isabelle. She chases the thought away.

Striding to the door, Isabelle looks back at the group. Lily hopes that her gaze will settle on her like soft snow, but it falls across the other tables. "Happy Christmas, everyone. Try to have fun."

And then she's gone. The front door closes, and her steps crunch away.

Even with Tom and Ronnie here, Lily feels alone.

"Are you going to drink that?" Sara asks, nodding toward Lily's untouched glass of champagne.

Lily shakes her head. "Help yourself," she says.

Sara takes the glass and sips, closing her eyes. "Touch of lemon, shot of sherbet fizz. And just the right amount of yeast."

Funny how yeast in champagne is good, but in an infection, it's bad. That'd be another good reply, for someone braver than her.

Mrs. Castle glooms into the room. "Your rooms are all ready. Liliana assigned your bedchambers; your names are on the doors. Miss Lily, you're in your old room."

Lily feels the glances of her cousins slide her way.

"Your luggage is on your beds," Mrs. Castle says, rubbing her arm. "I took it up myself. Good job it's snowing, otherwise all those clothes you've brought would be wasted." She stares at Ronnie, who bursts into giggles. His laughter dies under her dowsing glare. "I'm sure you are all old enough and ugly enough to unpack your own suitcases. Cocktails will be served at seven, dinner at half past. Be prompt, if you please."

Lily climbs the staircase, fingers tracing the familiar finials on the banister. The carpet has changed since she was last here—the corporate gray from when Endgame was a conference center has been replaced with plush hotel red. The creaks are still present, though, from the floorboards underneath. They whisper that nothing changes, not deep down. They *crack* as she steps on the fifth step, *sigh* on the seventh. She used to avoid those steps while playing hide-and-seek, or tread on them on purpose to send Tom looking the other way.

On the second-floor landing, she looks down the corridor leading off to the right. Some doors are open, some closed. A flash of her walking into Grandma Violet's room comes into her mind, of holding her moth-soft hand. She turns, trying to blink away the grief.

As she makes her way up to the third floor, the flashbacks keep coming. The Sunday she and Mum strung a violin on the landing; the night she couldn't sleep and crept around the silent house; the time she and Isabelle…every step sets off memories, like slinkies falling down stairs.

Her bedroom is, and was, on the third floor, in the East Wing. She stops by her door. On the other side of the corridor is Liliana's room and the old nursery. Flashes of memory spark of playing in the nursery with her cousins. It's like seeing little ghosts: her seven-year-old self trying to teach Ronnie object permanence by hiding a ball under a blanket. Ronnie blinking at her and toddling off to look in the airing cupboard. "It's under there," Lily had said to him, pointing at the blanket. "It never goes away, even if you hide it."

Opposite the nursery is her mum's old room. Lily walks along the corridor toward it. It's hard to catch her breath. She feels like someone is squeezing her lungs shut like an accordion. There are bare floorboards in this corridor, unchanged since Endgame was a private house in the

1920s and the third floor reserved for staff. The Armitages kept the same arrangement when they took on the house and turned it into a conference center—this time, it was the owners that were kept out of the way.

The rug is the same, too. A dark red streak running along the hall like blood down a spine.

She turns away. She can't go in Mum's room. Not yet.

Instead, she opens the door into her old bedroom. She feels something like a hand on her throat as she gasps. The room is almost exactly the same as when she left it. She's playing spot-the-difference with her own past.

One wall is covered in posters. The Spice Girls pose next to Eternal and Hanson, as if they've merged into one almighty nineties supergroup. Tori Amos smiles with her lips closed. Christian Slater slants an eyebrow. There's a smudge on Gillian Anderson's lips from where Lily once practiced kissing. Madonna stares down at her with blonde ambition, as if asking Lily what she's done with her life. Lily doesn't answer, instead turns to her old bed, tucked against the wall. On the pillow sits Christina, the doll her mum had made her one Christmas. Christina is a rag doll, with a dress made up of Lily's old baby clothes cut into strips and sewn together by hand. Mum had always said that nothing was wasted, that you can make patterns from anything.

Lily doesn't remember leaving Christina on her bed; in fact, she's sure that, after Mum's death, she'd placed the doll in the wardrobe so she didn't have to look at her. Looking at all those embellishing stitches her mum had sewn had felt like a needle passing through Lily's heart again and again, but with no thread to unbreak it.

Liliana must have left instructions to leave Christina on the bed. Liliana was as soft as the Medjool dates she loved at Christmas. Lily loved them too, although she never forgot the stone inside.

That bit of stone inside her aunt is what summoned Lily here. It's cruel, when she thinks of it, to ask her to return to this house, with its secrets written on walls and she's the one who has to strip back the wallpaper. If Liliana had wanted to expose the truth, she could have done so at any time. Why wait till now? Why leave it up to Lily? She could've just told Lily what happened to her mum. It's not fair to put her through this.

Anger swells inside Lily like the crescendo in a forty-part motet, voices within her crying out. She doesn't have to do this. The secrets can stay hidden as far as she's concerned. She won't unpack; she'll just leave.

There's still time to drive back down to London and be in her teeny flat by midnight. Or she'll find a Premier Inn on the way, if there's room. Anything but staying here.

Unless the snow stops her.

She moves over to the window, avoiding looking directly at the maze. Dusk has given way to winter dark. Victorian-style lamps cast haloes of golden light onto the grounds to the back of Endgame House.

The snow is already deep. It's up to the knees of the statue on the lawn. It's of a woman, naked but for a stone toga. As a kid, Lily had felt sorry for her and once dressed the sculpture, which she had called Mary, in a parka and woolly hat. Is it more or less dignified to be covered in snow when you're so exposed all the time? Doesn't matter. The snow's falling even as she thinks. She'd have to leave now. The roads round here get hazardous quickly. Aunt Veronica and Uncle Edward died in an accident on a night like this.

She turns to go, then stops. There's a pull in her, making her look back. She knows she shouldn't, but she can't stop herself directing her gaze at the maze. Her heart picks up speed, urging her to run, but she's stuck still, like Mary the statue. Maybe she too got frozen by looking back and now is forced to stay that way.

The maze is huge, at one time the biggest in the UK. It was built to be the same size as the house, before the East and West Wings were added. Its twists and false endings are picked out in snow. The tops of the tall hedges are white, the paths shown up in shadow. The way through the maze is not as clear as it used to be, though, the hedges not cut as sharp.

Her eyes, though, can still follow the route to the hidden section where Mum was found. And then she sees her, as she does every night in dreams that leave her sheets twisted: Mum slumped against the hedge, her neck all wrong. Her eyes staring straight ahead, unblinking.

Lily grabs the heavy curtain and pulls it across the window. Even so, she can still feel the maze behind the velvet. Her breath is sprinting, hard to catch. A panic attack is at her throat.

She tries to focus on sensations that root her in her body—that's what her therapist told her. She closes her eyes. Feels the worn rug under her feet. Her old desk against her legs.

As her breathing slows, she opens her eyes. Her desk is also as she left it. Her fountain pens and Biros are in a neat row, ready to be picked out of the lineup. Scissors sit next to a triangle ruler. Blue ink fingerprints still stain the wood. Two child-safe knitting needles hold the beginnings of a woolly scarf. A colored pencil bouquet sprays out of a Simpsons mug. She can still remember the last time she sat at the desk. She had written a goodbye note in Isabelle's favorite color—red. The pencil had needed sharpening and the shavings still lie curled up on the desk, like lipsticked wood lice. She takes the red pencil from the mug. All this time it's been waiting, not doing what it's meant for.

"I kept the note, you know," Isabelle says from the doorway.

Lily turns, heart pounding. The pencil drops onto the floorboards and rolls toward the baseboard. "You can still creep up on me, then," she says.

"You always were off in your own world." Isabelle walks in, briefcase in her hand, and closes the door, but not before checking there's no one in the hallway.

For a moment, Lily is ten again, and her mum is down the hall, singing to herself, and Isabelle is in the doorway with her book and a bag of apples as they're off to the attic to both pretend to be Jo from *Little Women*. They'd then do word searches and crosswords together, making their own language, composing silly songs. She has a strong urge to grab the cushions and blankets from the bed and climb up to the attic with Isabelle, make a fort as they used to with the boxes, the ottoman, and the dressmaker's doll. Under there, canopied by Grandma Violet's holey crochet, they'd dust off the years that had settled between them until their friendship shone again.

And then she remembers. She's leaving.

Isabelle moves over to the window, a few feet away, and peels back the curtain to gaze over the snow-smothered lawn. "You'll have to hurry if you're going. The road out will be impassable within an hour."

Lily takes a step back. "How did you—?"

"You're not exactly making yourself at home," Isabelle interrupts, nodding at Lily's still-full suitcase. "I get it, there are memories everywhere. I'd say you got in here, had a head-to-head with the past, and decided you couldn't be arsed to stay."

Isabelle is seeing her for the second time today.

Even more reason to go.

Lily moves off to get her luggage, but Isabelle stops her, placing a hand on her shoulder. She feels warmer under her touch. "Liliana said in her letter that if you came, she'd let you know more about your mum's death."

"I've lived without knowing so far."

"Are you really living, though? Or just playing at it like you used to play the Christmas Game—keeping close to the wall, hoping no one will see you mouth the answers? Do you live as you should, as your mum wanted you to?"

Lily knocks Isabelle's hand away. "Low blow, Izzy." She pushes past and grabs her suitcase.

Just as she opens the door, Isabelle calls out, "It wasn't just your mum who was murdered."

Lily stops. Her stomach clenches and she has to hold on to the wall. "Who? Liliana? You think they were both killed?"

"I know it. I just can't prove it. And I tried to get the police to investigate, but there was no evidence. They say it was simple. Liliana had an asthma attack and, as a result, her heart failed."

"Then why do you think someone killed her?"

"She was convinced someone would murder her before the game started; that's why she had me enshrine the rules and everything else in the will. Liliana may have been frustratingly cryptic, but she wasn't delusional. It's too much of a coincidence that she died when she did."

"And she never believed in those."

"'*Look for the pattern,*' she always said." It was true. Liliana believed that words repeated, whether in a book, a poem, or someone's drunken monologue after dinner, reveal everything if you look hard enough. She'd have made a great detective.

"So, who did it?" Lily said after a while.

Isabelle closes her eyes. "Wish I knew." She looks older suddenly, as if all the years between them have just caught up with her. "I'd have killed them myself already."

Lily believes her. If Isabelle would do that for Aunt Liliana, then the least Lily can do is help. "I'll stay, for a day or so anyway," she says. "If the clues lead nowhere, then I'll leave with the snow."

Isabelle's grin is huge. "Fair enough," she says. "Then I won't see you when I come back on the fifth?"

"I'll be long gone." Lily remembers then what Izzy said earlier. "Why did you come back? You said you had to leave."

"I had to talk to you first. Tell you what I was going to earlier before we were interrupted. I didn't want the others to know I was still here. I could do without Sara pestering me."

"I thought you said you were a rule follower?" Lily says.

"This *was* in the rules, the ones given just for me." Isabelle takes a folder out of her briefcase. "Liliana wanted me to give you this. Her Christmas present to you. And before you ask, no, it's not cheating."

Lily runs through the rules in her head. "Any papers in the house!" she says. "It's there in the rules." Opening the folder, she glances inside. It contains a blueprint of the house from before the East and West Wings were added.

"This gives me an advantage, I assume?" Lily asks.

Isabelle's eyes shine. "Bending rules so that they stretch but not break is part of their appeal. You should remember that when you play the game. Your cousins certainly will." Isabelle's face grows solemn again. "One last warning. I'm certain that whoever killed your aunt is after the house, so please be careful."

"I will. And I'll bend the rules till they creak but won't break them. Like corset bones."

They smile at each other, and Lily feels their old connection begin to knit together.

She feels a pang, a tug on the wool, as Isabelle moves toward the door. "Is that it, then? I'm left here on my own with, potentially, a murderer and I have to find them out?"

"You've got Ronnie and Tom." Isabelle points to the desk. "And Christina will keep you company. I thought she might remind you of the home you once had here. Good luck," she says, and walks slowly out as if she too wants to keep the connection between them for as long as possible. She stops in the hallway and leans against the door. "I meant it, you know. The note where you said goodbye. I still have it."

"I should have come to you before I left. Said it all in person," Lily replies. She swallows back the next bit: *maybe then you'd have replied.*

"When I was older, I realized you had to get out of here and not come back," Isabelle says.

"But you didn't at the time."

Isabelle stares down at the floor, but even from across the room, Lily can see the flash of pain crease her forehead. Isabelle then shrugs, a half smile forming. "We were kids," she says, as if that covers those years like snowfall on a stone path.

Lily knows, though, that unsaid hurt also has object permanence. Just because you can't see it, doesn't mean it goes away. The unuttered has been growing inside her ever since Mum died, and even more so now. She'd love to be honest with Isabelle, tell her everything.

"You know what you said about me having an heir?" Lily says.

Isabelle nods.

"If I have one, in the future, they're not eligible to inherit, right? Because of what I signed?"

"Technically, according to Liliana's will, your heir could inherit. Although you'd have had to be pregnant when you signed the papers. If a child was already conceived, then your aunt's old will would stand." Isabelle laughs. "She always did like a technicality."

Lily laughs too, shakes her head as if her being pregnant is the least likely thing in the world. Her hand, though, floats to her corseted belly and strokes back and forth. She tries to stop herself, but Isabelle has already seen.

"Tell me you're not," Isabelle says. She's no longer smiling. "Because that could make things very difficult. Dangerous, even." Without the light in her eyes, that sounds almost like a threat.

"I'm not," Lily replies.

Isabelle nods as if reassured. But she's still staring at Lily's tummy. "You can trust me, you know?"

There's nothing Lily wants more than to trust her. She imagines what it would be like to be open with her. With anyone. She'd be vulnerable, squishy. A date without a stone.

"Can you imagine if I was?" Lily says, keeping her voice light. "What would I know about being a parent? I'd be terrible. I'd have no idea how to be a mother."

Isabelle laughs but she's still not smiling. The connection between them lies frayed on the floor. "Be careful anyway," she says. "If anyone in this house thinks you're a threat..." She leaves the sentence without casting off, then walks out of the room, not once looking back.

Lily waits till she can hear Isabelle going downstairs before closing the door, lifting off her dress, and scrabbling with the hooks on the front of her corset. When the last hook is released, and the laces loosened, she breathes out. She goes over to her bed and lies down next to Christina. Her hand goes again to her rounded belly, and the fetus fluttering inside.

Chapter Seven

Lily's in the Endgame maze. The walls are made of frozen blood. Above, the sky is a blue ink smudge, the clouds painted on, like the sheep-shaped ones of a child's picture. As she walks through the cold corridors, bare feet burning on the snow, she hears singing. *"In the bleak midwinter, long ago."* The voice shivers with vibrato. It has sadness stitched into it. Mum's voice.

Following the singing like a skein of silk, she runs through the maze until she reaches the center. Mum is encased in one of the walls of the hidden section. Trapped in ice, her bloody hands press against it like she's on the other side of a mirror. Her singing pinches into screams.

Lily hammers at the walls, fingers pressed to her mum's. Mum's mouth opens and closes, her eyes urgent. She's trying to tell Lily something, but her words condense and can't get through. Lily scrapes her fingernails into the ice, but she can't tear her way in. She claws so hard that her nails shatter, revealing previously unseen skin. For one moment, Mum smiles, then freezes in place. She slumps to the ground like her strings have been cut. Her head is at that wrong angle. Her eyes are open, but they no longer see Lily, or anything else.

❄

Lily lurches out of sleep, hands grabbing the duvet. Her heart is still racing round that maze, hoping for a different ending. She checks her fingernails. They're still here.

The dinner gong moans throughout the house. Lily shivers, trying to blink away the dream. It holds on, not letting her go. She can still feel the ice on her skin, smell blood, hear her mother's screams. Dreams, now that she's pregnant, are as hard to escape as corsets.

Swinging her legs over the side of the bed, Lily stands up. The room shifts. Her vision is foggy. Bile rises up her throat. She shouldn't have had a big meal before she lay down. She must have been asleep for nearly two hours.

The gong goes again.

Doors open on the floor below. Voices call out. Feet clomp down the staircase while the strident voice of Mrs. Castle climbs up the house. Never has the word "cocktails" carried such threat.

Lily opens her suitcase and tips out the clothes till she finds her dark blue dress. She then scrabbles with the corset hooks, yanks the laces tighter, and fights the dress over her head. That'll have to do.

A few minutes later, Lily joins the rest of the house guests at the bottom of the stairs in the grand reception hall. Speakers high on the walls play carols.

"Got you out of bed, did we?" Sara says, pointing at Lily's face. A smirk runs under her lips like a rat beneath a red carpet.

"Just a nap," Lily replies. "It was a long drive."

Gray shuffles over to her, and subtly slides a small round mirror into her hand. He then touches his own cheek without meeting her eyes.

Lily thanks him and turns away. She glances down at the compact. Her eye shadow has slumped from her lids to join the already dark pools under her eyes. There's a red mark on her right cheek where the lace of the pillow slip embossed her cheek. She hadn't looked closely at it before, assuming it was the same swooping pattern as when she was growing up. It's the maze. It's everywhere—maybe it was the insignia of the hotel. The labyrinth etched on her psyche is now scored on her face.

"Here," Rachel says, coming over to hand Lily a baby wipe. "I always carry these with me now."

Lily thanks her, takes the wipe, and swipes it over her face. It's refreshing, even if it takes up the rest of her makeup and leaves her feeling more exposed. "How is Beatrice?" she asks, of Rachel and Holly's baby.

"About time someone asked," Rachel says.

Holly joins them, drink in hand. "She's brilliant. This is the first time we've left her for more than an afternoon. My mum's looking after her. Can't believe we've got to be without her for nearly two weeks. That's ages in baby time. Feels like I've left half my heart at home."

"You could always go back early if you miss her that much," Sara says, voice as arched as her eyebrow. "I'm sure she means more to you than a house."

Rachel snaps her head round to look at Sara. "We're doing this *for* her."

Holly's voice is quiet as she says, "I grew up in a one-bed flat in a tower block. I'd love Beatrice to be able to run around the grounds."

"But what about our Samuel?" Philippa says. "Or any other children we have? Do they not deserve to grow up here, too?"

"Let's not get into a fight so early in the evening, eh, everyone?" Ronnie says from behind a table where he's scooping up and handing out drinks from a punch bowl. "Drama before nine is just soap opera."

Mrs. Castle comes forward with a tray. "White Lady, Miss Lily?" she asks, offering her a coupe of foamy drink.

"Bit insensitive, don't you think, Mrs. Castle?" Tom says as he comes down the stairs, eyes twinkling. "Serving a cocktail with the same name as the Endgame ghost."

"What ghost?" Holly asks, looking behind her as if a specter is peeking over her shoulder.

"Ghosts aren't real," Ronnie says. "And even if they are, they definitely don't live here."

Lily agrees. She'd know if they did. She'd feel Mum's presence.

"Maybe you've never seen one, but I have," Philippa says. "Right here in this house when we looked round last month. Came out of the wall as if it was a door." She shudders.

"Sure," Sara says, the saracasm strong. "Course it did."

"You've got no reason to doubt her, Sara," Tom says.

"I know for a fact there are no ghosts at Endgame," Sara says, jabbing a finger at him on the word "fact." "Mum enlisted me to stand in for a sick waiter at one of those ghost-hunting parties in the hotel a few years ago, trying to find cold spots and orbs and other nonsense. Scariest thing they found was a hotel guest sleepwalking in her nightie."

"So, that was the White Lady, then," Ronnie says. "Glad we cleared that up. Now, can I interest you in my special concoction?" He points proudly to the crystal bowl of dark red liquid in which orange skin bobs and cinnamon sticks jostle with falling star anise.

"What's in it?" Lily asks.

"The only thing that isn't is booze," Ronnie says. "I've given up."

"How many times have we heard that before?" Philippa says, crossing her arms.

"At least twenty," Ronnie says with a grin. "But I mean it. One too many mornings waking up on the front lawn, waving at Mrs. Rogers as she tuts off to work."

"Samuel woke up in the middle of the night last week when Ronnie got back from the office party. Saw his dad stumbling out of the Uber singing 'The Twelve Days of Christmas,'" she says.

"I was serenading you," Ronnie replies. He's still smiling. Just.

Phillipa doesn't look at him, though, just turns to Lily. "Then he fell flat on his face and knocked himself out. Blood all over. Samuel screamed the place down. 'Daddy's dead!' he said."

Pain crashes onto Ronnie's face. He closes his eyes. "So, yeah. As I said. I mean it this time."

Lily touched his arm. "Then I'll join you," she says, reaching for a warm glass. She tastes it, determined to make a face that says she likes it, even if it turns her stomach. The smell of the spices hits her nose first, then she tastes honeyed plums. "It's delicious," she says, and means it. "Cheers." She raises her glass, and everyone lifts theirs in return, some reluctantly, some with genuine good will, others with an enthusiasm that's more to do with the promise of more alcohol.

All of her family take a sip of drink. Because that's what they are, she realizes: bar the little cousins left at home, these are the remaining members of her family. All she has left. Liliana was her mother figure when Mum died, and now she's gone, too. Lily feels another wave of grief. Growing up is one long game of Guess Who?—one by one, the family is laid down until there's only one left.

Lily already feels full by the time she's sat down in the dining room. The afternoon tea still sits squeezed somewhere in the middle of her stomach. Only five courses to get through.

She looks round the dining room. Hardly anything has changed in here. The old tapestry drapes have been replaced by green velvet curtains, but otherwise, everything's the same. Mirrored wall sconces create an infinite echo of candles. Wooden floors dip in the middle of the room. Ivy, carved into the dark wall panels, wraps the room in a choke hold.

Maybe that's what's stopping everyone's tongues as Mrs. Castle ladles out the tomato and tarragon soup. She doesn't spill a drop or a word as she moves around the table. The bread rolls steam as they're split open, but that's all that's released. Maybe everyone's heeding Ronnie and waiting till nine o'clock for the real talk to start, but Lily isn't going to hang around for that. Bitterness is already mulling in the room, resentment spiking the air like poison in a punch bowl.

When Mrs. Castle has finished serving everyone, she stands in the doorway. "Enjoy your soup," she says. "You've got fifteen minutes until the main course."

Soup spoons clink on china. Salt is sprinkled, pepper is grounded.

As Lily shakes out her napkin, she has the childlike urge to tuck it into her collar. It feels weird coming in here. She always had to avoid this room when she was little as it was used as a meeting room by the conference guests. She had to be as invisible as a black star. Sometimes, though, she used to sit in the kitchen next door and listen to laughter, swearing, and boring training videos winnow through the sides of the serving hatch while she and her mum made them lunch.

Lily can recall it so clearly it's like she's still sitting in the past, swabbing slices of bread with margarine, right up to the edges, then creating a bread Jenga tower. Mum would then grab a slice, place the cheese, ham, or dollop of egg mayo on top, and slam on another piece of bread. One morning, the pile of bread had teetered too far and fallen on the floor. Mum had been quick but TC, Isabelle's cat who used to come and play when she visited, had been quicker, walking across the slices like they were a butter-slick Giant's Causeway. He'd then used one as a cushion while licking his paws. Liliana had come in then and laughed so much she'd cried.

Tom gently prods her shoulder. "Where have you gone?"

She physically shakes off the past as if she were a dog getting out of the sea. Good memories tide you over, but they also tug you under. "I got caught up in memories." She takes a spoonful of soup. It's rich, complex, and acidic. Like Aunt Liliana herself.

Tom nods. "Same here. I keep doing all the tricks I teach my clients—mindfulness and stuff—and then I walk into a room here and all I can see is Mum and Dad. Must be so hard for you, you lived here far longer. Must be like opening a time capsule."

Lily nods. She can't reply without crying, so doesn't.

Tom looks at her, then places his hands on the table. "Let's change the subject, but know that you can come and talk to me about it anytime. We're here for a while, might as well make use of the time."

"You're on holiday," Lily replies. "You shouldn't have to counsel me."

"It'd help me to chat. This is weird for me, too. Other than Sara and Gray, we're the only ones not coupled up, so we'll be twiddling our thumbs otherwise. And it's not as if Sara will let her brother out of her sight."

Tom looks down the table to where Sara is fussing a napkin over Gray's lap. He sees Lily watching and his cheeks turn mullet red. Poor bloke.

"We're a team, then. Deal?" Tom extends his hand.

Lily shakes his hand and nods. "Deal. And now to change the subject. What have you done with that Christmas tree you brought?"

Tom laughs. "When I saw that downstairs has been dressed like the Bloomingdale's festive section, I took it up to my room. It's now standing in the corner, leaning to one side and feeling sorry for itself. Looks like me as a teen at an indie disco. I'll string some lights on it later, boost its confidence."

"Even trees get the patented Tom Self-Esteem Treatment," Lily says, remembering how he always made her feel good about herself.

"What can I say?" Tom says, opening his hands. "I can't bear to see them pine."

"Oh, mate," Lily says, shaking her head.

"Some things have got to stay the same," he says. His smile fades, and he looks away. Lily is about to ask what he means when Ronnie taps his spoon on his water glass.

"I propose a toast," he says, standing up. "We have much to be thankful for. A warm house, an abundance of food and drink, and each other. We owe all this to Aunt Liliana, so let's raise our glasses to her memory."

Crystal glasses are raised, reflecting a constellation of flames. Sara's glass remains on the table.

"To Liliana!" Ronnie calls out. Lily and most of the others echo him, some louder or more heartfelt than others. Gray says "Mum" and closes his eyes.

"Not joining in the toast to your mum, Sara?" Tom asks.

"Ignore her," Lily whispers to him. "No point antagonizing her."

"Why should I share a toast when she didn't share with me that the house has a secret room?" Sara asks.

"Presumably she didn't tell Gray either," Tom says, "and he hasn't got a problem with it."

Gray shrugs very slightly. He has tomato soup all round his mouth.

"Did any of you know?" Sara asks, glaring around the table. She stops when she gets to Lily and jabs a finger toward her. "You *lived* here. You must know where it is."

Lily shakes her head. "Only till I was twelve, and I would've loved to find a secret room. I never did, though."

"Sure," Sara says, saracasm dripping like melting ice. "And I suppose you don't know any of the other cryptic shit Mum said in her rules and that letter to us."

"I want to know the secrets of this house as much as you," Lily says.

"What I want to know," Philippa says, "is how Isabelle will have any knowledge of us looking for clues. Have they got CCTV in the house as well as round the perimeter? In our rooms, maybe? 'Cause that's an invasion of privacy."

Holly glances toward the ceiling. "I haven't seen any cameras," she says.

"And you should know," Philippa says.

Rachel twists round to look at Philippa. "What do you mean by that?"

"We all know your wife is well aware of cameras pointing at her." Philippa gives a smile as she scrapes the last spoonful of soup from her bowl.

"There's no need to bring that up," Tom says.

"It's OK," Holly says, quietly.

"It fucking isn't, baby," Rachel says, standing up and pulling Holly up with her. "She has absolutely no right to be so smug." She points her butter knife toward Philippa. "My wife has absolutely nothing to be ashamed of. You wish you looked that good on screen."

Philippa gets to her feet, too. Ronnie tugs at her arm, but she shrugs him off. Their shouting rises up to the cornices of the room.

"Stop it!" Gray shouts, slamming his hands on the table.

Everyone turns to look at him, mouths open. No one has heard him shout before. Sara looks the most stunned of all.

Gray points to Mrs. Castle standing in the doorway with a platter of meat. "Time for the main course."

"I thought I'd be too full for karaoke," Tom says, flicking through the list of songs. "But there's something about seeing other people sing that makes me want to join in." They're in the games room, tucked away under the stairs. Disco lights flash to the beat of "I Wish It Could Be Christmas Everyday." Ronnie is trying to get Philippa to sing along with him, but instead she walks away and sits in one of the armchairs by the chess table. Ronnie shrugs and sings louder.

Lily watches as he closes his eyes, his grin huge as he croaks out the chorus. Lily used to love singing that much. Maybe she still would if she let herself. She shuts down the thought, and a burgeoning sneeze at the same time. The insides of her ears itch as if she's allergic to off-key singing.

"Come and do a duet with me. I can tell you're dying to."

"I can't," Lily replies.

"Go on. I know you've got a thing about singing. Maybe if you had a drink to loosen you up?" Tom says.

"I don't fancy it tonight," she replies. She hears his unbelieving laugh and resolves never again to coax someone to drink.

"If you're off the booze in solidarity with Ronnie, he won't notice. He's in the karaoke zone."

Lily looks back to Ronnie and his beatific smile. She feels a pang of sadness at not being able to access that place. It seems blissful.

"Come on, it'll be good for you." Tom does his pleading look. "We'll do 'Fairytale of New York.' It'll be great."

Lily folds her arms. "Even if I wanted to sing, I would *never* do that one. And please don't you sing it either."

Tom frowns. Then remembers the lyrics. "Oh," he says. "Sorry, I didn't think." He may be flushing or it might be the lights. "Then how about 'Baby, It's Cold Outside'?"

She's about to explain to him why that also might not be a good idea when she feels a wave of nausea. The room is suddenly too hot, pressing in on her. No windows to open for snow-fresh air. The sounds make it worse—karaoke clashing with the pinball machine, pool balls dispensed, darts hitting the board with a dull thud. Lily stands, steadies herself. Tom's mouth is moving but she can't pick out the words. She's got to get out. She's going to be sick.

Moving toward the door, her vision spins like the red spotlights spattering the floor. Just as she heads toward the library, Lily stumbles. She reaches out but there's nothing to hold on to. Her hand goes to her tummy as the floor hurtles up to hit her.

And then everything goes dark.

Chapter Eight

"I saw her eyelids move," Tom is saying, his voice close to Lily's ear. "I think she's coming round."

"Thank God," Philippa says. She sounds genuine, emotion running through her voice.

Lily's head is pounding. She reaches her hand up to her forehead. Her hand hurts, too. She must have landed on it. She looks around. They must have carried her into the library, laid her on the chaise longue. The vaulted ceiling recedes above her. Books seem to be swaying in their shelves. Lily tries to sit up.

"Don't move yet," Tom says. "You might be hurt."

Lily feels plunged into ice. The baby. What if she's hurt her in the fall? And then her heart hurts as much as her head. This is the first time she's called her a baby. Up to this minute, Lily's tried to keep the terms medical—implantation, zygote, fetus—and used nonmedical ones—like blob—to stop getting too attached. Because what if she *doesn't* attach? What if she goes? What if she's going right now?

"Shall we call an ambulance?" Philippa asks.

Tom's hand goes to his pocket and feels around. Then he says, "Shit, I forgot she took our phones."

"What are we supposed to do in an emergency?" Philippa asks.

An emergency. Lily feels a wave of panic as she thinks of having to go into a hospital. "I have to go to the loo," she says.

"Steady," Tom says, reaching for her hand.

Lily grabs on to him, but still her head reels as he pulls her up. She takes a deep breath, then stands.

"I'll go with you," Philippa says, holding out her arm. Lily takes it, and together they slowly leave the library.

Lily doesn't pray; she's not sure there's anyone to pray to. But she talks to her baby in her head, and she can't believe she's calling it that, saying, "Stay with me, little one." What can she call her now? Lily thinks of the first scan, at twelve weeks. Of hearing the super-quick *bow-wow-wow* of the heartbeat. Of seeing, for the first time, the butter-bean-shaped lodger in her womb. Lily will, for now, call her Bean.

They go through the fire door into the West Wing, and turn left into the women's toilet. Philippa helps her into a cubicle, then steps away.

Locking the door, Lily holds on to the wall. The tiles are cold under her palm as she lifts her midnight-blue skirt and sits down on the toilet. She knows she'd look ridiculous if anyone saw her. Like a gothic loo roll holder.

But she doesn't care. Crumpling her skirt, she pulls down her knickers. It's the move so many pregnant people know. The check for blood, for clots. Either longing for blood or fearing its arrival. Either way, blood holds power over those with wombs.

But, right now, there's no blood. No cramps.

Lily breathes out, then realizes she can breathe more deeply than usual. Looking over her shoulder, she sees her corset cord coiling down next to the toilet like a black ribbon snake. Someone must have loosened it while she was unconscious.

"Are you all right in there, Lily?" Philippa asks. Sounds like she's by the door. "Do you want me to come in?"

"I'm fine," Lily replies. "I'll be out in a minute. You can wait outside if you like."

She waits until Philippa leaves, then flushes the empty toilet and leaves the cubicle. As she turns on the taps, she looks in the mirror. A bump is growing just over her left eyebrow. Lower down, the baby bump is also just visible through the loosened corset. She hopes neither Tom nor Philippa noticed.

When Lily feels ready to move, Philippa insists on taking her into the kitchen for a restorative cup of Yorkshire Tea.

Philippa fusses about, putting on the kettle, finding biscuits. Mrs. Castle sits at the table, watching everything through narrowed eyes.

"Don't mind me," Mrs. Castle says, the very model of an affronted woman. "Just taking a break before I feed you all again. Bet that lot will want a midnight feast." She looks at Lily, and for one moment Lily thinks she sees worry in Mrs. Castle's eyes. And then the moment passes and Mrs. Castle is glaring at the rind of some Stilton.

"Before we go," Philippa says to Mrs. Castle, "if there's an emergency, have you got access to a phone so we could call an ambulance?"

"What's the emergency?" Mrs. Castle asks. Her palms slam on the table as if reassuringly poised to act.

"Only hypothetical," Lily says.

"Lily had a fall," Philippa says.

Mrs. Castle half rises. "Are you hurt?"

Lily says, "I just fainted. I'm fine."

Mrs. Castle's eyebrows arch. "Liliana told me that you keep too much to yourself. If you're hurt, tell me."

"Honestly," Lily replies. "You don't have to worry about me."

Mrs. Castle humphs.

"But what if there *is* something urgent?" Philippa asks. "What do we do?"

"There's a house phone in my room," Mrs. Castle says. "All the others were taken out of the old hotel rooms to prevent you lot from trying to cheat."

"You don't have a mobile either?" Lily asks.

"Isabelle even took mine," Mrs. Castle says. "In case one of you was a thieving little so-and-so and tried to use it."

"When do we get them back?" Philippa asks. Her thumbs tap on an invisible phone as if they don't know what to do without one.

Lily is surprised how little she misses having her mobile at hand, or the iPad she normally takes everywhere. She definitely doesn't miss the app where she's supposed to log every time she feels Bean move. You're supposed to stay as calm as possible and somehow carry on with your life while counting swishes and, later on, kicks. What's too few, what's too many? As if Lily doesn't have enough to worry about.

Mrs. Castle folds her arms. "The will stipulates that they're kept in the safe at Stirling Lawyers' office till the game is over. Now, if you'll excuse me," Mrs. Castle says, closing her eyes. "I intend to nap for forty minutes. You should go to bed, too, Miss Lily."

Grateful for the out, Lily nods and gets up to leave. Philippa comes with her, and they climb the stairs slowly, with Philippa's arm under Lily's. When they get to Lily's door, she gives Philippa a quick hug. "Thanks," she says. Philippa looks as if she wants to say something else, but Lily is already closing the door.

Going to bed on Christmas Eve used to be a magical ritual. With all the conference goers gone for the holidays, Endgame House was all hers. After dinner, Lily would drink hot chocolate with marshmallows while she wrote a note for Santa. She'd then hang her stocking on the living room mantelpiece and place the letter on the black tiles of the hearth below. Next to the note went a carrot for Rudolph, and for Santa himself, a mince pie made earlier in the day while carols played. Mum also poured Santa a tankard of Baileys, which she was certain was his favorite, no matter what anyone else said.

Upstairs, Lily would find a new pair of pajamas and a book on her pillow. Tucked up by Mum, who always sang the same song, Lily then went to sleep listening for sleigh bells. Even when Lily no longer believed in Santa, she still hung up her stocking, and on to the magic.

Until that last Christmas. Finding your mum dead on Boxing Day will have that effect. On that New Year's Eve, she'd thrown her new pajamas into the fire and swore she'd never read *The Subtle Knife*, the book she'd been delighted to receive only seven days before. And she hasn't. It still lies at the end of her bookcase, next to Jacqueline Wilson's *Girls in Love*.

This Christmas Eve, she's in the same room, but instead of sleigh bells, she's listening to the wind outside and, from two floors below, someone shrieking along to "Last Christmas." George Michael advises keeping one's heart safe this Christmas. And Lily always listens to George Michael. His mother had died the same year as hers, and she'd wished that she could feel and express the same eloquent grief as him. Maybe losing someone to cancer is different to when they take their own life. Maybe. Lily can still taste the shame she felt at not being enough for Mum.

Only, someone else may have taken her mum's life. Taken her from Lily.

Lily cracks open the front of her corset, lets the carapace fall to the floor, and moves over to her bookcase. *Smash Hits* stickers still cling to the shelves. She takes *The Subtle Knife* down and carries it over to the bed.

Placing Christina on her lap, she snuggles into the pillows and opens the book. On the inside cover is Mum's message in her signature green ink.

To my darling daughter,

May we never be parted. And if we are ever worlds away, let's tear down their walls till we're together again. I love you.

Mum
Xxxxx

Reading that message on the night she'd received the book had made Lily feel hot-chocolate warm. Reading it a few nights later, she'd thrown it across the room, scalded by the hypocrisy. Tonight, she reads a message from a woman not far off the age Lily is now, who pledges to always be there for her daughter.

Lily curls up, lying like a comma on the bed. When the sobs stop, she takes a deep breath. She's older now; she can do something. Time to find out who wrenched her mother from this world.

She turns over to try to get herself comfortable, stuffing a cushion under her burgeoning bump and propping another behind to keep her lying on the left. Someone on a parenting forum said that switching to the right could result in a lack of oxygen to the fetus, and woe betide you if you went onto your tummy, which is how Lily used to sleep. Same as her mum. Most of these rules didn't exist when Mariana was pregnant with her. She could drink a little, smoke slightly more, eat all the cheese, although even the thought of it makes Lily feel sick. At least Lily's morning, afternoon, all-day, and all-night sickness is subsiding, although it could come back, like a monster at the end of a horror movie.

There's *so* much to worry about as a pregnant person. So many things to take, to not take. What if she can't remember it all? What if her body takes over and turns her onto her tummy by habit? What if she wakes in the morning to find she's lost Bean after all?

Just then, she hears a tap at the window. That'll be the tree outside, knocking on the glass. Mum used to say that it was the tree telling her to go to sleep. It'd be reassuring to see the tree, see the branch that links her to her past. She shifts until she's sitting up and reaches to pull back the curtain. But, when the window is revealed, no spindly twig fingers tap their knuckles on the glass. Then she remembers that the tree was cut down just after Mum died.

The tapping comes again, but this time from inside the room. As if it's in the walls, scratching to come out. And now there are whispers. Sibilant shushes. Like wind through reeds. And then nothing. The clock ticktocks, scoring time into silence.

She wonders then if she had been dozing, or in that state of half in, half out of sleep, and imagined it all.

And then she hears her name. "Lily."

The voice is too faint, too feathery to recognize. But it feels familiar. It makes her bones ache and yearn to be held.

"Lily, I am here for you," the voice says.

She doesn't think it's her mum's voice. And it couldn't be. She doesn't believe in ghosts, of course she doesn't.

"Lily," the voice says again.

The ice-cold certainty that there is no such thing as ghosts is based on the fact that she has never felt her mum's presence, or heard her talk. And she still hasn't. She can't have.

And yet.

"Lily." The voice again.

Her certainty is in danger of melting.

She tries to reply but can't. Her throat's frozen. For a moment, she thinks that she can't move either, and that maybe this is sleep paralysis. But then her hand moves at her command.

Removing the covers, she gets out of bed, feeling the winter air on her skin as she goes over to the wall that she shares with Mum's room. Lily hopes the cold will wake her up, let her speak, but her mouth still feels as dry as years-old fruit cake.

She places her hands on the wall, feeling the ridges on the wallpaper. She waits for the voice to say something again.

"Lily, do not trust them," the voice says. The sound comes from beyond the wall. It's as if someone is tickling the wall as her mum used to tickle her back to help Lily go to sleep.

Lily swallows, trying to unstick her voice. "Mum?" she's able to say at last.

The clock ticks on, but the voice has stopped. The scratching has subsided, leaving only the silence of the night.

Chapter Nine

December 25th
Christmas Day—The First Day of Christmas

"Happy Christmas!" Tom says as Lily walks down the stairs. He's wearing his kilt, a festive red and gray tartan in honor of his mum's clan. His legs are surprisingly tanned given he spends most of his days in his office, nodding while his clients tell him their problems. "How are you feeling?" he asks, gesturing to the small bump on her head.

Her hand goes up to it. "Bit tender, but otherwise OK," she says.

"Excellent," Tom says. "May I say, that's another amazing dress."

Lily looks down at the dress she'd made for today. It's in a deep red velvet, with many hours' worth of hand-embroidered cocoa truffles scattered on the knee-length skirt. A haute couture chocolate box of a frock.

"You look pale," Gray says to Lily. He's leaning against the wall by the dining room door. "Didn't you sleep well?"

"Why, did you hear something?" Lily asks, suddenly worried that he'd overheard her calling out for Mum in the middle of the night. She'd woken herself up several times, and Endgame House's walls are thin.

"Should he have?" Sara asks, appearing from the living room. She's wearing another designer number. How does she afford all these clothes?

Lily gets sample sizes from friends sometimes, and adds panels to fit. But Sara's are made to measure, not usually something you can afford on a teacher's wage.

"I was restless in the night," Lily says. "Went for a wander. I didn't mean to disturb anyone." She smiles, hoping that will do. Sara, though, doesn't seem appeased.

The dining room door, hidden within the wood paneling, opens into the hall. "Are you coming in then or not?" Mrs. Castle asks, stepping out. She has a sprig of holly tucked into her hair but not even that gives her any hint of merriness. A less festive bearer would be hard to find.

Lily goes in, glad of any distraction to get her away from Sara. What happened in the night lies heavy on her, and leaves her feeling shivery, like fallen snow.

The dining room looks different by day. The dark curtains have been tied back and the walled kitchen garden is visible through the stained-glass windows. Morning sun reflects off the deep snow, making it look ultrabright outside. The table is different, too. There are small red Christmas stockings at each place setting, names sewn onto the white velvet trims. Platters of croissants, pains au chocolat, and other pastries have been placed on a runner spanning the table's length. Lily's tummy rumbles. Now that she's pregnant, she's always full and always hungry.

"When do we get the first clue, Mrs. Castle?" Philippa asks once they've all sat down at the breakfast table.

"No clues about the clues," Mrs. Castle replies. "Those are the rules I was given."

"You must be able to help us a little bit?" Philippa tries a Princess Diana–type plea, looking up through her heavy fringe. Rather than shy doe-eyed, she looks cross-eyed.

Mrs. Castle stares at Philippa, eyes stewed in something nearing enmity. Without breaking her gaze, she tips the teapot. Philippa's cup fills right to the brim. The steeped meniscus shivers. Philippa won't be able to pick up the cup without spillage. Tea has never been served with more aggression.

"Things happen in their own time, love," Ronnie says.

Philippa makes a sound somewhere between a snort and a whinny. "That's what you told me when you set up the restaurant."

"Some things, and people, never have their time," Ronnie replies, quietly.

Lily wishes she was sitting next to Ronnie rather than opposite him. She'd have given his arm a squeeze, a lean-in to the shoulder. She should speak up, she knows. As it is, she just gives him a smile that she hopes says, "I'm on your side."

She then points to her stocking and says, "It's traditional to open stockings before breakfast, right?" Anything to distract from another argument. And even her lame detection skills can work out what they might find inside.

"I never saw you as traditional," Sara says, smirking. "The opposite, if anything."

"What does that mean?" Holly asks, quickly.

"Just that Lily's lifestyle can't be described as conventional."

"That's enough, Sara," Tom says. His voice is cracknel brittle. He always did stand up for her. Lily wishes he didn't have to.

"Lily's right," Rachel says. "Time to open our stockings. Get this game started, eh?"

No one speaks as they each pull out a piece of coal from the stockings.

"Looks like we've all been bad," Gray says, quietly.

Sara, however, is already rummaging again in her stocking. There's a look of triumph to accompany her smug "Ah!" as she pulls out a folded piece of paper. Her hands are covered in coal dust as she opens the document. She frowns, mouthing the words as she reads them in her head.

Lily feels for her copy, and reads it, too. She can hear everyone else doing the same. There's a sense of occasion, a certain solemnness. As if everyone is feeling the impact of Liliana's words.

"Can I read it out loud?" Gray asks. He's holding the clue reverently, as if handling the communion goblet at mass.

Everyone looks at him. Mouths fall. Gray speaking up is as much of a surprise as a party popper at a funeral and, by the look on Sara's face, just as welcome.

"I think your mum would have liked that," Tom says, gently.

Gray takes a breath. His hand trembles but his voice is steady as he reads, slowly, as if drinking in the words.

> *Elephants are said to remember, I'm*
> *The same, I never forget. Whether it's*
> *Chamber music, aria moans, mor n rise,*
> *Or sun set, in my memory it sits.*
> *When people hurt those that I love, the sting*
> *Stays beneath the skin. This Christmas I will*
> *Draw it out, and, in the endgame, you'll sing*
> *A song of strangled death and pilfered bills...*
> *But enough of this, for now. The first key*
> *Is easy. It lies deep in the forest,*
> *Surrounded by bleak briars and twisting trees,*
> *Where animals are stiff and laid to rest,*
> *Where bones are picked and locked in cloth-lined wood*
> *And evidence remains of trunked falsehood.*

Silence for a moment. Lily only just stops herself from sobbing.

"This is a clue?" Holly asks. Her eyes are wide, looking at Rachel for backup. Her wife, though, has already gotten out a pen from her bag and is circling words.

"What are we supposed to do with this?" Philippa says to Ronnie. Ronnie smiles. "It's one of Aunt Lil's sonnets," he says. "She used to write her clues as poems. Aunt Mariana, Lily's mum, would have music clues, and Grandma Violet could make a code out of anything."

"She was at Bletchley Park," Gray says. "She was a genius, and so were her daughters."

Ronnie laughs. "Are you saying my dad was the only child of Violet who wasn't a bona fide brainiac? Well, you're probably right."

Holly points to one part of the sonnet. "We passed through a forest on the w—"

Rachel places a finger over Holly's mouth, stopping the next words.

"Aren't we all going to work together?" Holly asks.

Rachel looks at her with such love it makes Lily's heart hurt. "I doubt that's what anyone wants," she replies.

Sara doesn't say anything. She just scrapes her chair back and strides out of the room. Lily can hear her pulling on her coat and wellies. The front door opens and then slams shut.

Ronnie grins. "Looks like Sara's already solved it. Maybe the genius gene passed down to her."

Rachel taps Holly on the shoulder. "I've got it, too," she whispers, tugging at Holly's arm. Rachel whispers in Holly's ear as they hurry to the door.

"Really?" Holly says, shuddering. "Urgh."

Rachel shushes her, and they both leave.

Philippa gets up, looking worried. "Shouldn't we go, too?"

"Have you solved the clue already?" Ronnie asks. His raised eyebrows suggest it's unlikely.

"Don't need to if they've already got it. We just follow them."

"Isn't that cheating?" Ronnie asks.

"I don't remember anything in the rules that says we can't piggyback on people solving things," Philippa says. "And Sara has an advantage— her mum set the clues. Only fair that she helps us." She bustles to the front door, calling back. "Are you coming or not?"

Ronnie shrugs at Lily, then follows Philippa out of the room.

"Aren't you going, too, Gray?" Tom asks, his voice gentle.

Gray shakes his head. He's stroking the paper on which the clue has been printed.

Lily also looks down at the words, reads them again, slowly. Excitement and anticipation course through her. She'd forgotten how much she loved the clues, and solving them. Only this time, she knows there's a code beneath the code. She mouths the words, feels the poetry in her mouth. There's a bittersweet taste to the lines, a hardness too, like blackened raisins in a burned cake.

Liliana isn't being subtle in this first clue. It deals with death and remembrance. It suggests that the truth will come out by the end of this festive time, like a splinter working its way out of skin. Funny how no one mentions that side of the sonnet. Either they're too busy trying to work out where the key is, or they don't want to mention the accusations that spike the sonnet. Lily's hand goes to her throat. Does the "strangled death" refer to Mum? Is that how she really died? Maybe the "evidence" for it lies with the key.

Lily scans through the poem after its turning point one more time, and a sudden image comes in her mind.

"Lily!" Tom says, clapping his hands in front of her face.

Lily focuses on him.

"You were off somewhere again," Tom says, his brow creasing with concern.

"Sorry," Lily replies. "Got lost in the poem."

"I was asking if we should follow them, too? I get terrible FOMO— what if they find the key and we're not there?"

"Don't worry," Lily says. "You won't miss out. I know where they're going. And they're wrong."

Chapter Ten

"Can you see them?" Lily calls out to Tom from the staircase.

Tom is already at the end of the landing on the floor above, looking out over the woods and drive. "Not yet," he says.

She walks toward him, puffing slightly. She's glad she wore her red sneakers, weird as they look with her dress. Her feet hurt enough as it is without walking around the house in heels.

"You sure they're wrong? The clue said the key was in the forest," Tom continues.

"And that's why it isn't," Lily says, reaching for her breath. "Liliana would never be that straightforward." She swallows a burp. Heartburn is climbing her esophagus much more quickly than she ascended the stairs. She should have nabbed a croissant to line her stomach.

"There! I saw a flash of Sara's red coat," Tom says as she joins him in front of the window. "And again! She never moved that quickly when we used to play rounders. There she is, in the clearing." He pauses, scanning the woods for the rest of them. "And there's Ronnie!"

"Do you remember what that clearing is?" Lily asks when she gets her breath back. Couldn't they have put in a lift at some point in the house's history? She sits down on the window seat. She can feel her pulse in her swollen ankles. So much for pregnancy glow.

Tom turns to her, head cocked. Then his brow unfurrows. "Of course." He looks down at the clue in his hand. "'Where animals are stiff and laid to rest.' Then there's the 'bones' and 'cloth-lined wood.' It's the pet cemetery. Although 'trunked falsehood'? Did someone bury an elephant there? Or is it that we shouldn't forget?" His smile fades. "Not sure I really wanted to be reminded of that place. Hamish is buried there."

Lily remembers a letter she received from Tom, after his own mum and dad died in a car crash a few miles from Endgame House. His dog, Hamish, a lovely and licky Labrador, had been in the car, but somehow, he'd survived the terrible accident and limped home. It was Hamish who'd led the housekeeper to the smashed-up car. Hamish died a few years later, but Tom told her in his letters that Hamish wasn't the same dog again.

"We should go to the cemetery later," Lily says. "Say hello to Hamish." And to the other resting pets, including TC, Isabelle's cat, who'd made Lily laugh as much as he made her sneeze.

"They're not going to dig up the graves, are they?" Tom asks. He looks like a little boy again, worrying about his dog.

Lily thinks Sara or Philippa could be absolutely capable of digging up a pet cemetery. These are the people she's spending Christmas with.

Tom sees her hesitate. "Shit. Of course they would. What's a few bones to them when there's a house up for grabs?" He moves away. "I'll go and stop them, tell them they're looking in the wrong place."

"I'll go," a voice says from below them.

Gray is standing halfway up the staircase, looking up at them through the finials. His face is specter pale. "Sara won't listen to anyone else. She might not even listen to me." Gray then turns and walks silently down the stairs.

"How does he move so quietly?" Lily asks.

"You're the same," Tom says.

Lily turns to him. "What?" She always sees herself as lumbering, especially now.

"You always won grandmother's footsteps when we were little. And you always knew which stairs to avoid when we played hide-and-seek."

"True," Lily says. So many things to re-evaluate.

"So, where do you think the key is?" Tom asks.

"Liliana loved anagrams, as well as outliers and oddities," she says, "so first you look for anomalies, things that stand out. Something that could be a mixed-up word or phrase." She points to "aria moans, mor n rise." She takes out one of the colored pencils from her pocket and underlines the "n." "This is out of place."

"Could be a typo," Tom says.

"Liliana doesn't make mistakes."

"I'd say this whole thing was her making a massive error," Tom says. He looks so sad. "Why couldn't she give the house to blind cats, if that's what she wanted?"

"Why are you here then?" Lily asks.

Tom looks thoughtful. "Honestly? I liked the idea of us all being together, in a place where we've all been stuck in some way for so long. I thought it might be cathartic, and we could all move on." He sighs. "Judging from dinner and breakfast, I was horribly naïve. Not for the first time."

Lily squeezes his hand. "You're perfect as you are. And I'd like catharsis, for both of us," she says.

Tom smiles back. "So would I, so we'll get it. That's kinda how it works."

"Like Gray's rituals."

Tom nods. "Invest meaning in something, and it helps it become real."

"Liliana always said that there's meaning in everything." She looks back down at the clue. "'Chamber'—could point to one of the bedrooms."

"But the hotel must have loads of bedrooms. Where do we start?"

"It wouldn't just be a random room. And, if I'm right, she let us know exactly whose bedroom it is."

The mentioning of music and aria means there's only one person it could be. But she needs to be sure.

On the back of the clue, she splits the line up, so the letters lie far apart:

ARIAMOANSMORNRISE

And there it is. If she removes the letters, "n rise," as they are separated from the rest, it spells out exactly where to look.

"Are you OK?" Tom asks. He's staring at her in concern. "What's wrong?"

Lily doesn't reply. She just rearranges the anagram, writing it down in red:

MARIANASROOM

Chapter Eleven

"I'd forgotten that Aunt Mariana had sung in operas," Tom says when they're outside Lily's mother's room. "What was it she sang at one of Dad's shows?"

Lily closes her eyes and can still hear Mum's silver voice soar over the terrace and Endgame's summer-kissed grounds. "A Mozart aria, I think. I don't know it in German. Something like, 'Gently Rest, My Dearest Love.' It was her favorite."

When she opens her eyes again, Tom is looking at her with such compassion that she has to glance away.

"You should be the one to get the key," he says. "She was your mum. And you solved it."

"We don't know if I'm right yet."

"Course you're right. I'd almost forgotten that she had that overgrown forest for her wallpaper. Please—of all people—you deserve the key."

Lily shakes her head. She feels sick at the thought of going in. "I can't. Not yet. I'd rather you went in for me."

Tom looks utterly miserable.

Lily feels her hands trembling and holds them out to him. "I'm a mess, I wouldn't be much use in there. Anyway, think how much it'll piss Sara off if you get the first key."

"Excellent manipulation, Lily," Tom says. "You should be a psycho-analyst. Right. I'm going in." He rolls up his sleeves as if going on an archaeological dig. Which, she supposes, he is. Digging up the past so she can build a future.

"Try in the wardrobe first," Lily says. "I think that's what the clue means by 'cloth-lined wood'—Mum's wardrobe was lined with cotton she dabbed with lavandin oil to keep moths away. And…" Lily pauses, swallows rising bile. "And there's a trunk of photos in there."

"'Trunked falsehood,'" Tom says, "of course!"

He checks with her one more time that she doesn't want to go in, then opens the door. Tom steps into a dance of dust motes. Lily turns away, heart pounding. She'll go in, just not today.

She can hardly breathe as she listens for the wardrobe door opening and then the trunk unlocking. The lid lifts with a creak.

"There are no photos in the trunk," Tom calls out. "But there is something else. Hold on." A rustle of fabric. A clatter of metal on floor-boards. "I've got it!"

Tom rushes out holding a brass key. He offers it to Lily. "Take it, please—you solved the clue."

Lily steps back, holds her hands up. "I told you, I'm not here to get the house."

Tom looks down at the key, then tucks it into his jeans pocket. "Thank you," he says. "Without you, I'd be in the cemetery, trying to stop my cousins from digging up dead pets." His hand flies to his head. "God, I hope Gray got to them in time."

Lily feels suddenly tired, and has an overwhelming urge to slip into her room and shut the door. She can't rest, though; she has to work on the deeper levels of the clue and find out what it's telling her about Mum. "Go and see the others," she says. "Tell them today's search is over."

"I will," Tom replies. "Though it's tempting to let them keep going till lunchtime." Tom's eyes twinkle. "Wait a minute."

Tom darts back into her mum's room and comes back out holding a balding teddy bear. "Thought you might like this," he says, holding it out to Lily.

"That's Ada." She points to the label on the teddy's side. "My mum's Steiff bear. I think you got your love of puns from her."

Tom thinks for a second, then gets it. "'Where animals are stiff and laid to rest'! Steiff and stiff! And it was on her bed!"

Lily nods, trying to close the flickbook of memories that just opened, running through moments spent in the room. Having tea parties with Mum, Christina, and Ada. Rescuing Ada from the twisting trees on the wallpaper. Standing by the window, watching the ambulance take Mum's body away.

She then remembers the first clue. How does it help her work out what happened to Mum? She turns to Tom. "Was there anything else in the trunk? Sounded like there was fabric."

Tom runs back into the room and re-emerges with a swathe of green fabric draped from fist to floor. "The key was wrapped inside." He folds the material and hands it to Lily.

As Lily examines the buttons on the fabric, her heart clenches. More images fall like torn leaves around her. "It's a coat," she says. Her voice is so thin, so quiet, that Tom has to duck to catch it before it slips down the gaps in the floorboards. "It belonged to Mum."

"Shit," he says. "Do you want me to put it back?"

Lily brings the coat up to her face. She takes a deep sniff but even her pregnant supernose can't smell any trace of Mum's perfume. A sob tries to break free but she manages to trap it in her throat.

In her peripheral vision, she sees Tom's fingers tap against his sides. "I'm supposed to be the professional, ready to help with healing words, but seeing you like this…" He stops, shrugs. "All I can think to say is how brave you are."

Lily, though, is looking at the coat's sleeves. Both are covered in dark stains, as if the cuffs have rusted. The stains are the color of dried blood. And with that, Lily is slung back to stumbling through the maze and find-ing Mum slumped on the ground. This was the coat her mother died in.

And Lily doesn't feel brave at all.

Chapter Twelve

Lily stumbles from Mum's bedroom to her own door, clutching the coat and Ada. "I'm going to lie down," she says to Tom.

Tom follows, hand to his forehead. "I'm not sure you should be alone," he says.

"I'm used to it," Lily says. And means it. Solitude is the cloak she wears round her to stop people coming near.

"Even so," Tom replies. "Come down with me for a while. Just to see Sara's face when I tell her you solved it."

"Could you say that it was you? Who worked it out, I mean?"

Tom frowns again. "Why?"

Because she doesn't want to stand out. Because she doesn't want to be looked at. Because she doesn't want to speak. She just shakes her head.

"If that's what you want," Tom replies. "But, you know, at some point it'd be good for you to take your place. To shine."

Lily must be making a face that shows how hackneyed she thinks that is as Tom laughs.

"Yeah. I know. Cheesy and corny. I mean it, though. You can't keep quiet forever."

Wanna bet? Lily's mum has been quiet for a very long time.

Lily gives Tom a hug, if only to stop the psychobabble. "You go and gloat," she says. "I'll be down soon."

When she can no longer hear Tom's footsteps on the stairs, Lily slips into her room, cradling her mum's coat. Very carefully, trying not to touch the stains, she lays the coat out on the bed.

Against the duvet, the coat is a silhouette that shows up the absence of her mum. And bears her blood.

Lily's heart feels stabbed by holly.

Why did Aunt Liliana keep the coat? And why direct Lily's attention to it? Cruelty ran through Liliana like tannic raisins in tea-soaked bread, but it couldn't just be that. Could it? Liliana wouldn't punish Lily because she didn't want to come here for Christmas. Would she?

Lily thinks back to the day Aunt Liliana drove her away from Endgame House. Lily was in the back seat, squished between Sara and Gray. Sara had her arms folded and was jabbing her elbow into Lily's side, but Lily could barely feel it. She hardly felt anything at all. It was as if her whole body was left in the house and the rest of her was being taken down south, far away from the home where her mum had lived and her mum had died. Lily was a reverse ghost: she was still alive but not in her body. It was numb, as if placed in the icehouse ever since she found Mum dead.

Aunt Liliana hadn't said anything for the first few miles. She had driven with her shoulders up near her ears. Didn't look in the rearview mirror once.

Lily reached for the key to Endgame House that still hung around her neck. She pressed it against herself to feel its cold teeth against her skin, to feel something. Everyone in the family had a key. They were all given one on their fifth birthday, presented in a ceremony on the terrace. Each key was threaded onto twine and tied round their necks. It was a symbol of how they belonged to Endgame, and Endgame belonged to them.

Grandma Violet had given Lily hers. She'd held Lily's hand afterward, as they had walked barefoot through the wildflower field. "Keys give you freedom, Lily," Grandma Violet had said. "But they also protect you. Keep you safe."

The key hadn't kept her safe. Mum's hadn't either. All twine does is keep things tied—runner beans fastened to sticks so they can't run, sunflowers cuffed to bamboo so they can't search out to another sun. The key's teeth were pressing deeper into her skin now. She scraped it against her collarbone. Dug its incisors into her skin until she felt something, and she went deeper and harder until she felt something wet on her fingertips. She touched the hot spot on her chest. The splodge of blood on her finger showed her that, despite her numbness, she was still alive.

"What are you doing?" Sara asked, leaning over Lily and peering at her chest. "Mum, Lily's bleeding!"

Aunt Liliana then looked back through the rearview mirror. Her eyes met Lily's. They were as cold as the frost that rimed the car windows.

"She used her key to cut herself," Sara said.

Lily felt hatred for Sara, and it felt good. She hugged it to herself. If she couldn't feel anything on the outside, at least she could on the inside.

"Take it off, Lily," Aunt Liliana said.

"But it's mine," Lily replied. She had left so much behind, the key felt like her last connection to Mum.

"You don't need it. You won't be going back to Endgame House."

"Never?" Lily asked, and a weight dropped inside her that was either grief or relief. Maybe they were two faces of the same feeling.

Grandma Violet had always told her, "Fear and excitement are twins; they live on opposite sides of the same door. It's up to you which room you live in."

"Give the key to Gray," Aunt Liliana said.

Lily felt Sara stiffen next to her.

Gray glanced across at Sara before turning back to his mum. "Why me?" he asked. "I don't want another key. I've got one."

"I want the key," Sara said. "I'll look after it better than Gray could."

"It's because you want it that Gray must keep it," Aunt Liliana said. "You need to learn you can't have everything you want. Life is not going to be kind to you, Sara. You don't have brains, looks, or charm. You're going to have to use something else to get on."

"That doesn't seem fair," Lily said. She turned to Sara and gave her what she thought was a consoling look. What Aunt Liliana had said to Sara must sting, getting under her skin like a knife.

Sara, though, glared at Lily. Maybe she knew that it was good to feel hatred, too.

"You should know better than anyone, Lily, that life is not fair. Fair happens to other people. We have to get what we can and make our own kind of justice."

Aunt Liliana had then concentrated on the road, gnawing on her lip. She was frowning and seemed lost in thought. Lily would have liked to be lost, too. She would have liked to be a snowflake in the drifts that lined the road. An individual lost among many. She would have liked not to be seen ever again in a whiteout of her own life. If she always felt cold, then she wouldn't know when the sun wasn't shining.

Lily took the key from around her neck and handed it to Gray. His silver eyes held hers for a moment and were full of softness, like the gray pelt of a cat rubbing against her face. His kindness made her feel just as allergic. She looked away and could feel hurt radiating off him. She put walls up against that, too. She would be her own maze, construct wall after wall and get lost within it, then no one else could get in, and she couldn't get out.

Lily felt Gray slide the key into his pocket. A sob romped up within her, and she swallowed it back down. She wouldn't let Sara know what was going on inside. At least without the key to Endgame House, there would be nothing tethering her to the place that killed her mum. Because that was all she can think of, that something inside Endgame twisted around Mum until she couldn't see herself, or Lily, anymore. Because if Mum had loved Lily, she wouldn't have killed herself, would she?

She didn't know what had happened to make Mum so sad. She'd seemed fine the day before, had brought out the Christmas pudding and laughed as everyone clapped and cheered at the flames. She'd loved the present Lily gave her—a handmade snow globe. Lily had glued a plastic polar bear to a jam jar lid, then filled the jar with glitter and vinegar. Mum had seemed enchanted when she tipped her gift and silver snow fell. But maybe that was as much of a show as the pantomime matinee they'd seen in York on Christmas Eve. On stage, Buttons had been full of love, smiles, and joy as he helped Cinderella; at the stage door, when Lily had gone to get his autograph, his smile never reached his eyes and he smelled of cigarettes and whisky.

If Mum had been acting, Lily should have known. There *had* been a moment on Christmas night when Mum said she wanted to tell Lily something. Her eyes had been serious, and Lily felt excitement, but then Aunt Liliana and Uncle Edward had come in and Mum froze. Lily had then crossed into the other room, fearful, though she didn't know why.

Branches hit the car windows, hammering like paparazzi, demanding to know why she hadn't saved her mum. She wanted to know, too.

"Aunt Liliana," she said, and her voice sounded strange in the car, strangled like vines were wrapped round her neck.

"What is it, Lily?" her aunt replied. Once again, she glanced in the mirror to meet Lily's eyes. They seemed angry, hard as the ground that her mum was placed in.

Lily knew that she needed to ask, even though everything inside her told her to keep it locked up inside. But she needed to know. "Why did Mum do what she did?"

Liliana looked like she was chewing words as if they were the round toffees in a box of chocolates, the gold ones left to the end along with the strawberry creams. "I don't think you want to ask that question, Lily."

"I do," Lily said, screwing up courage into a ball and throwing it into a fire to fuel herself.

"Your mum left us because no one was around to stop what happened to her. No one listened to her."

"I tried," Lily said, then remembered Christmas Eve night when Mum had come into her room to tuck her in and how she had insisted that Mum read to her "The Night Before Christmas" and not talk about whatever it was on her mum's mind.

"You didn't listen hard enough," Liliana said. Her eyes were shiny. Frosted ground glinting in the sun. Her tears didn't fall, though; they were stuck, frozen. "None of us did. It doesn't make sense, and I don't know if it ever will. But we all need to find out what we could have done, and what we'll do to make it up to her."

They were all silent as the road widened, the trees backing away as if afraid of Liliana's fury. When Liliana spoke again, her hands were gripping tightly onto the wheel as if it was the only certain thing. "You should ask yourself, Lily, and I'll be asking myself the same thing: What could I have done, and what will I do?"

It's a question that has been there for the last twenty-odd years, hanging around her neck like a door key that can't be removed.

Lily shivers. Sometimes when old memories appear, it's as if she's standing behind a window, watching the past from the other side of the glass. At other times, she's thrown through the window into her younger self. Right now, she feels the same numbness she did on that long journey to Grantchester. As if she is hardly there, just the impression of a snow angel, lost in a drift.

Liliana's cruelty, though, her abrupt statement that Lily could have done more, and should in the future, reads differently now. She was blaming herself, not Lily. And maybe all these clues she has written, and maybe died for, are her attempt to make it up to her sister.

There must be a reason Liliana specified that the key be swaddled in the coat. It'll all be in the clues. Liliana always communicated in code.

Taking the sonnet from her pocket, Lily reads through it again. "Trunked falsehood," its last line says. The coat was in the trunk. So, what's false about the coat? She bends over the coat as it lies on the bed and looks in the pockets, like a detective searching a dead body.

There's nothing, only lint.

So what was Liliana trying to point out?

Must be something to do with her mum wearing that coat. But that would mean hauling to the surface images of her mum's last day rather than drowning them. Liliana had said in her letter that she'll have to remember everything.

Heart stuttering, Lily closes her eyes and tries to welcome her past.

Memories break over her, dragging her under. They'd played outside, her and Mum. She remembers running over frost-tipped grass, laughing. She remembers tripping on a tree root and landing splosh in the snow. Mum pulled her up and cuddled her. Lily can almost feel the coat's buttons against her cheek, the ice on her eyelashes. It hurts so much to be in the memories that she cries out.

Opening her eyes, she moves over to the window and looks out, trying to center herself in the present. But everything looks like it did twenty-one years ago. Snow sleeves the branches of the trees and coats the ground. The memories don't want to be dammed anymore. She can see herself throwing snowballs at her mum. She can feel the sides of her cheeks burning from the cold and grinning so much. She can't remember when it last hurt that much to be happy.

Other memories of that day mill like ghosts in her peripheral vision. She can almost taste the spice cookies that Uncle Edward made for tea that day. Almost hear Aunt Veronica chopping firewood with Tom. Almost smell and feel the bonfire they'd sat round that Christmas night—mulched leaves spitting, marshmallow skin crisping, newspaper sparking into ink-colored smoke.

Something in that conversation makes her want to draw closer. An instinct that there's something there she needs to remember. Mum had said something to Lily while she was wearing her green coat. Her eyes had been fixed on Uncle Edward as she leaned over and whispered to Lily. But what had she said? All Lily knows is that it had something to do with lace.

Lily shakes her head. Enough of the past for the present.

The others are back; she can hear them trudging through the front hall, peeling off coats, shouting to Mrs. Castle for refreshments. Sara is calling the loudest. Lily wonders how Sara reacted when Tom told her that he had solved the riddle and found the key. A picture of her scowl comes to mind and Lily holds a smile to herself.

She doesn't want them to see her, though, quiz her how Tom worked it out. Lying doesn't come easily to her. And she can't bear to see their flushed faces, treating all of this as if it's just a game.

Her coat and hat are downstairs, right where her cousins are milling. She looks back at her mum's coat on the bed. Heart beating fast, she goes over to it and, holding it like it were made of skin, places one arm inside it, and then another. A shiver passes through her. Along the corridor, a door slams shut.

No one is up here; she'd have heard them. The wind is picking up, though, and icy draughts pickpocket the house. The coat fits her perfectly. It's as if her mum is cuddling her close again.

Slipping down the corridor, past Liliana's room, Lily enters the old nursery. She fights back memories as if they were cobwebs, and heads straight for the stone back staircase that leads up to the attic and down to the pantry. She's about to descend when she hears a noise. Floorboards rasp above her head. There's someone in the attic.

Lily climbs the stone stairs. She can almost feel the ghosts of her younger selves running past, skipping every other step.

At the top of the staircase, she reels with the strange sense of being the wrong size. When last in the attic, she hadn't had her sunflower-style growth spurt, from short to five feet seven, in the space of a summer holiday. Here now, it's like entering a doll's house version of the attic she once knew.

Shoulders hunched, head down, she looks around but can't see anyone. She takes in the smell of dust and damp linen, of wood that could start to rot at any minute. Even though nothing is moving, someone must have been up here recently. There's a handprint in the dusty lid of Mum's old upright piano. She hovers her palm just above. The hand is bigger than hers, with slender fingers. Maybe Isabelle's, or Mrs. Castle's, placing one of the keys up here.

Would this count as looking for the key? Hardly. And it's not as if she wants to win. What would she do with a huge house like this, filled with memories, strange noises, and dust motes?

Turning her back on the attic, she goes down the back stairs. No plush carpet here, only echoing stone all the way to the bottom. No one will hear her come down. The point of the servants' staircase is that the household doesn't know they are there, carrying their drinks and food and dirty laundry, like blood cells around an oblivious body.

She emerges in the pantry, allowing her to slip out into the kitchen garden. At one time, when this was a grand manor house, the laundry had been done out here. There's still an old clothesline strung from one peeling brick wall to the other, and a rusting washing board that the conference guests used to find charming—and throw up on when drunk. Mum had shown Lily how to wash clothes on it, taking Christina and rubbing her dress against the slats. Lily had cried—she thought Christina was going to be grated like a rag doll carrot. Now washboards are kept to stomachs and skiffle bands, although Lily would rather not see or hear of either.

Lily looks at the sleeves of the coat. The brown-red blood on the cuffs seems out of place here. You'd think blood and nature would be simpatico. The light, though, makes it look different. She peers closer, holding the sleeve up to the sun. Lily has had to remove many fluids from costumes she's made before. Everything needs repairs, but so does everyone. Her costumes are returned after a masked ball, or themed wedding or fancy-dress party, with petticoats torn or corset fastenings stretched, popped a little too quickly, either from ardor or simply a need to stop ribs being squished. Maybe she should wash it. Bring it down here later, put the sleeves to the washboard and make the coat feel new.

She steps onto the snow-covered path that winds past gangly rosemary and spikes of lavender plants that fill the space with scent in summer. Her mum used to come out here and cut mint and chives and nasturtium leaves for the guests' meals. Going by what was left on conference goers' plates after dinner and supper, Lily had gleaned that they were more into slabs of meat and fists of potatoes than the ingredients which gave Mum's food its flavor. But they were most interested in the wine.

The door out of the kitchen garden used to be painted blue. Now, rotting wood peeks from underneath. Patches of paint hold on, which is either admirable or a case of extreme denial. Rot will take over unless something is done. Decay is the natural state.

Lily opens the door with her second shove. It's warped, and now has to work its way through the snow, scraping against the flagstones beneath.

"May I ask what you're up to, Miss Lily?"

Lily jumps. Mrs. Castle is standing behind her in the pantry doorway. Her arms are folded. A red scarf is draped around her neck.

"I was going out for a walk," Lily replied.

"Usually, guests consider themselves too important to use this door. Usually, guests don't even know it's here unless we show them."

"Not many of them grew up here," Lily replies.

Mrs. Castle's appraising stare makes Lily feel as cold as the wind chapping her lips and chafing her cheeks. "Reckon not," she replies. She's silent for a moment, staring into space, and Lily wonders whether to leave her to it. Then Mrs. Castle says, "I heard you wandering about in the attic."

"I heard someone up there. It's why I went to look."

Mrs. Castle frowns. "Everyone else is in the drawing room, having a brew."

Lily shrugs. "There was no one up there, not that I could tell. Liliana used to say noises like that were the house shifting around us."

"Liliana could be reassuring at times," Mrs. Castle says.

Not many, Lily would like to reply.

"You should be careful up there," Mrs. Castle says, unfolding her arms. "Or anywhere on the grounds."

"Why?" Lily asks.

"This place does funny things to people."

"Such as?"

"You'll find out," Mrs. Castle replies. "I'll just say, though, that I've no idea why anyone would want this house." A shiver ripples through her. "Houses wear history like skin. And this one has layers of epidermis, built up into calluses."

"Just one reason why I don't want to win it."

"So you keep saying," Mrs. Castle says. A smile is trying to part her lips but her teeth bite them closed.

"I just want to solve the clues."

Mrs. Castle nods, slowly. "Tom did what you asked. Came down and said he found the key." Mrs. Castle pauses. "But he didn't, did he?"

"Why would you think that?" Lily asks.

Mrs. Castle can't help smiling now. She places a finger on her lips.

Lily shrugs. "I don't see how it matters who claims they solved the clues." Her heart, though, is beating overtime. She'll have to be more careful not to be overheard.

"So, falsehoods don't matter to you, then?" Mrs. Castle asks.

"I didn't say that, I—"

"No need to say any more, Miss Lily. I understand. Not everyone can be as good as your mother."

"You knew her?" Lily asks, coming closer, as if being in Mrs. Castle's orbit could ever bring her closer to Mum.

Mrs. Castle nods. "I used to play here with her and Liliana. I was older than them, but my parents lived in the village. I came here with Mum when she helped out with the laundry on changeover days."

"So, you're part of Endgame's history, too?" Lily asks.

"I'm part of its skin, yes," Mrs. Castle says. "Why else would I agree to be here?" A troubled look crosses her face, then leaves as if it had never been present. "Mariana was the loveliest girl. Such a terrible shame what happened to her. That's her coat, I believe," she says, pointing a bony finger at Lily.

Lily self-consciously hugs her arms to her chest.

"It suits you," Mrs. Castle says, simply. She turns to go, then unwinds the scarf from her neck and throws it to Lily. "Take care out there. Ghosts walk everywhere here, and you don't want to be alone with them."

Lily catches the scarf and winds it tightly around her neck, as if it could stop Mrs. Castle's cold words being taken to her heart. The last thing she needs to think about is ghosts.

Out of the shelter of the kitchen garden, the wind makes itself known. It tries to sidle up the sleeves of Lily's mum's coat, so she curls her hands into balls like she did when she was little—only the knuckles showing over the cuffs.

Her trainers are no match for the snow as she makes her way past the East Wing. It makes its way through the mesh, her tights, drawing up the cold and holding it to her toes. She knows she won't feel them soon and that's a welcome thought. Numbness is a comfort. It's feeling that causes problems.

To her far right, she can hear the bickering whicker of horses from the old stables. But that's impossible. No horses have been on the estate in many, many years. If Endgame House had any nearby properties, she'd say the wind must be carrying the sound from there. But Endgame has no neighbors.

Lily tries not to think about it. She concentrates instead on the fountain before her. In summer, plumes of water leap from its wide stone basin into a wet fleur-de-lis; now, in winter, its mechanism has been stopped, the well of water frozen in its basin. What does a fountain feel if it cannot flow? From the other side of the grounds, the chapel bell sends out its mournful call for rare prayers.

As she approaches the maze, something twists inside her. This is where she'll find things out. More memories are held inside. Something that will trigger what her mum said on that last day.

Lily stands at the entrance. Hedges loom on either side. In front of her, the snow is a white path that leads into twists, corners, and shadows. Her mum had often said, "You always find answers in a maze. You don't even have to know the question; the search will tell you." And she'd been right in some ways. Wandering around the maze had let Lily think about things; concentrating on getting to the center meant that her brain could go off in other directions. Maybe it's because it's not linear, thoughts turn back just a little bit more advanced than they were.

But now she can't go in.

It's as if her feet have frozen to the ground. Fear has hold of her and won't let her cross into the other room where excitement lies.

She extends an arm and touches one wall of the maze, soft fir spiked with needling holly. Ivy finds its way through like gossip.

Offcuts of memories tumble around her, like the time the maze was trimmed back and she and Isabelle stood nearby, leaves falling on them like green confetti.

Like the time there was an open day for the conference center, and she saw two women kissing, stumbling into the maze with their lips joined, and thought for the first time, consciously at least, that she liked girls as well as boys.

Like the time she found Mum in the maze arguing with Aunt Veronica about something to do with…but she couldn't remember what they were talking about. The words are stuck on the inside of the maze, and she can't go in.

Whatever is in there, waiting for her, she's not going to find it today.

The French doors open on the terrace. Philippa's laugh spills out onto the snow along with the smell of Christmas lunch cooking. Lily still can't face them, so she heads away from the house.

Behind the willow that wept over her and Mum lies the icehouse. A thrill passes through her when it comes into view. When she was growing up, she was never allowed to enter, in case she got locked inside. It was the only part of the grounds that had been forbidden to her. She had, therefore, obvs, gone in frequently. Isabelle and Lily used to time each other to see how long they could sit on the ice. Lily had called them bales of ice, as they seemed the winter equivalent of the sun-soaked hay bales that would line the fields at harvest time.

The icehouse door is frozen. Her fingers stiffen as she tries to jolt the bolt into opening. She huffs on it, breath billowing onto the rusted metal. She works it back and forward until at last it gives, and the heavy door opens with a forbidding creak.

She reaches for the light switch and turns it on, but nothing happens. On searching outside for a remnant of the nearby rock garden, she finds a large stone, and uses it to wedge open the door. Even so, it's dark in the icehouse. And so cold.

Footsteps outside crunch in the snow. Slow, measured steps that stop outside the door. They must be able to see her own prints in the snow, leading right to where she stands. She hopes they'll leave her alone, that she won't have to make small talk with one of her less friendly cousins while surrounded by ice. That'd be a bit on the nose. And there is no chance of ice melting in here; it has kept families replete with cold for centuries and it won't stop now.

The stone moves. The door swings shut. The bolt moves back. Darkness takes over.

Heart drummer-boying inside her chest, she calls out. "Someone in here!"

There's no sound outside. Maybe they didn't hear her. It's possible that, with the door closed, it traps sound inside just as it keeps heat and the warm-blooded outside. Then the footsteps walk slowly away. And if she can hear steps in snow, then they must have been able to hear her.

She hammers on the metal door, hard. She stops but can't hear a reply, other than her own heart telling her to run. But there's nowhere to go. Panic moves through her, freezing her in place as it did at the entrance to the maze.

She holds out her hand but sees nothing at all. This is the kind of dark that encompasses you, making you part of its darkness. It doesn't cloak her, doesn't even swallow her, it's as if she has disappeared within. There's something reassuring about that. Not existing has its temptations. She pushes the thought away.

Think, she says to herself. *Keep legs and mind active. Find your way out.*

Moving forward, she walks into something sharp. Reaching down, she touches ice. She smooths her hand across its surface. When she was little, she had been confused by the way that ice burns. She had asked, out loud at an Endgame dinner party: "If fire and ice were opposites, then did fire give you frostbite?" After all, the flicker around a flame is a cold blue. Uncle Edward had chuckled and said she was too clever for her own good, and she should try putting her hand in fire and see how cold it was.

She hasn't thought of that in a very long time. She touches the bales of ice again, counting the seams that separate one from another. There are many of them, stacked across one side of the shelter. Her hand now feels as if it's on fire. She stuffs it into the coat pocket, opening and closing her hand. For a moment, she hopes that maybe there's now something in the pocket to help, a message from her mum, some magic aid from the past to assist her. Still nothing but lint.

With her other hand, she stretches over the table of ice to touch the far wall. She can't remember another door in here, but memory is a funny thing. She doesn't know why Liliana has set her this task of remembering something. Memory distorts facts like a fairground mirror.

"Ouch!" She's pricked her finger on something. She picks it up—an ice pick. If she wanted ice, that'd be useful. But what she needs now is her phone. If she hadn't come back to Endgame, she wouldn't be in here at all—she'd be in London, having a quiet Christmas with Netflix. How can she look after a baby? She can't even get herself out of an icehouse.

She returns to the door and whacks the ice pick against it, hard.

Thwack. Thwack. Thwack.

Lily gets into a rhythm, hitting the door and letting its thick metal resound like the dinner gong across the grounds. The silence in between feels cold.

She's hammering at the door for ages, it feels like, although it could only be a minute, before she has to sit. The stone is cold under her hand as she eases herself down. Sitting on the floor in a corset is not easy. As she crouches, she hears the coat rip at the shoulders. She couldn't even keep her mum's coat safe for a morning. Tears form. This is how they'll find her, if ever they need to come here for ice. A frozen lolly of a onetime Lily, tears of grief stuck to her blue face.

Tiredness drapes over her like another coat. It's warmer than being awake. She feels the tug, the cord that will pull her into a sleep from which she may not stir.

Chapter Thirteen

Half covered in a drift of sleep, Lily wakes as the bolt is drawn back. The door opens with a scrape.

"Here you are!" Tom says. His cheeks are red, his long hair out of place. He's sweating as if he's been running. "I've been looking all over for you."

Lily steps out of the icehouse, away from its tomblike womb. Outside, the air feels sun warmed despite the snow. The smell of woodsmoke drifts from the house, making it seem almost welcoming. Almost.

"You're shaking," Tom says, taking off his coat and placing it around her. His worry for her warms her from the inside out, giving an oatmeal glow to her middle. She wonders if Bean can feel it, too.

"How did you find me?" Lily asks as they trudge back through the snow to the house.

"It helped that you were hitting the door like you were an aggressive member of the timpani section," Tom says, laughing. "I went up to your room to check on you, but you weren't there. I then went through the house, worried that Mrs. Castle might catch me and think I was looking for tomorrow's clue!"

"Someone locked me in."

"Of course," Tom says, stopping suddenly. "The bolt was across. But they couldn't have meant to, surely?" His eyes are wide and as blue as the sky behind him. It's amazing that something so clear could yield snow.

Lily shrugs. "I was asking them to let me out. Can't see how they couldn't have heard me."

"True. I heard you as soon as I got outside." Tom is silent for a moment. "Are you going to ask the others who did it?"

Lily shivers again. She does *not* want to have to talk to her cousins about this.

Tom inspects her with one of his understanding looks and it makes her want to turn away from him and cry, and not in that order.

"I should, I know," Lily says.

"Tell you what," Tom says, "I'll say I was in there."

"You can't keep rescuing me," Lily says. "I'm no princess."

"Could've fooled me, sweetheart," Tom says, putting on his best—and by that, she means really bad—Humphrey Bogart twisted grin. He looks more like Columbo. But then that's who's needed in any crisis. She should be more Columbo. Or Bowie. Whenever Aunt Liliana gave advice, it always came down to: "WWBD, darling. What Would Bowie Do?" But David Bowie, as luminous as he was and always will be, was not known for solving crime. Or maybe he was. Maybe he's the best undercover detective of them all. Maybe his role in *Twin Peaks* was reality played out on the celluloid stage.

"Ground control to Lily," Tom says. He's standing in front of her now, waving.

"What is it?" Lily asks.

"I've been talking to you for whole minutes—really good, fascinating stuff, I can assure you—and you're just staring into space and smiling!"

"Sorry, got lost for a minute."

"Could you stop doing that?" Tom asks. "I've got enough to worry about here without you wandering off in your head." He's rubbing his forehead, now crosshatched like a crossword puzzle.

She puts her hand up to his brow. It uncrinkles like paper being smoothed. "You don't have to worry about me," she says. "I can take care of myself." She really can't, but he doesn't need to know that.

Tom nods. "I know. It's my fault. I get too involved. Always been my problem. I manage it with my clients just fine; it's my family that gets me every time."

"What are you worried about at Endgame?" Lily asks. An instinct tells her that there's something she should know, something that ties in.

Tom shakes his head. "Nothing in particular."

So much for her detective instinct. Columbo would never have gotten that wrong.

"Sara is being horrible," Tom continues. "Gray needs help, but I'm too close so I can't give it to him. Ronnie needs to stand up for himself, Rachel is the happiest I've ever seen her and I don't want that to change, and—"

"And me? You're worried about me?" Lily asks. She doesn't know if she wants him to say yes or no.

"Oh, only always," Tom replies, smiling.

"Are you going to tell me why?"

"Because you keep everything locked up in an icehouse," he says. "If I didn't know better, I'd say you shut yourself in there so you didn't have to talk with any of us. But you couldn't have, could you?"

"Don't think even I'm capable of that."

"Quite. It's being here, surrounded by ghosts and people who are crying out for help and screaming at me to stay away. It's nothing and everything at once. I worry. But nobody needs or asks for my interference. So, I'll say this once: Is there anything you'd like to tell me?"

"Like what?" Lily says, hoping he can't see her face. What does he know, if anything?

"Kinda defeats the question if I have to say." Tom's laugh is crystallized by sadness. "I just want you to let me in."

"I will," she says. "When I can."

They walk on in silence until they reach the bottom of the terrace. Leaves have fallen onto the snow like punctuation marks. They've held on for so long, but winter gets to us all in the end.

As they climb the steps, the living room and library come into view. Several of the guests are standing in the living room window, mugs raised. There is laughing, mouths open, heads thrown back. From here the silence makes it macabre.

"Ghosts," Lily says. "You said you were surrounded by ghosts." She thinks of the voice she heard in the wall last night.

"Aren't we always?" Tom says. His forehead is creased again. "I can just hear them better here."

"Your mum and dad?" Lily asks.

Tom nods. "I went into their room," he says, "the one they had after you left. Everything had changed. It had been made into one of the swanky suites in the hotel. I hadn't realized. I hadn't wanted to visit since."

"At least you were able to go in," she says, remembering that feeling as she stood at the entrance to Mum's room. The pull to go inside, and the force field of her own making that kept her out.

"Wait till you hear what happened," Tom says. "I was sure I heard Dad's voice."

"Uncle Edward?" Lily asks. Images of Edward come into her head. Of him smiling and winking as he handed out presents. Of him running to find chocolate eggs in the garden, the strings of his handmade Easter bonnet flying behind him. She had loved him, and he had died not long after her mum. Not being close to Sara, Gray, or Rachel, Lily had been left with only Liliana, Ronnie, and Tom. She didn't even see Isabelle.

"And then I heard Mum," Tom says, his voice breaking, nut brittle snapping. "And ran right out, crying."

Lily nods, although she was never as fond of Aunt Veronica. She had rarely smiled, and was so cold. The last memory Lily has of Veronica before her death was at Mum's funeral. Veronica had rearranged a petite pair of earrings as she said, "I'm sorry for your loss, Lily." Words that anyone could say and ones she clearly hadn't meant.

"I'm so sorry," Lily says. And *does* mean it. She knows better than most what it's like to lose your parents. And she never knew her dad, or even who he was. Her hand goes to her stomach. She wonders if Little Bean will ever know, too.

They go in together, and a cheer comes from the other side of the living room. "Where have you two been?" Ronnie asks. He's standing in front of the fire, then comes over to them and puts a hand on both of their shoulders. The look of relief on his face makes Lily feel warm again.

"I found Lily in the icehouse," Tom says. "Then someone locked us both in."

Lily looks at him, turning her head sharply. He said he'd tell them *he* was locked in. Not that it matters.

"What were you doing in there?" Sara asks Lily. Her eyes are canal narrowed and just as murky. Lily can't see what's at the bottom of them. Probably silt and several lost shopping trolleys' worth of bitterness. "Tom hasn't gotten you looking for other clues for him to solve, has he? That's against the rules."

"Because we all know how much you like tradition and playing by the rules," Rachel says.

"I think the better question is who locked us in?" Tom says, successfully diverting attention from Lily.

"I hope you don't think I did it," Sara says. She's puffing her chest out like an indignant French hen.

"I've no idea," Tom says, stretching his hands out in a display of openness Lily recognizes from her own therapist. "Otherwise, I wouldn't be asking."

"I've been in here with Rachel, Holly, and Ronnie the whole time," Philippa says.

They all turn back to look toward Sara.

"It was me," Gray says, quietly, from his seat next to the fire. He stands and holds up a pair of earphones. The leads dangle from his hand. He walks over to Lily. "I went for a walk and was listening to music. I saw the door was open and closed it. I should have looked inside, I'm really sorry." He looks straight at Lily. His eyes shine like the ten-pence pieces that Grandma Violet used to give out to her grandkids as pocket money. She would bathe them in vinegar—the coins, not her grandchildren, although her tongue could be acetic at times—and buff them till the Queen looked five years younger.

"No harm done," Tom says. "And now we know that the icehouse still works. Lily was freezing when she came out."

"But you weren't?" Sara asks. "Even though you gave her your coat?" Her gaze is not as shiny as her brother's. It's tarnished by time and meanness. Lily makes a mental note to slip away before Christmas dinner to change. She's not sure how she'll explain her mum's bloodstained coat to her cousins.

"You know me," Tom says, grinning, "hot whatever the weather." He waggles his eyebrows in a clownish come-hither.

Sara humphs. She turns to her brother. "You'd better be listening on your old iPod," she says. "And not something you should've handed in to Isabelle."

Gray holds up an early model iPod Shuffle. Lily used to have one just like it. Liliana had given one to all of her children, which she included Lily as one of, something that Sara has never really gotten over.

"Good," Sara says. "Because you're useless to me if you have to go home."

Gray's head lowers. Lily goes over to him and places a hand on his back. He leans into her like a greyhound putting its weight on someone visiting a dogs' home. "I'm sorry," he whispers.

"You didn't mean it," Lily says quietly back.

"No, not for the icehouse," Gray says, so much under his breath it's practically vapor.

"What then?"

Sara comes over and Gray is left with his mouth open like a fish on a hook. "How did you get out, then?" she asks. "If Gray locked you both in?"

Lily feels Tom freeze next to her, as if he's been left in the icehouse overnight. "I managed to force the door," he says, eventually.

"You're a terrible liar, Tom," Sara says.

Mrs. Castle comes in, holding a tray of canapés. "Christmas dinner will be served in an hour," she says. She plonks the tray down on a table. "I've stuffed some vol-au-vents. You can get your own drinks." She looks at them all as if she wishes they would disappear up the chimney and not come back, then turns quickly and leaves, boots stomping across the tiles.

Silence is held for a moment, then Tom says, "Well, isn't this a Christmas party to remember?"

Chapter Fourteen

"Where are the crackers?" Ronnie asks as they sit down. "You can't have Christmas dinner without crackers; it's like not having turkey, or family arguments. It's the hat I like. My head was made for hats." He demonstrates by turning his head from one side to another.

"You must be pretty pleased with yourself, Tom," Sara says. "For getting that first key. Hope you've got it in a safe place."

Tom smiles. He taps his top pocket. "Right here."

"I'd be worried someone would take it," Philippa says.

"Why would anyone want to nick the key?" Tom asks.

Gray laughs. Everyone looks at him. He slams his hand immediately over his mouth as if ashamed of making a noise.

"We all want the keys," Philippa says. "Otherwise, we wouldn't be here. No point being disingenuous."

"That's a long word for the Christmas table," Sara says.

"Sorry, didn't mean to baffle you, Sara," Philippa says. "It means being deceitful, misleading, dishonest—"

"I know what it means," Sara says.

"This is getting a bit serious," Tom replies. "It *is* Christmas, you know? Can't we enjoy it—crackers or no crackers, key or no key?"

"That's all right for you to say," Philippa says. "You've got one. And you're in a much better position than us to win more."

"Take it then," Tom says, plucking the key from his pocket and holding it out to her across the table.

Philippa's hand reaches toward it.

"You can't just give it away, Tom," Sara says.

"Why not?" He places the key in Philippa's hand. "I'm here for the fun, not the win."

Philippa smiles at the key with pride, as if she had found it herself. She then turns away from the table as she secretes it in her handbag.

The door opens and a whole side of smoked salmon is carried into the room by Mrs. Castle. Lily can smell it from across the room and turns away, as if not looking would stop its stink.

"Mrs. Castle was telling me earlier that the salmon is cured on-site," Philippa says. "In the old smokehouse, just like it has been for centuries. Wood chips, from fallen trees on the estate, are lit and left to smolder for days. The smoke slowly works its way into the fish."

"Bit like you," Sara says. "Trying to get your hands on our family money."

"Sara, love," Tom says, gently. "It's not actually our, or your, money."

"Don't you dare 'love' me, Tom," Sara says.

They stare at each other. It's so quiet you could hear tinsel drop.

"Can I put this bloody platter down now?" Mrs. Castle asks.

The silence now broken by Mrs. Castle's mouth and boots, everyone leans back in their chairs. When the plate is placed in front of Lily, she sidles one of the lemon wedges off the plate and holds it in her fist. She raises it to her nose and breathes in. The citrus blast chases away the smoked fish, until everyone at the table raises their forks and peels a piece of salmon off. She can't see how she'll ever eat it again. Even the look of it is wrong—flensed flesh flaked onto plates. It's too human.

"Now, I suggest we all tuck in and enjoy ourselves," Tom says, rubbing his hands as Mrs. Castle exits, the door slamming behind her.

Once the turkey has been carved by an insistent and triumphant Philippa, and eaten along with its vegetable accessories—with some spared, at

Gray's request, for Boxing Day pie—the party waddles as one out into the hallway. Lily doesn't want to see another sprout for a really long time. Not that she's eaten much. Just enough to keep the nausea at bay.

"Christmas pudding will be served in ninety minutes," Mrs. Castle says.

"God, no," Ronnie says, holding his stomach.

"For once I agree with Ronnie," Sara says. Lily is not unpleased to see that Sara's face has turned to the ashen-gray state of her brother's name.

"I think I speak for us all when I ask you to save it for tomorrow, Mrs. Castle," Rachel says.

Sara looks at her cousin as if she most definitely does not speak for them all, but she's so full, speaking seems beyond her. For once.

Lily spends the rest of the afternoon trying to get away from her family. It's not easy, for anyone. Around the country, millions will be playing the same waiting game, along with charades, Monopoly, and other excruciations.

Despite earlier protests that everyone is full, two dozen mince pies are somehow eaten, complete with brandy cream, brandy butter, and chasers of brandy. Ronnie whips up his own maple syrup cream, which lets Lily join him as a point of camaraderie, rather than one of avoiding alcohol. She's amazed no one has noticed that she hasn't drunk anything since she got to Endgame House. That can't last long.

When *The Muppet Christmas Carol* is shown in the games room, projected against one wall, Lily manages to sneak out to the orangery to be by herself. She settles into an armchair at the far end, puts her pulsing feet up on a stool, and looks out over the grounds. From here, she can adjust her field of vision so that the maze isn't in sight. Instead, she looks out over the lawn to the wild garden. The steeple of the chapel in the distance points up to a cloud-heavy sky.

Philippa walks in and places a far too milky cup of tea on the side table next to Lily. She pulls her shawl over her shoulders while checking that no one else is here. "Can we talk?" she whispers.

Lily nods, because what else can she say in this situation?

Philippa pulls up another chair and sits a little too near Lily. "I just wanted to say that I know why you're here. And I can help you."

Lily's heart starts beating as fast as Bean's. "What do you mean?" How does she know that Lily's looking into her mother's death? And how could she help? Does she have information on what happened?

"What I don't understand is why you're bothering to play the game," Philippa continues. "You could've just told Isabelle Stirling that you're pregnant and the house would be yours."

Realization and disappointment slink over Lily. "You saw when I fell over," she says, her hand going to her tummy.

"It was when I loosened your corset," Philippa says.

"I'd hoped you and Tom hadn't seen. But how could you not?"

"I don't think Tom did. He looked away."

"Ever the gentleman."

"You really shouldn't wear that corset when you're pregnant, you know? It'll hurt the baby."

This is another reason to keep the pregnancy hidden. Avoid the unasked-for, and dubious, wisdom people can't stop themselves from dispensing. "Historically, women used to wear them to hold the bump" is all Lily says. Stick to facts. "They were advertised as producing 'better babies' as it supported the muscles in the stomach and back. They were intended to reduce the high mortality rate for babies, not add to it. I designed the corset with the bump in mind. When I take it off at night, my tummy hurts."

"You can't be more than eighteen or nineteen weeks?" Philippa says. "Wait till you get over thirty. That's when it gets *really* uncomfortable." Her hand goes to her coccyx. "And your back will never be the same again."

"Right. Thanks," Lily says. "I'll bear all that in mind. I'm twenty-one weeks. Had my latest scan last Monday." Lily thinks of seeing her daughter playing with the umbilical cord that linked them. The awe she felt. The terror.

"I was scared, too," Philippa says. "With Samuel. Right up until he crowned, then I was swearing in Ronnie's face for giving me such a big-headed baby."

"He does have a head for hats," Lily replies. She then remembers what Philippa originally said. "What did you mean by being able to help me?"

"I was thinking you could keep the house as a hotel—as is your right as you're pregnant with the heir—then Ronnie and I could run it. Well, I'll run it, Ronnie will have free rein in the kitchen. Apart from the budget. I'd best keep control of that. Save us going bankrupt. Again."

"It's a lovely idea but—"

"It's a *great* idea," Philippa interrupts. Her eyes shine, glazing over as she sees a possible future wild-blooming. "Think about it. Your little one could play with Samuel, you'd be able to leave that shoebox of a flat—don't make that face, Ronnie's been and told me about it—you'd have room to make the things you really want. Set up a proper business making your own clothes." She points at Lily's dress. "More people should see these frocks. You're hiding your talent away, as well as a baby."

"Now you're sounding like Aunt Liliana," Lily says. Lily pictures living here, with Ronnie in his element, launching herself properly into the fashion world. Near to Isabelle, too. But in the corner of her mind, the maze looms. She'll never get away from the memories if she lives here. "I'm sorry, but I can't. I'd still be tied to the house in my head."

"Then why are you here? Not just because an old woman asked you to?"

"Well, yes. Mainly."

Philippa folds her arms and gives Lily a skeptical stare. "You've got the same look on your face Ronnie has when he's hiding something."

Lily looks away and says nothing. White lies won't cover the dark secrets she's seeking.

"Think about it," Philippa says. "You wouldn't have to be involved. I'm good at this stuff, and it would mean everything to Ronnie. Please?"

Lily hesitates, then nods. "I'll think about it." She won't, but at least it'll keep Philippa off her back.

The sound of a glass falling comes from the open door into the living room. "You don't think anyone heard us, do you?" she asks.

"I hope not," Lily replies.

❄

It's early evening by the time Lily spots an opportunity to get away again. When yet more food arrives in the form of a slate of Yorkshire cheeses, Lily heaves herself up. "I'm off to bed," she says. "The journey and the bad night's sleep have caught up with me." Tom bumps his hand to his chest, and Ronnie walks over to give her a hug. Holly waves goodbye, her cheeks made as red as the berries of her namesake by a long-cellared wine. Nobody else even looks at Lily.

Lily climbs the stairs, and once more memories tumble. One in particular, though, stays with her. Going up to bed on that Christmas Day, before Mum died.

She'd wanted to stay up. Who didn't want to stay up late when they were eleven? She'd crept down and sat on the stair that didn't creak. Her nightie pulled over her knees to keep her warm, she'd listened to the drunk-fuzzy conversations and the snap and giggles as the adults played Ronnie's Hungry Hippo game. He hadn't even had a chance to play it himself. She'd been thinking of how unfair that was when she heard Grandma Violet's stick tap-tapping on the hall floor. Lily had been about to call out, as Grandma wouldn't have minded her hiding there—she'd probably have smiled and applauded her, kept her secret—but then Aunt Liliana emerged. Lily could tell from the snap of her feet on the tiles that she was angry.

Lily made herself as small as she could, tried to keep still, like a statue when no music is playing.

"Did you hear what that snake said to me?" Liliana said. Through the banisters, Lily watched her aunt's face. She'd never seen her so angry.

"I saw her sneer as she leaned over Mariana. That was enough," Grandma replied.

Lily couldn't help leaning forward to catch the next sentence. Her feet were on the next step down. It creaked, giving her away.

Liliana looked up and saw Lily. Lily was sure she saw fear cross her aunt's face with such heavy footsteps it left marks on her forehead.

Grandma Violet, however, didn't look up at all. Yet she still said, "Lily is good at listening. People shouldn't underestimate her."

"I don't," Liliana had replied.

"People underestimated me throughout my life," Grandma said. Only then did she look up to see Lily hunched on the stairs. "I've always found that very useful."

"Didn't hold you back," Liliana said, with what Lily had thought at the time was a touch of envy. But maybe it was pride, too.

"You pay for it in other ways, but it means you can slip through the gaps. Like wind in the walls, like ghosts in a house, hearing everything, saying nothing until the time it will scare people the most."

Lily had crept down the stairs. Grandma Violet held out her arms, and Lily sidled into them. The floorboards could make as much noise as they wanted now. Grandma was small, but as squishy and warm as a plushie without the seams, and able to hug back. She felt so strong. As if even the cancer running through her like dry rot couldn't take hold and cause her to crumble away.

Mum had walked into the hallway then, and Grandma had let Lily go. "This one should go back to bed," she said.

Mum nodded. She looked tired. Her eyes were shadowed. She took Lily back to the bottom of the stairs. "Up you go, Lily," Mum had said after kissing her on the top of her head. "I'll be in to say goodnight again soon." And so, Lily had climbed up these same stairs, slowly, one after the other, until she'd reached her room. She got into bed and pulled the duvet up to her neck and waited. And waited. But her mum hadn't come up.

And Lily never saw her alive again.

Thirty-three-year-old Lily lies in bed, the same duvet pulled over her. Underneath, she's holding her mum's coat close. Fabric arms cradle Lily in a ghostly embrace. Part of her feels ashamed, and hopes no one ever finds out about this. But another part knows there's been something missing in Lily ever since that night. She's still waiting for Mum to come up and say goodnight.

If the bloodstains weren't there, she could go to sleep like this. But she can't stop thinking about them. They cover the sleeves, with some on the hem of the coat where it must have dripped as she died. Why did no one get it cleaned? Lily sits up and turns her bedside light back on. She stares at the stains, as if being close to her mother's blood could help her feel it in her veins.

Before she can stop herself, she bends to lick the blood. There's nothing to taste, of course.

Disgusted with herself, she gets out of bed. Maybe removing the blood will leach away what she has been stained by.

Lily goes into her bathroom and runs the bath. Needing salt, she throws on her dressing gown and tiptoes down the stairs to the pantry. Murmurs come from the living room, but otherwise, the house sleeps. On her way back up, saltcellar in her pocket, she hears someone moving on the second floor. She hurries up the next set of stairs before they see her.

Fifteen minutes later, Mum's green coat is soaking in Lily's tub. It looks as if it's waving, sinking into the salted water. The saline should start to work on the blood—like taking the top off a scab—then she can try detergent and soda paste. Bleach is a last resort, as then she'd have to dye the coat green again, and she'd never match the color. Bloodstains never really go away.

Chapter Fifteen

December 26th
Boxing Day—The Second Day of Christmas

Lily wakes to the sound of keening. At first, she thinks it's her own, screaming out from her bad dream. She'd been trapped in ice this time, and Mum had been trying to reach her.

Then she hears it again. A loud, mournful groan rising from the floor below.

It's still dark. She could still be in a dream. One of those recursive nightmares where she dreams she wakes up, over and over again. "Nooooo, please, no." Loud and urgent, the moan roams the house.

This isn't a dream.

Lily fumbles for the light and scrambles out of bed, sleep dropping its shroud from around her. Her corset is barely laced up when she runs across the cold floor. The sound keeps coming, from downstairs. Lights crash on, making her blink. Other doors open and slam, footsteps match hers as she hurries down the staircase.

She slows when she sees Tom at the bottom of the stairs, his hand over his mouth. Holly and Rachel are next to him, Holly buried in Rachel's arms. Rachel glances over Holly's head and catches Lily's eye. Tears are rolling down her face.

Lily walks past them, then she sees him.

Ronnie kneels on a black square. "No, please, no," he says, rocking backward and forward, holding something.

Lily can't understand what she's seeing. Images snap into focus: Ronnie's hands covered in blood. Blood smeared down the corridor from the entrance to the library. An arm slipping from his lap. Philippa's head lolling back. Her eyes open and unseeing.

A knife sticks out of her, her back a macabre knife block.

Lily finds herself moving forward and crouching next to Ronnie. He turns away from her slightly as if not wanting comfort. Holding Philippa's body tighter, he rocks harder. "Get an ambulance!" he shouts, craning round to look at everyone. "Why are you all standing there?"

"I think she's gone, Ronnie," Lily says, gently.

He shakes his head and then shakes Philippa. Lily looks away from Philippa's lolling head. "No. She wouldn't leave me," he says. "She knows I can't cope without her."

Lily slowly reaches past Ronnie for Philippa's wrist. She presses two fingers into the underside, in the vulnerable spot between tendons. "There's no pulse, Ronnie," she says.

Ronnie curls over his wife's body. His keening returns, echoing up to the minstrel gallery. Lily remembers where she heard that sound before. It came from her, when she found Mum. Hearing Ronnie cry in the same way salts the scab of old wounds.

"What are we going to do?" Sara asks. Lily looks up. Sara stands over them, her eyes wide, as if needing to be open as much as possible to take it in. A human reaction at last.

Next to Sara, Tom's mouth keeps opening and closing, as if trying to speak but unable to.

"No way can she have done that to herself," Holly says.

The silence is fully loaded. Lily looks round the hallway. Everyone is here—Ronnie, Sara, Gray, Rachel, Holly, Tom, Mrs. Castle, and Lily herself. Whoever stabbed Philippa could be in this house.

"It's the carving knife," Gray says, his voice so quiet. "The one

Philippa used to cut the turkey." His eyes are dulled by what they're seeing, clouded silver pieces.

"Call an ambulance," Ronnie cries again.

"Too late for that, mate," Sara says. She bends and awkwardly pats him on the shoulder.

"Shut the fuck up, Sara!" Ronnie shouts.

"Don't worry, I'll call them," Lily says to him. She has spun round the inner tube of grief many times and knows Ronnie will keep circling back to the safest, darkest place: denial.

Ronnie nods at Lily. "Thank you." He then bends close and whispers into Philippa's ear. "Get up, sweetheart. Time to go back to bed." He is clinging on to hope like ivy to a haunted house. Any moment now, he must be thinking, Philippa will dust herself off, rise up, and do something really annoying and everything will be back to normal.

But nothing will seem normal to Ronnie again.

Lily gets up, motions to Tom to take her place next to his brother.

Tom nods. Then he puts on his therapist face and sits by Ronnie's side. "Don't worry," he says. "We'll look after her."

Ronnie keeps whispering in Philippa's ear. The love in his voice sticks a pin in Lily's heart.

Lily walks into the kitchen where Mrs. Castle is filling the kettle, her hand shaking. "We have to call the police," Lily says.

"You can't," Mrs. Castle replies. Her voice hitches, as if she's trying not to cry.

"Philippa's dead and someone killed her," Lily says. "We need to get help."

"Not by phone, you won't. The snowstorm's brought the lines down."

"What storm?" Lily asks. She looks out into the garden. The light from the kitchen shows how much snow must have fallen overnight. It's a third of the way up the rotting door, and still falling. The top layer of snow is whipped by the wind into white gauze petticoats.

"I tried to get through to the police as soon as I saw her. Poor love. She was only asking about what to do in an emergency the other night."

"Didn't anyone think of this happening?" Lily asks.

"Someone getting murder for Christmas instead of a present? Funnily enough, no, we didn't," Mrs. Castle replies. She then covers her mouth as if trying to shovel the words back in.

"We? Did *you* plan the Christmas Game with Aunt Lil?" Lily asks.

Mrs. Castle shakes her head. "Liliana insisted on writing the clues and rules by herself. You know what she's like. Isabelle and me, we were only involved in logistics. No one was supposed to get hurt."

"Well, they have. We'll have to drive to the police ourselves."

"If things don't get any worse," Mrs. Castle says.

"How can it get worse?"

"Never ask that question," Mrs. Castle replies. "Fate has a tendency to answer."

Chapter Sixteen

Tom is by the front door, hurrying his coat on. "Where's the nearest police station?"

"Bedale, maybe," Rachel says. "Or Ripon?"

"I'll check," Gray says, reaching into his pocket, presumably for his phone. He closes his eyes. "Sorry, keep forgetting we've handed them over."

"Why did we agree to that again?" Tom asks, looping a scarf around his neck.

"Because of Mum's precious rules," Sara replies. "Rules that also say that anyone who leaves forfeits their right to the house."

"You can't think we'll carry on with the game?" Lily asks.

"Why would we stop?" Sara says, eyebrows raised.

"Philippa's dead," Lily replies, as quietly as she can to avoid hurting Ronnie. She looks back to where he still sits with his wife's head on his thigh. She tries not to see the knife, the blood.

"And I'm sorry about that. But there's nothing we can do for her now," Sara says. "I'm just being pragmatic."

"You're being cruel and obtuse," Tom says. His voice vibrates with anger.

"Maybe," Sara replies. "But I'm staying. The phone lines will be back up at some point; I'll call the police then. By all means, the rest of you go. And then I'll get the house."

Rachel hovers in the hallway, stuck somewhere between Tom and Sara. Mrs. Castle leans against the wall as if she needs its solidity. She stares at the picture of Liliana on the wall. Probably wondering how she got herself mixed up in this family.

"Wait," Sara says, her finger raised. "What's happened to the key Tom gave Philippa?" She raises her voice, turns toward Ronnie, who still sits on the floor with Philippa's body. "Ronnie, did you see what she did with that key?"

Ronnie doesn't turn round. He's stroking Philippa's head as if sending her to sleep. Lily hopes he didn't even hear Sara.

"How can you ask that?" Holly demands. Rachel holds her closer.

"It's not like she needs it, is it?" Sara replies. "And, let's be honest, Ronnie won't have any use for it."

"You're disgusting, Sara," Tom says.

Sara shrugs again. But Lily is standing close enough to see her shocked intake of breath. Maybe even Sara has feelings.

"Right," Tom says, pulling his car keys from his pocket. "Anyone got snow tires?"

Heads shake.

"Call yourself from Yorkshire, you lot?" Tom says. "All right, then— anyone got an atlas, a map, a bloody globe? I don't care what as long as it takes me to the nearest police station!" His voice echoes in the hall.

Mrs. Castle seems to wake up at this volume. She marches over to the bureau in the reception hall and opens a drawer.

Tom's voice gets through to Ronnie, too. "Ssh, Tom," Ronnie hisses. "Philippa's sleeping." He strokes her hair over and over.

"It's all right, Ronnie, love, we'll keep quiet," Rachel says, looking over at her brother with so much love it hurts.

Mrs. Castle rummages through the drawer, muttering to herself.

"Have you got GPS?" Rachel asks Tom.

"I use my phone," Tom says through a clamped jaw. "Only I don't have it."

"I'll get my GPS from my car," Lily says, wrapping her scarf around her. "It's a bit old, though. Kept freezing on the way up. Doubt the connection will be better in a snowstorm."

Tom nods, as if he wouldn't expect anything else from a night like this.

Lily hopes she'll be able to read the other clues later—there's nothing in the rules to say she can't. Right now, though, Philippa has been killed and Ronnie needs help. That's far more important than a decades-old mystery.

Tom hugs her, really tight. She's not sure if he's shaking or if she is.

Mrs. Castle shouts out "Ha!" and waves a road atlas over her head. "I'll come, too," she says, smiling at Lily. "The map will get us where we want."

Ten minutes later, Lily and Mrs. Castle are in Tom's car. Rachel and Gray shovel snow from the driveway while Tom douses the front and back windscreens with deicer. Snow keeps falling, mocking their attempts.

"Maybe I spoke too soon," Mrs. Castle says.

"Thought you were all for not tempting fate," Lily replies.

"I'm hoping it'll prove me wrong," Mrs. Castle says, but there's not much hope in her voice.

Tom gets in and places the key in the ignition. "Come on, Kristeva," he says, "work for me, would you?"

"*What* have you called your car?" Mrs. Castle asks.

"Julia Kristeva," Tom replies. "She's a psychoanalytic critic."

"I know who she is," Mrs. Castle says, folding her arms.

Julia Kristeva revs, trying to get her tires into the gravel. "Come on," Tom says. "You can do it."

Lily huddles into the back seat. The heated seats are beginning to work. Imagine that in her old Mini. There's a drink holder, too. She'd kill for a coffee.

No. She wouldn't.

The engine kicks in and the car starts to move. She thinks she can hear Gray cheering, but it might be the wind in the trees. Tom leans forward in his seat, trying to see out of the window. The wipers are on, but his vision must be almost zero.

"I'm not sure this is safe," Mrs. Castle says.

"I don't know what else to do," Tom says. There are tears backing up his voice.

"It's not like we're safe in the house," Lily replies.

"Aunt Liliana should never have brought us all together," Tom says.

"She couldn't have known someone would die," Mrs. Castle replies.

But Liliana knew that someone had been killed at Endgame before. What if that has something to do with Philippa's death?

Mrs. Castle catches Lily's eye in the rearview mirror. She places a finger to her lips.

As they start down the steep driveway, the car slips. Tom keeps it on course, but the car slows. The snow is getting heavier and heavier. Snowflakes cover the windows like intricate lace.

On either side of them, the woods press in, as if trying to climb into the safety of the car. Maybe it's for the best that Lily's leaving. Even Aunt Liliana would agree that she's given the Christmas Game a fair chance. She wouldn't expect Lily to stay in a house where yet another person has died. After all, Liliana had left when her sister died, taking Lily with her.

And then a thought occurs to Lily. Maybe her aunt had been taking Lily to safety, away from whoever had killed Mum. But then why now bring her back into danger?

The car has stopped. Tom revs again, but the wheels are just chewing up earth, ice, and gravel. They're stuck.

Tom tries to open the car door but it's wedged in by a snowbank. Lowering his window, he leans his head out as far as possible. The storm barges into the car, spitting sleet into their faces.

"Can't see much," Tom shouts. "But it looks like a tree has fallen over the road. We'll have to shift it!"

Lily undoes her seat belt and opens her door a fraction. "There's more room this side!" she shouts. "Mrs. Castle, if you get out, then Tom can climb over."

They nod, and she hopes they've actually heard her. The wind is trying to keep the door closed, whether to keep her out of danger or in it is not clear.

Using her legs, Lily pushes against the door. It swings open just long enough for her to get out, placing her back toward the door to protect her tummy. Her face feels lacerated. Even with her coat and layers of clothes, she might as well be out here in a nightie.

Mrs. Castle bundles out of the car, followed by Tom. Heads down, huddling together, Lily, Tom, and Mrs. Castle edge around the car to see what's blocking the way. Every few gusts of wind, the fallen tree becomes visible for a moment. One of the huge oaks, severed at the knee, lies prone across the road. Its branches reach out under the wheels of the car. It creaks and rustles and flinches, dying in front of them.

"Must have come down in the wind," Mrs. Castle says.

Tom doesn't say anything. Holding his arms in front of him, squinting against the sleet, looking out for roots, he works his way down to the base of the felled tree. Lily follows, twigs scratching at her limbs. Tom points to the trunk, salami sliced, rings showing its final age. She's no tree surgeon but Lily doesn't think a storm could cut an oak smoothly in two.

"We can't move that tonight," Tom shouts. "Too dangerous."

Lily nods. The three of them turn and link arms, just as Lily did with Philippa less than two days ago. She doesn't know if this is the best way to face the storm—three abreast rather than single file—but it feels more comforting.

Together they trudge back up the driveway. She didn't think she'd ever be happy to see Endgame House rising through the snow. Then she remembers what she's returning to: a murder house, that someone has stopped them from leaving.

Chapter Seventeen

"You're shaking," Holly says as Lily steps back into the house. She rubs Lily's arms, hugs her tight. Lily looks to the floor, and finds strange joy in seeing Holly's pom-pom-topped slippers.

"All right, all right," Sara says, frowning. "It's not Lily who needs comforting here."

"Her teeth are chattering, Sara," Holly says, snapping for the first time in Lily's company. "What's your problem?"

Sara steps back. She frowns, but doesn't seem to know what to say.

Lily hears, then, her own molars snapping against each other, like the windup plastic teeth you get in crackers. She must have been this cold before. The day she found her mum, she'd walked through the snow in bare feet. Now she can't even feel her toes, and is grateful. She raises a hand, and she can see it shaking. "I don't know what's happening," Lily says.

"It's the shock," Mrs. Castle replies.

"We need to get her warmed up," Holly says. She puts her arm round Lily and guides her toward the living room. As they go, though, Lily can't help looking toward the library. Ronnie still sits there, on the floor. Although now he's not moving. It's as if he's one of the statues in the garden.

"He won't get up," Holly says in as soft a voice as she can manage.

"And he won't let us take Philippa," Rachel adds.

"Nor should he," Mrs. Castle says in a whisper. "It's bad enough that he held her. Don't blame him, mind, poor love." Her face softens, just for a moment, then stiffens as if starched into its normal state. "But she shouldn't be moved an inch more till the police arrive. Not that they'll get here anytime soon."

"What happened?" Rachel asks.

"A tree fell across the driveway," Tom says. "No way we can get out, not by car, not tonight."

"Oh, no," Holly says as she settles Lily into a chair. Once again, Lily has a blanket tucked round her. Philippa had looked after Lily in a similar way, and now she's dead. "The poor tree, it was so big. Must have been here a long time."

"Right. And that's our priority right now," Sara says. "One tree that can't take a little storm."

"It was cut down deliberately," Mrs. Castle says, her voice sharp enough to cut down the tree itself.

"Who'd do a thing like that?" Holly asks. Her eyes are as round as berries, red from tiredness and crying.

"Maybe the same person who'd kill Philippa," Gray replies. He's standing by the fire, his hands behind his back as if trying to stop himself from gesticulating.

No one can find a reply to this. The fire fills the silence with a low-level hiss. The wind shakes the sash windows. The house creaks around them.

"Is anyone going to get us tea? Or coffee? Preferably something stronger," Sara says at last. "Or does Mrs. Castle have to do that too, despite what's she been through?" She stares straight at Holly.

"Of course," Holly says, looking confused. "I'll do it." She stands up, her face a display of bafflement, and shuffles out of the living room.

Sara waits until Holly's footsteps are out of hearing. "I didn't want to say this in front of an outsider, especially a sweet and naïve one like Holly—"

"She's my wife, and part of this family," Rachel interrupts, eyes flashing. "And you've got no idea what she's like. Although I suppose anyone seems sweet and naïve compared to you, Sara."

"I'll take that as a compliment," Sara replies, rolling her eyes.

Rachel stands. "You can take it and shove it right up your—"

"I don't think we need to go into biological details, Rachel," Tom says. "And Sara, for God's sake, just say what you want to say."

Sara looks across at Gray for backup, but he's staring into the flames as if he wants to disappear with the sparks up the chimney. "Fine. Well, we clearly need to get our stories straight for when the police actually get here."

"The only reason to get our stories straight is if one of us did it," Tom replies.

"One of us did, cousin dear," Sara says. "Either that or someone broke in during a storm, killed Philippa while we all slept, and then felled a tree to make sure we couldn't get out."

"That's not impossible," Gray says, hope lacing his voice.

"Improbable, though, wouldn't you say?" Sara says. "I thought you studied logic at university."

Gray looks as if he's about to say something, then stops. Lily knows exactly how he must feel. All those words bottled up for decades, oak aged and waiting to be decanted.

From the hallway, Ronnie starts sobbing. Lily stands up quickly but feels faint, darkness encroaching on the edges of her vision like an old photograph.

"I'll go," Tom says. He moves quickly out of the room. "Coming, mate!"

Lily takes a deep breath. If Philippa's death is connected to both her mum and Aunt Liliana dying—and she can't see how it isn't, unless the house itself is cursed—then she needs to step up. Without drawing attention to what she's doing. This is where she has to prove herself. If she can.

"If we're going to get our 'stories' straight," Lily says, slowly, trying to think as she speaks. "Then we need to know what everyone was doing around the time Philippa died."

"I was asleep," Sara says, quickly. "First thing I knew about it was hearing Ronnie."

On mentioning Ronnie, everyone is quiet for a moment, listening to his hushed crying and Tom's reassuring whispers from the hallway.

"And me," says Lily.

Mrs. Castle, Rachel, and Gray all state the same thing. They were asleep and were woken up by the sounds coming from downstairs.

"So, either one or more of us is lying," Lily says. "Or Tom or Holly did it, or someone from outside."

"Or Ronnie," Gray adds.

"Can you hear him?" Sara asks. "Does he sound like he murdered someone he loved?" Ronnie is roaring now. It sounds like his pain can't be contained by his skin.

"I wouldn't know," Gray says, meeting his sister's eye. "And I'm just using logic, as you suggested."

Lily tries to picture the driveway. "There might be CCTV footage on the perimeter gates," Lily says. "But we'd need to get a message to Isabelle to see it."

"If we could let her know, then we'd be able to contact the police," Rachel says.

"There's something else we should talk about," Sara says. "What we're going to do with Philippa's body."

"I told you, she shouldn't be moved," Mrs. Castle replies. "And we shouldn't go near the library entrance either. Forensics won't want anything changed."

"You said yourself that Ronnie already moved her."

That's true enough. From the blood on the floor, it looks to Lily like Ronnie dropped to the floor on seeing her lying in the doorway, and dragged her into his arms.

The low murmur of Holly's voice comes from the hallway, followed by the slow shuffling of her slippers on the tiles. She enters, carrying a tray. Her eyes fix on the stacked cups and the huge pot of tea until they are placed safely on the table. Tom follows her in with another tray—this one is topped with coffee and mounds of biscuits. Lily's tummy rumbles.

She covers the sound with a cough. Feeling hungry at a time like this feels disrespectful.

"I'm worried about Ronnie," Tom says, moving back into the doorway so he can keep an eye on his brother. "He refuses to leave her. I mean, he's still trying to wake her up."

"It's shock," Mrs. Castle says again. "Finding your wife dead." She shakes her head. "How can he possibly react any other way? It's the most devastating thing that could happen." Holly moves even closer to Rachel.

"I think we should move her," Tom says.

"For once we agree," Sara says. "That's what I've been saying."

"Now I wish I kept my mouth shout," Tom replies.

"We should leave her where she is," Lily says. "Moving her could ruin an investigation. We've no idea what we're doing."

"We can't leave her, not on the floor," Holly says. "It's so uncomfortable."

"I don't think she's in a position to care," Sara says, not unkindly. "But there's another reason to remove her. Not being funny—" Sara adopts her "I'm just saying it like it is" face. "But she's going to start to smell soon."

"God, Sara," Tom says. His face is scrunched up in disgust. "I thought you couldn't surprise me anymore, and then you say that."

"True, though," Sara replies. "We all know that it's a fact. Tell them, Gray."

"Leave him alone, Sara," Tom says. "What would Gray know?"

"Undertakers tend to know a lot about death," Sara answers. She smiles at everyone's shocked faces. She loves knowing things others don't.

"I only started training in September," Gray says, staring at the carpet. Lily feels a flush of peace at the thought of someone as gentle as Gray dealing with the dead. If she were to die, she'd want Gray to be present, head bowed, hands behind his back.

Sara pokes her brother in the arm, and he recoils. "Tell them, Gray— how she'll start stinking the house up if we leave her."

Holly places a hand over her mouth and turns her head to rest on Rachel's shoulder. Lily wishes she had someone she could do that with.

"And you used to be such a nice little girl," Mrs. Castle says.

"No, I wasn't," Sara says. And she's right.

From the hall, Ronnie starts crying again. Lily's heart hurts. She needs to hold him. And that must only be a sliver of what he's feeling toward Philippa.

Lily stands up slowly to prevent reeling. Inside her, Bean twists and turns like the conversation. It feels reassuring. Glad to leave the group, Lily walks away. Tom grabs her hand as she passes and squeezes it.

Ronnie looks up when Lily places a hand on his shoulder. "I know what you're going to say," he says, wiping his face of snot and tears with the back of his hand. "I know she's gone, but I can't let her go."

"I understand," Lily says. She eases herself down next to him. "I'm not going to ask you to do anything you don't want to."

Ronnie leans into her. She feels his sobs shake through her. She wonders if Bean can feel them, too.

"Tell me about Philippa," Lily says. "Tell me everything you love about her."

Lily knows not to place the past tense onto the situation. It's up to Ronnie to do that.

"I love all the big and little things. How she knows the end of a film before it's hardly started. Her love of yellow roses after the rain," Ronnie says, gazing down at Philippa. His eyes are soft, his voice softer.

"Tell me more," Lily says, stroking his head.

"She loves Samuel with such ferocity. I always tell her that she's not going to be any old helicopter parent—she's going to be a Chinook. She soothes him to sleep by reading the weather forecast. She likes fruit and nut chocolate, but takes out the nuts and gives them to me. She only sits in the front row of the cinema as she likes huge people to make her feel thin. She sucks the sugar off popcorn; she can skin a fish in under thirty seconds; she will eat the same meal I make her time and time again and still give me notes on how to make it better, and that's good, that's great, as I want to make it the best I can for her." Ronnie breaks into a sob that makes him start rocking again.

"It's OK," Lily says. "Keep going."

And he does. He talks for what seems like hours on that hard floor about every tiny and massive thing he loves about the woman lying dead in his lap. He doesn't seem to notice the knife in her back, only what he loves. Lily aches to feel this kind of love, but then look what happens when you lose it.

"She was so excited about coming here," Ronnie continues, shaking his head and smoothing Philippa's hair so it doesn't cover her eyes. "She's been studying hotel management, asking me loads of questions about the family…she even started doing crosswords when I told her that Aunt Liliana liked anagrams. I'd never have brought her here if I thought this would—" He breaks off. He's racked with sobs again and all Lily can do is hold him.

"She told me she'd be back," he says. Lily has to hold on to his words, she can hardly hear him through the sobs. "That's what I can't get out of my head. If I'd only gone down with her…"

"Why did she go downstairs?" Lily asks, her heart beating faster.

Ronnie shrugs. "I was half asleep. She said she wanted to check on someone."

"Someone? Or something?"

Ronnie closes his eyes and screws up his face. Then lets out a sigh of frustration. "Someone, I think. But I don't know." He turns to Lily, eyes wide, nostrils flaring. "Why don't I know? They were her last words to me. I should have listened harder, should've kissed her. Gone in her place."

Lily can do nothing but hold him until, eventually, his tears dry up. Ronnie collapses in on himself, chin to chest. He seems small. His cracked lips move but no sound comes out, as if in silent prayer to Philippa.

Hearing soft steps nearby, Lily looks up to see Gray standing by the staircase. "He should get some rest," Gray says. "It's going to be a long day for him."

Lily nods.

Ronnie's eyes are closing. "Do you think you can come with me to rest for a while?" Lily asks.

Ronnie hesitates, then nods. "But what about—"

"We'll look after Philippa for you," Lily says.

Gray is now standing next to her. His face as he looks down on them is full of empathy and compassion. How did he become like this when Sara has none of these qualities? Where did Liliana go so right and so wrong? Or is it nothing to do with how you are as a mother?

Lily doesn't know whether to hope for nature or nurture as the biggest influence on Bean. Both are suspect.

"I'll make her comfortable," Gray tells Ronnie. "I'll get a cushion for her head."

"One of the festive red ones," Ronnie says. "She loved Christmas."

Chapter Eighteen

It's light by the time Lily wakes from her nap. Bean is awake too, swishing in her cozy suite. Lily hadn't thought she'd be able to get back to sleep, but the white noise of wind against windows had slowly lulled her away from thoughts of mortality.

But not for long. It's Boxing Day. The anniversary of Mum's death.

Lily pulls back the curtains and looks out over the white-laid land. She can't escape it. The maze and the events of twenty-one years ago today are as fresh and cold as the overnight snow.

Lily goes into her bathroom and turns on the light. She steps back, startled. A human shape lies still in the bath. Then remembers—her mum's coat. Still soaking. The water has a pink tint to it. But the coat is green.

And then she notices the stains on the sleeves, or rather the lack of them. The bloodstains have almost all gone. Which means they weren't bloodstains at all.

When she's changed into her dress for the day, a black Victorian-style mourning gown, she stops on her way downstairs to check on Ronnie.

Opening the door gently, she calls his name. In the curtained dark, she can see him curled up on the bed. Still asleep, properly knocked out. His duvet and blanket are crumpled at the bottom of the bed as if he's been fighting them. He's cuddling a pillow as if it were his wife.

Lily looks over to the other side of the bed. Philippa's eye-mask, hand cream, and paperbacks are laid out. What will be referred to by the police as her "personal effects." No sign of the key.

The drawers, though, are open in her bedside cabinet. Lily walks softly over and tries to see if the key is in one of them, but can't see anything amid the tumble of knickers, tights, makeup, headbands, and moisturizers. When Ronnie had visited Lily's flat the first time, he'd said that Philippa would freak at the chaos. So, either Ronnie has been rifling through his wife's things as if her personal effects contain something of her, or someone has gone through Philippa's things, maybe looking for the key.

Ronnie whimpers in his sleep, and Lily carefully pulls the duvet back up over him. He clutches the pillow tighter. May he stay asleep and dream of Philippa.

At the bottom of the stairs, she hears a kettle boiling in the kitchen. It's weird how life carries on when someone dies. It's then that she notices Philippa's body is gone. And her blood has been cleaned from the floor.

Tom walks out of the dining room, rubbing his eyes. He hasn't shaved. Dark shadows under his eyes make him look older.

"What's going on?" Lily asks. "Where's Philippa?"

"She was gone when I came down. I only went for a quick nap, but in that time Sara and Gray carried her to the icehouse."

Lily looks around as if seeing everything for the first time. The hallway, strung with switched-off lights and dying pine, seems even more foreboding. Yesterday it was a simulacrum of a celebration that never happened, and now it's the site of a wake. She imagines Philippa lying in that dark icehouse. Lily shivers, as if she can feel the hard cold on Philippa's skin. "What's Ronnie going to say when he wakes up and she's out there? He'll want to go to her. We can't exactly strap him down."

Tom shakes his head. "He should be out for another few hours at least. But I've no idea what to do when he wakes. I'm trained in this stuff, but I don't know what to say to him."

"Maybe we'll be able to get out by then. Between us, we should be able to move the tree."

"And that's the other bad news," Tom says.

"What now?"

"Mrs. Castle heard on the radio. The whole area is officially snowed in. No chance of getting through any of the country roads. The police can't get to us, and we can't get to them."

"We're trapped," Lily says. And neither of them says it, but she knows they're both thinking it: they're trapped in Endgame House with a murderer.

All of them—apart from Ronnie—are sitting in the morning room upstairs. Coffee cups cool in their hands. Only in houses like this are there rooms for different times of the day. Guests move about the house like shadows round a sundial.

The name of the room is appropriate. Winter lilies drop tears onto the table. Even the light streaming through the window can't stop the funereal gloom. Lily had intended to wear this dress to honor Mum and Liliana. She never thought it would have a more immediate use. If she doesn't have the words, at least her clothes can show Ronnie how she feels.

Tom comes over and sits on the arm of Lily's chair. "How are you feeling?" he asks, so very quietly. He points toward her black dress that she'd handsewn to look like a thousand raven feathers cascading around her. "I know this must be difficult. Philippa's death on the same day as your mum's."

Lily winces at his openness. She feels difficult tears welling and tries to dam them. She will not cry, not here. That won't help. "I'm fine," she says.

Tom nods. He touches her arm lightly. "I'm here if you want to talk."

Lily can't even nod as the tears will tip out. "OK," she says instead.

"Have you seen Ronnie?" Lily asks.

Tom nods, his face serious. "I gave him another sedative."

"I can't even imagine how losing a spouse feels."

"You'd have to be close to someone to know that," Tom replies. He sees her darting glance. "I'm talking about me as much as you. Neither of us have allowed anyone under our skin."

Lily looks away and says nothing. What can you say when someone pins down the truth?

Sara is watching them. Lily can feel her cold stare from the other side of the room. She wishes she knew why Sara didn't like her. It makes her want to appease her, make it OK, especially on days like today. Smooth everything over like marzipan on a dark, bumpy cake. It's not a side of herself that she likes. It can help make situations go better, but it also costs.

Tom has noticed Sara, too. She feels him tense up next to her, the muscles in his arm contract. "You look like you're going to say something, Sara?" Tom says.

Lily nudges him, hoping it can convey her need for him to shut up, to not make things worse. It does. She hears him breathing out slowly, can feel his muscles relax. He's doing the breathing exercises they learned together at the mindfulness class last year. He's much better at it than her. She's only mindful of how minutes drag their feet in the classes, that she's supposed to let thoughts go like balloons and watch them drift across the sky of her mind without any attachment to them, their strings hanging free as they float away. She's holding on to the strings. She can't let go.

"I was just thinking how lovely it is that you two are so close," Sara says. Lily isn't always great at picking up her saracasm, but that one lands like Santa falling down the chimney.

Tom tenses again. "And what's wrong with that?" he asks.

"Oh, nothing. I believe it's fine for cousins to carry on with each other. I just wish Lily would make up her mind."

Lily feels sliced like salmon. She opens her mouth to say all those phrases that come late at night but they are stuck, itching at her throat.

She never can say anything whenever someone comments or threatens violence in the street when she's holding hands with or kissing a woman. Or when she's with a man and assumed to be straight, leaving her privileged and safer, yet erased. Speaking up is beyond her. She's letting everyone down, a whole community, as well as herself.

Rachel and Tom, though, don't seem to have the same problem. As if sharing a protective breath, they speak at the same time: Rachel says, "What do you mean by that?" and from Tom, "Wait a fucking minute, mate."

Lily can feel Sara bristle from over the other side of the room. "Mate?" she says, as if spitting out a bad almond.

"Lily likes who Lily likes," Tom replies. "She doesn't have to make up her mind or make up anything for you. And as for your snide insinuation, you're ridiculous." He's vibrating against Lily's arm. He's clutching one hand with the other, as if trying to stop himself from jabbing it toward Sara.

Gray places his hand on Sara's arm and gently shakes his head.

She stands up and goes over to the fireplace. Grabbing a pomander from the display on the mantel, she picks out cloves as if removing Tom's words from her skin. "If we had the next set of clues," she says, "we wouldn't have to be in each other's company."

"You could go outside," Rachel says. "See if the fresh air cleans out your bi-phobic mouth." Lily feels a flare of gratitude to Rachel. Holly smiles at her.

Gray is pacing up and down, rubbing his head. "Someone's died," he says. "We shouldn't be doing this."

"Doing what?" Tom asks.

Gray looks over to Sara. "Arguing," he says, quietly. "It's not respectful."

A sneer veers across Sara's face. "You're all pathetic, you know that?"

Mrs. Castle walks in. "Lunchtime," she says, with all the warmth of a grate that hasn't seen fire in years.

"But we've only just had breakfast," Holly says. She still has croissant crumbs in her hair. Lily has to resist the urge to pick them out.

"That's what Christmas is all about, isn't it?" Mrs. Castle says. "Someone spends all their time making food, others spend all their time eating it. Then it's over, bar the antacids."

"So nothing changes?" Lily asks.

"Just doing my job, Miss Lily." Mrs. Castle looks like she'd rather be doing any other job but this. And Lily can't blame her.

"Liliana wouldn't expect the Christmas Game to continue when someone has died," Lily says.

"Nothing gets in the way of your aunt's agenda, Lily. You should know that. The Christmas Game continues." She holds Lily's gaze and Lily can't help feeling that Mrs. Castle is trying to tell her something.

Chapter Nineteen

A traditional Boxing Day lunch has been laid out in the dining room—platters of steaming pie sit next to serving plates stacked with slabs of turkey and cola-roasted ham. Jars of homemade chutney stand in a line down the center of the table, made from ingredients from the Endgame estate.

"Dad would have called this 'funeral baked meats,'" Tom says, surveying the table.

Lily reaches for the chestnut and Ribston Pippin chutney and opens the lid. The smell of spiced apples and smoked chestnuts tugs at a memory that feels good, for once. Of walking, wrapped up, in the Endgame orchard, picking Ribston Pippins and ripe plums for Grandma Violet's Yorkshire drop. It's a sugared version of Yorkshire pud, made with seasonal fruit. Eaten in silence at the kitchen table with dollops of cream and heavy-lidded smiles. If it weren't for Philippa's murder, she could see a time where these kinds of memories would make staying at Endgame House bearable. Instead, death has been laid on top of death. This house is a stacked grave.

In most houses on Boxing Day, pie will be popped down everyone's gullets and there won't be a squeak of ham left on the table. In Endgame today, the food remains untouched.

"We should talk about last night," Lily says, with some difficulty.

"Can we not?" Sara says.

"Lily's right. We need to find out who killed Philippa," Holly says.

"And how do you propose we do that?" Sara asks. "Go round and demand to know where we all were at the time of death and whether we saw or heard anything?"

"Well, yes, I suppose," Holly says, looking to Lily, who nods.

"That'd be a start," Lily says.

"All right, then," Sara says. "Did anyone see or hear anything unusual last night, including the murder of Philippa Armitage?" No one replies. Heads shake. "There you go, then. As if anyone is going to admit anything."

"Maybe it's not one of the family," Gray says. Hope lights up his eyes.

"Do you think it was Mrs. Castle, with the carving knife, in the hallway?" Sara says, her saracasm so heavy it could weigh down a body in water.

"That tone really isn't necessary, Sara," Rachel says. "It's incredibly distasteful to talk about Philippa like that."

"I was more thinking it could be someone from outside the house," Gray replies. "A stranger."

"Wouldn't that be convenient," Rachel says, looking at Sara.

Mrs. Castle reappears to turn off the lights. The door closes. The whole room is in the yellow half-light of midwinter afternoon, with everyone taking on a sepia tinge.

The door opens again, and Mrs. Castle walks in with a flame-lit Christmas pudding. She carries it like an Olympic torch, the fire dancing like a Bond silhouette round the dark dessert.

"You wanted it today, so here it is," Mrs. Castle says, plonking it on the table. "Watch out for something inside. It's not edible."

"I'll cut it up for everyone," Sara says, quickly, presumably guessing that the clues are hidden inside. She's staring at the pudding as if she wants to gouge out its heart.

"I have to serve it. Another clause in my contract." Mrs. Castle takes a knife and squidges it into the Christmas pud. Lily can smell the spices and see the pecans and posh cherries from halfway down the table—no clown-nose red glacé cherries for Endgame's puddings. Everyone, including Lily, leans forward as pieces of pud are dolloped into bowls. Sara picks up her dessert spoon. She elbows Gray to do the same. He does so, holding it up in front of him like a lollipop man.

When the bowls have been handed round, Lily carefully breaks open her treacle-black pudding. Everyone is doing the same. When no one finds a clue, most lean back in their chairs.

Holly, however, surrounds her pudding with a moat of brandy custard and tucks in.

"Ouch," she says, her mouth scrunched up. She reaches into her cheek and pulls out a silver thimble.

"Told you to be careful," Mrs. Castle says.

Sara grabs it, turns the thimble around as if checking for a hidden clue. She finds nothing. "I think this was meant for you and your little sewing enterprise," she says to Lily, throwing it to her.

Lily catches the thimble without thinking. It's embossed with the Endgame maze, and the graze marks of Holly's teeth.

Half an hour later, Mrs. Castle pushes in the follow-up course on a hostess trolley.

"Please, no more food," Holly says. Lily doesn't blame her after the adventure of the Christmas pudding.

"Cheese and crackers!" Tom says. No one even groans at his pun. There is, indeed, cheese, but the crackers are the pulling kind.

Mrs. Castle places one next to each guest. They're shiny gold and huge, with the Armitage crest in the center and a yellow, red-dotted ribbon round each end's neck. "Given the circumstances, I thought Ronnie wouldn't mind if we went ahead," she says. "I went in to ask, but he's still sleeping."

Tom offers Lily one end of his cracker, and they both pull. The cracker snaps, and Lily jolts back. Tom, left with the larger end, tips it up. A hat, a rolled-up piece of paper, and something heavy falls onto the table. "You'll win next time," he says.

Lily picks up the pack of cards that fell from the cracker and hands it to Tom. "Your loot," she says.

Tom puts on his pink hat and unrolls the motto. He reads through it, frowning. "I think you should open the other crackers."

All of them grab the end of a cracker. They pull on the count of three. Mottos, hats, and gifts fly across the room to the sound of snaps. When they each have a motto in their hands, Tom reads out the message.

> *Do you feel safe as hot brandied cocoa?*
> *As bones in snow? As secrets lie beneath*
> *T'stories told; the Christmas songs; and bows*
> *Made with yellow ribbon for a pine wreath.*
> *Lies aged in barrels, stoppered forever,*
> *Or at least till frosty grapes weep to wine*
> *Served with summer-sweet regret. However,*
> *I cannot wait months—there's no longer time:*
> *This winter, my secret will be revealed*
> *And yours. You're not safe. Like pressed leaves, your spines*
> *Will show, their weakness clear; your cover peeled,*
> *Sins stacked, your lies cracked like leather binding*
> *You to your past. At great volume, you'll cry*
> *The beginning and end mark of the line.*

Holly retrieves a pencil case from her bag and three pencils—one red, one blue, one black. She's learning, quickly. Her tongue sticks out a little as she starts circling words.

Lily turns to the sonnet. It feels wrong. Ronnie up there, devastated, while they play this stupid game. But the sonnet is a step closer to knowing the truth. What else can she do?

She reads through slowly, sipping the words like a fine whisky. She tastes the bright citrus top notes of the poem and then the syrupy middle. An anagram unravels itself on her tongue. The base notes, though, the heart of the poem and the clues Lily is supposed to be left with, take a while to come through. She holds the words in her mouth, warming them till they burn her gums. There is so much flavor in those lines, such peat. Such smoke. Why does nobody else notice the darkness at its heart?

"Aunt Liliana's obviously trying to make us go down to the cellar," Rachel says. "All those references to brandy and wine, aging in barrels, and stoppers. So, given yesterday's wild-geese-a-laying chase, I bet the key's not down there."

"Obviously," Sara says, but looks annoyed that Rachel, and everyone else judging by the way they're all nodding, has noticed.

"And I think it's clear where it's actually pointing to," Rachel says, staring right at Sara without blinking. The challenge is clear. Her hands press down on the table, her bum pushing the chair back.

Sara jumps up from her seat and runs out of the dining room. Rachel is close behind, followed by Holly, who leaves spilled pencils and pens and erasers in her wake. Gray gives Lily a ghost of a smile, shrugs, and follows.

"Shall we?" Tom says, pointing to the door. "I really don't want to miss this." Lily stands, and Tom pulls back her chair and takes her arm in a parody of gallantry. They walk slowly to the door, and the floorboards creak as if applauding the pageantry. The house must miss this, Lily thinks, the grand occasions, the frocks and the balls, the coquettes and banquets.

Tom and Lily enter the hallway. "It seems a bit too obvious again," Lily says. "The library, I mean."

"I know what you mean," Tom replies. "But 'stacked,' 'volumes,' 'leather binding,' 'spines'…What else could it be?"

As they approach the library, they hear the heart-ripping sound of books being thrown on the floor. Lily quickens her step. Sara is pulling row upon row of books down at once, sending them scattering onto the floor. The yellow smell of aged pages is written in the air.

"Don't you think we should be more careful?" Lily says. She bends to pick up some of the books, smoothing their spines, trying to resist the urge to kiss them better.

"Shut up, Lily," Sara says, flicking through books, then tossing them to one side. "We're here to find a key, not be librarians."

"Lily's right," Gray says. He's standing in the corner, holding a book to his chest, trying not to look at what's going on. "There are precious books in here." He pauses, as if searching for the right page. "Valuable ones."

He seems to have found the right words, at least, because Sara now looks at each book as if it's a check, and makes sure they don't bounce when she drops them.

This library was the sanctuary for the elder women in the Armitage family. Grandma Violet used to sit in the red, tatty armchair by the fireplace, looking out on the bookshelves like it was a sea view. Aunt Liliana would sit at the long desk down the center of the room, her fingers tracing lines of poetry. Mum sat cross-legged on the floor with Lily on her lap, teaching her to read. This is a sacred place, and Lily won't see it deconsecrated.

She moves closer to see if Gray's found the right book. It's not the one she's looking for, but it's one she loves. *The Hitchhiker's Guide to the Galaxy*. Gray's favorite book, audio drama, TV show, and film. His guide to life. For two of his teenage years, he wore nothing but pajamas and a dressing gown.

Lily, trying to ignore the carnage, the fallen books, the wounded words, walks slowly toward the poetry section. She thinks she knows where the key is, but the last thing she wants is Sara getting it. Anyone but her. Sara wouldn't know how to look after this house; she'll turn it into flats, bulldoze it down herself if she has to, in a Prada hard hat.

Not that Lily cares what happens to the house. It could burn, or be demolished, and she wouldn't care. It probably *should* be destroyed. Its pages torn out. It contains too much sadness to be left intact and extant. She just doesn't want Sara benefiting from its loss, or from Liliana's death.

The poetry section is at the back. This was Aunt Liliana's favorite place.

It's full of her poetry books, and some of her own poetry pamphlets. If Lily's right, she should be looking under "R." It was the hokey "T'stories" that alerted her. Liliana would never write that unless it was pointing to something important.

And then she saw the reference to "Winter, My Secret," a poem Liliana read every year, by her favorite poet, Christina Rossetti. And Rossetti is an anagram of "T'stories."

Lily places her hand on the poetry books and travels down to "R," feeling the spines rippling under her fingers. It is as if they flex under her touch, like a cat arching its back up to her hand. Lily feels a tickle in her nose, as if just thinking of felines makes her sneeze. Racine, Rich, Rilke, Rimbaud, Roethke…but no Rossetti. Not even Christina's brother.

Lily must have gotten it wrong. She's seeing clues that aren't there. And if that's the case, she'll never work out what happened to Mum.

Lily joins the others in looking through the books, if only to stop any more from getting ruined. Gray is going round the walls, pressing all the panels as if this is *Indiana Jones* and a secret passage might be revealed. After all, according to the Christmas Game rules, there *is* a secret room that Lily has never seen. She'd learned about priest holes when she was young and went searching for one, but Endgame House had never revealed to her so much as a hidden cupboard. It keeps its secrets well.

When all the books in the library—and there must be thousands—have been looked through, Rachel says, "Maybe it was a double bluff. Maybe it *is* the wine cellar."

"Wouldn't put it past Mum," says Sara.

Both of them head into the hallway. Rachel and Holly follow. The door to the cellar is next to where Ronnie held Philippa for so long last night. Lily listens as their footsteps slow, then disappear into the basement. Last time she went down there, Gray had locked her in when all the cousins were playing hide-and-seek. She'd counted to a hundred, then, when she found she was trapped, counted all the bottles, too. The walls had been damp, as if they were sweating.

When she'd eventually been let out, she'd asked Gray why he'd done it. He had shrugged, hair falling over his silver eyes. "Sara didn't want you finding her." He seemed to think that was an adequate explanation. Maybe this was the real reason he locked her in the icehouse. Maybe, once again, Sara didn't want Lily to win.

Tom's sitting in the chair that his dad, Edward, used to sleep in of an evening. It's also by the fireplace, with its back to the books. Tom is staring into an unlit fire as if his memories are making their own flames.

Lily goes over and places a hand on his shoulder. He jumps, then looks round. His eyes focus on her. "Sorry, miles away," he says.

"I wish I were," Lily says.

"If you could be anywhere, where would you be?" Tom asks, clasping his hands into what Lily reckons is his therapist listening stance.

"Australia," Lily says, without even needing to think. "Turn this winter into summer sitting on a beach in Sydney, a book close at hand."

"Just like Aunt Liliana," Tom says. "Always had a book within groping distance, and made sure we all did, too."

Lily nods. Liliana even kept a bookcase outside her bedroom, stocked with a selection of books she thought the kids would, or rather should, like. They were her favorites, though they changed every week. As it was opposite Lily's room, she'd pick them each day like orchard fruits. Sometimes sour, sometimes ripe. Often raw, always nourishing.

And if there was anywhere that she'd place her precious Christina Rossetti's poems, it'd be there.

"I've got an idea where the key might be," Lily says.

Tom looks around the library as if properly seeing the chaos for the first time. "Doubt we'll find anything in here."

"Come with me," Lily says, and walks out of the room.

As they go through the hallway, the clank of bottles being moved and boxes heaved across a stone floor bubbles up from the wine cellar. That should keep them busy for a while.

When Lily and Tom are at the top of the first staircase, however, Lily hears quick footsteps coming toward them down the hall.

"Is this where we run?" Tom asks. His eyes are sparkling.

"You try running in a corset and this dress," Lily says.

"Where are you two going?" Sara calls out from the bottom of the stairs.

"Just going to get something from Lily's room," Tom says, turning round. "No need for all of us to go." He presses a hand to Lily's back, urging her on. He's trying to give her time.

Lily walks quickly up the next set of stairs and turns right. Behind her, Tom is trying to waylay Sara.

"Out of my way, Tom!" Sara shouts.

Flooded with adrenaline, Lily hurries down the corridor. Bean flips inside her like an internal cheerleader.

As Lily reaches the bookcase, Sara huffs toward her. Lily scans the shelves. And then she sees it. Middle shelf. A green box, with a handwritten label marked "Rossetti."

The box is rough under her fingers. She's just about to open it when Sara snatches it away.

"Finders keepers," Sara says. She opens the box and a key lies inside.

"Yeah, and Lily found it," Tom replies, appearing behind them, out of breath.

"Losers weepers," Sara continues. She holds up the key. "And I'm not crying."

Chapter Twenty

Dusk is coming. Cygnet-gray clouds huddle above, ready to shed more snow. The Boxing Day shoot is going ahead, even though the house is in mourning, even if the substitute pigeon is indistinguishable from the sky, even if the snow is so deep it's up to their thighs. Mrs. Castle had marched outside in waders and galoshes to set it all up. "It's in my rules" is all she will say.

"Pull!" Sara shouts. Tom releases a clay pigeon into the air.

A gunshot shocks the sky. The clay cracks into pieces.

All of the cousins were trained in the art of culling clay from an early age. Grandma Violet had made sure of it, first teaching them herself, then getting Uncle Edward to step in when she could no longer pull the trigger. She said that it was a tradition in the country to shoot on Boxing Day. She just didn't want anything to die in the process.

Lily had never enjoyed it. But she doesn't want to be alone right now, so she's sitting on a garden chair, watching.

Sara reloads. "Pull!" she shouts again.

Tom sends up another. This time, though, Sara misses. The disc falls to earth intact, ready to clay another day.

"Again," Sara shouts, lifting the gun. Irritation is sewn into her voice.

"You've had three shots, Sara, love," Tom says. "Give someone else a go."

Sara marches over to him. In her Barbour jacket and Hunter wellies, she looks like she's about to tell him to get off her land. "I've told you before, don't 'love' me, Tom," she says. "And you can drop the accent, too. You haven't been back in Yorkshire for years. You've lost your right to it. And, if I had my way, the house as well."

"Tom's got as much claim to the house as anyone here," Rachel says, coming over to stand by her brother.

"Not *anyone*," Sara replies, looking at Rachel. "The spouses only get to help."

Holly looks at Lily, then lowers her head. She kicks down hard into the snow. "Although we're down to only one of those now." She glances up at Ronnie's room on the second floor. The curtains are closed. He still hasn't emerged.

"You're even nastier than when you were a kid," Rachel says to Sara.

"You just never got to know me then," Sara replies.

"Trust you to sink lower than even I thought possible," Tom says, looking at Sara in disgust.

"You shouldn't be so trusting," she says to him. "And you should never have trusted Philippa with that key. Oh, and keep any other keys hidden, if you're jammy enough to get to them."

"You are *all* trusted, love. Owt else leads to paranoia," Tom says to Sara, in a Yorkshire accent so thick you could use it to butter Botham's tea bread. He's smiling but his eyes are the iciest Lily has seen them.

"Where *did* Philippa keep that key, do you think?" Sara asks.

Rachel shrugs. "Probably in their room."

"I suppose it's Ronnie's now," Sara muses. "Unless someone took it from her when she was killed."

"You think she was killed for a key that may or may not be the right one to unlock a secret door that may or may not exist?" Tom says. His tone says exactly how unlikely he thinks that is.

Sara aims her gun at the sky. "Well, she was killed for some reason or other. By someone or other. Of course, it's usually the husband."

"No, Sara," Lily says, the words escaping her mouth. "Ronnie would *never* do that."

"Pull," Sara shouts and shoots into an empty sky.

"I'm going in," Lily says. She doesn't need company if this is what it brings. "Too cold for me, I'm used to London winters."

"But it's my turn next," Tom says. "You'll miss me being brilliant."

"You're always brilliant," she says. "But I'll watch from my window." Lily turns to go.

"We'll come with you," Rachel says, taking Holly's arm.

"Mind how you go, Lily," Sara calls out, her saracastic tone cutting through the air like salt in snow. "Make sure you don't fall again, eh?"

"I forgot to ask," Rachel says to Lily as they walk up the steps to the terrace. "How did you know to look in that bookcase?"

"Lucky guess?" she says.

Rachel raises an eyebrow. Even Holly looks skeptical.

"I saw you looking in the poetry section in the library," Holly says. "You must have known what to look for."

"It was the anagram," Lily says.

"Of what?" Rachel asks.

"In the sonnet, it mentions 'Winter, My Secret,' which was one of Aunt Lil's favorite poems, by Christina Rossetti. And 'T'stories' stood out as it doesn't change the meter, and Liliana's Yorkshire accent was never strong, so I thought it might be an anagram."

"Of Rossetti," Holly says, nodding slowly.

Lily nods and feels a shot of joy. With both of them looking at her, she feels like a Christmas tree whose lights have been turned on. And for once she doesn't want to turn them off.

"I wish we'd been closer," Rachel says. "As kids."

Lily nods. "Might have made things easier for both of us," she says.

"Come and see us, when this is over," Holly says, bobbing up and down in excitement. "We'd love Beatrice to know her amazing aunt."

"We'll need to bring the family together somehow, after all this," Rachel says. "Ronnie will need our help with Samuel."

"Hopefully the new generation of cousins will all be close," Lily says.

※

On the way to her room, Lily stops on the second floor and goes down the East Wing corridor to Ronnie's room. She knocks on the door but there's no reply. She opens the door slightly, and sees a huddled shape on the bed. Ronnie snores gently, murmuring in his sleep.

"I love you, Ronnie," Lily whispers, then quietly leaves.

Chapter Twenty-One

December 27th
The Third Day of Christmas

A knock on her door. "Are you up, Lily?" Tom shouts.

Lily opens her eyes and slowly swivels her legs out of bed. The whispers of ghosts that have chased her in her sleep fade away. "I will be in a few minutes."

"The clues are already here. In presents in the drawing room. Sara found them first thing, and she's gone off with Gray into the grounds."

"Give me five minutes. Ten, tops, and I'll be down."

"OK," Tom says, in a tone of voice that says it's not OK. That there's excitement to be had.

Lily smiles. Coming back here, Tom has regressed into a little boy in the best of ways.

In the drawing room, Lily holds the clue in her hand. The yellow ribbon with red spots that had wrapped up the present lies coiled like a measled snake. She reads it through another time, getting caught on some of the lines. Her heart aches once again.

We used to sing together, remember?
Weeping candles, mulling wine; you recall,
Perhaps, the ice-bound, snow-rimed December
Of '97, on the twenty-fourth?
Outside the house, rose cheeked, iron feet?
We sang as a family, the last time,
Then a duet till Eve fell into sleep.
Does it ring a festive bell? Does it chime?
It should. The next dark night my sister left
Us. Found by the valet inside the maze.
A strangely bloodless death. We were bereft,
Some even meant it. Today, the ache stays:
Faultline inside sedimentary rock,
Ready to crack open, never forgot.

Shame floods through her. How could Liliana do this? Spelling out her mother's death in a sonnet. As if death can be made pretty by poetry. As if clues should be shoehorned into apparent suicide. But then, isn't disproving that why she's here?

"God, I'm sorry, Lily," Tom says. "Can't be easy to read this."

"And it's not even true," Lily says. "I was the one who found her, not a valet."

Tom grabs her arm. "Maybe that's the point. In the first two sonnets, you pointed out areas that stood out as 'wrong.'"

"And this is definitely wrong," Lily agrees.

She reads it again, trying to calm herself. After all, Liliana told her that the answers would be revealed, and here she is addressing things head on. And what does this mean, "strangely bloodless"? She must have known Lily would try to remove the supposed blood and find it fake. Is it supposed to point to another method of her mum's death? If she didn't slit her wrists, why did everyone think that she did? And if not, how did she die? Strangled, as in the first clue?

"Lily, are you OK?" Tom is asking, waving his hands in front of her face.

"I was just thinking," she replies.

"Don't ruminate, if you can help it," Tom says. "I know it's difficult, and that sonnet's not going to help." He pauses, kinks his head to one side. "Maybe we should play the game. Try to take your mind off your mum."

"And how is reading and rereading about her going to do that?"

"For starters, we could work out what that bit about 'valet' means, and go from there. At the very least, you'll get to beat Sara again."

He has a point. Concentrating on the poem will help her find out who really did kill Mum, and how she died. And that in itself will help her move on.

Lily looks over at the remaining two presents on the fireplace surround. The labels are addressed in Liliana's handwriting to Philippa and Ronnie. She feels a pang—ghost handwriting to the dead. The gifts are wrapped in burgundy paper embossed with the maze, tied with those yellow and red-dotted ribbons. There's something especially poignant about presents that will never be opened. Ribbons that will never be undone.

Lily reads through the poem again. "I think there's something else in the poem that's off."

"What is it?" Tom jumps up and down, then stops himself. "Sorry," he says. "Not appropriate in the circumstances."

Lily smiles. "But it does take my mind off things."

"So," Tom says, "let's start with your odd part."

"There was one line that didn't scan right, but that's quite usual. Then I went back to it. 'Outside the house, rose cheeked, iron feet.'"

"I think it's referring to when we sang carols that last year before you left," Tom says. He's staring into middle distance as if he can see it. "We were all there. My mum and dad…" he stops. His eyes flick over to her, then away.

"And my mum," Lily replies, keeping her voice flat as if held down by pattern weights.

"I didn't mean to…" He rubs his hand over his face. "Told you I wasn't good at this."

"It's fine," Lily says, squeezing his arm. "Anyway, that line is one syllable short."

"You're going to have to take me through it—you were the one who listened to Liliana, not me."

"Sonnets are in iambic pentameter," Lily says, "which means that there are five beats in every line, with a rhythm of iambs."

"Yum. Cat food," Tom says.

Lily bites back a Sara-style sarcastic reply. "It's an unstressed followed by a stressed syllable."

Tom's eyes are wide. "How do you remember all this?"

Lily feels herself flushing again. "Grandma Violet said I had a mind like hers. I can remember most things I hear, see, or read, like in a video clip."

"You could be a spy, like her."

"Bit late for a new career," Lily says. "And Grandma was a code breaker, not a spy."

"Never too late. And that's what a spy would say," Tom says.

"Aunt Liliana made it easy, too—she was a great teacher. She told me to remember it as 'I *am*,' the stress on the *am*." Lily smiles at the memory. "She said that if I could state who I was with such emphasis, then I would always hold my head high."

"And can you?" Tom asks, gently.

"Not yet," Lily replies. She tries to smile again but can't.

"OK, so that line is missing some kibble," Tom says. He reads through it, counting on his fingers.

"It is, unless you count one of the words as two syllables."

"But that would be cheating; anyone could do that."

Lily picks up Tom's pen and adds an accent to one of the words, turning "rose" into "rosé."

"Shit!" He smiles. "Time to break out the wine."

The steps down into the cellar creak under their feet.

"Ssh," Tom whispers to them, "don't give us away."

Lily suppresses a giggle. She knows she shouldn't be enjoying this.

Upstairs, Ronnie is grieving, and outside, Philippa won't ever wake up, but part of Lily is reveling in solving the puzzle. And if she can solve the top layer of the clue, maybe she can find what's in its cellar.

"Whoa," Tom says as he scans the floor-to-ceiling wine racks. "There must be thousands of bottles down here." He takes out a few and looks at the labels. "And arranged in alphabetical order by wine and region. Bet that was down to Aunt Liliana."

"Sara's probably already had them valued," Lily replies.

"Sounded like they made a right mess down here yesterday," Tom says, "but if it weren't for the complete lack of dust, it looks as if nothing's been touched. It's all been put away."

"Which means that Mrs. Castle was busy last night..." She can't finish the sentence.

"She was cleaning before we found Philippa, too." He pauses, thinking. "You'd think she'd have heard something, being so near where Philippa died."

"You don't think she could have—"

"Nah," Tom says. "Can't see Mrs. Castle as a killer. Although we don't really know why she's here. And we don't know why Philippa was up in the night."

"Ronnie said something to me, before he went to rest. Something about Philippa going to check on someone."

"Some*one*?"

"That's what he thought."

"So, whoever she went to check on could have killed her?"

"It's possible," Lily replies. "She didn't tell him any more than that. At least not that he can remember."

"Maybe more will come back to him when the shock wears off," Tom says.

Fear rises in Lily. "What if Philippa was killed because she knows something? And what if Ronnie knows, too? Should we be keeping an eye on him, in case he's a target?"

"I think he's safe, unless he recalls something important," Tom says.

Something twangs in Lily when he says "recalls." She's read it recently.

In the sonnet. She separates the letters of the word RECALL out in her mind and rearranges them. And then again, until they form a word.

"What are you doing?" Tom says, waving his hand in front of her face.

"Reassuring myself that we're in the right place."

"I believe you—where else would you keep rosé in a posh country house?"

"In an anagram of 'recall.'"

Tom takes a moment, then claps his hand. "Cellar! You're brilliant, Lil. Any other idea where to look?" He walks into the next room that stores spirits. "It's pretty big." Tom picks up a bottle of whisky and whistles. "Bottled in 1963! That's ancient. Probably tastes terrible. Like old tires and piss."

"Some things get better with age," Lily says.

Tom starts talking about all the many things that do get better, then worse with age, then better, then worse again—like *Star Wars*—but she's focusing on the other line of the poem that stands out. There was no valet who found her mum. They didn't even have a valet at the conference center. There may have been one at the hotel, Lily supposes, she'd have to check. But that's not going to help her find the key.

Why are you so keen to find it anyway? Part of her asks. The rest of her replies that she's not keen, she's just distracting herself, helping Tom. Besides, the better she knows the poems, the better she can unravel their secrets. And she may have found one of them.

"'Ready to crack open,'" she reads out.

"You crack open bottles of wine," Tom says, breaking free of his monologue.

"And to do that you…" Lily waits for a reply.

"I saw someone on telly use a sword to slice off the top and not lose a drop," Tom says.

"And if you don't have a sword at hand?"

"Then I'd ask what kind of a country house this is?" Tom stands with his hands on his hips in mock disgust. Then drops his hands when he sees her face. "OK, I'll stop messing around. You uncork it."

"I think that's where we'll find the key—a 'faultline inside sedimentary rock.'"

"Wait, I get it," Tom says, getting out the poem from his pocket. "Sediment is found in bottles, and rock is an anagram of cork! It's in one of the corks."

Lily nods.

Tom reaches for her hand. "I don't think I've seen you this into anything for ages," he says.

"I know, I shouldn't be."

"Tragedy doesn't mean that you can't have joy," Tom says. "Sometimes emotions are back-to-back, connected. Like Grandma always said. Fear is the other side of the wall to excitement."

"I don't see how death can be the other side of joy."

"It helps us appreciate life," he says.

"You are very good at your job, you know?"

He lets go of her hand and gives a bashful grin. "Oh, shush, you. Now, let's get back to the task at hand. Uncorking all of this wine. We'll have to drink it, I'm afraid. It's the only way forward. Unless there's a reason not to drink?"

Lily searches his face for signs he knows she's pregnant, but there's none. "Not sure that's going to help us long term," she replies.

Tom pouts. "Fine. Presumably we're looking for a rosé, then." He paces along each section. Right at the back, in the third of the cavernous rooms, he says, "Ah-ha!"

Lily walks over to a wall of wine that looks like it's been poured out of her pink bathtub.

"Look at the poem again," Tom says. "Liliana would have given us something to go on. What about the valet thing?"

But Lily is already pulling out a wine right in the center of the wall. She shows Tom the label.

"Tavel," he says, frowning. Then he smiles. "Tavel!" He's got it.

❄

"I don't get it," Holly says.

They're in the kitchen, where Lily is digging the cork out of the bottle. She had tried using a corkscrew first, but it had gotten stuck on the key buried in the center.

"You mix up the letters in valet," Rachel says, patiently. "And you—"

"*That* I get," Holly interrupts, "but, Lily, why did you go down to the basement? There were clues pointing toward the cellar yesterday, and yesterday was a trick."

"That's my mother for you," Sara replies. "Try being her child. She liked to misdirect and then laugh at me when I ended up in the wrong place." She turns to Tom. "And you call *me* cruel and obtuse. She'd have loved seeing me trot down to the cellar yesterday, then reading the clue and assuming she was doing the same today." Sara folds her arms.

"Liliana can't be trusted, even when six feet under," Rachel says.

"Mum was cremated," Gray says. "She's in a pot at home."

"She's in a pot here, actually," Sara says.

Lily looks up to see Gray's face get even paler. "Why?" he asks in a voice that reminds Lily of when he was a little boy.

"I thought she should be scattered at her precious Endgame," Sara replies. "She's in my wash bag. I should get her out, pop her on the mantelpiece so she can see how her game is playing out." Sara, too, has regressed to the angry little girl she used to be. Summoning rage to stand in front of the tears. For the first time, Lily truly sees the impact Liliana's ways have had on her eldest biological child. Her aunt spent so much time with Lily that it's no surprise that Sara is resentful. She never could live up to Liliana's idea of a great brain. Now she never would. And Liliana could never now be the mother she should have been to Sara.

Gray also looks as if he's about to cry. "She didn't want to be in the ground," he says. "She hated being cold."

"Fine, then we'll stick her by the boiler in the airing cupboard. She'll love it. It'll be like that Caribbean holiday she never took us on."

Gray raises a hand to wipe away a loose tear. His sleeve drops back, showing a bandage around his wrist. Seeing Lily looking, Gray places his hands behind his back. He then walks away, trying to tug his jumper over his hands. Oh, Gray. Not again.

The knife slips while Lily isn't looking. It flicks up, nicking her other hand holding the rim of the bottle. Blood trickles onto the cork.

"Careful," Tom says. "Do you want me to do it?"

"She doesn't need a man to help, Tom," Sara says.

Lily gives her a smile, which is thrown back with a scowl. Fine. It's easier this way.

The cork comes out, piece by piece. At last, Lily is able to pincer out a part with the key in. Peeling off the remainder of the cork, she holds it up. "The third key," she says.

"I wish I had your brain, Lily," Holly says.

An unexpected feeling of pride bubbles up inside Lily. She's not used to thinking of her mind as anything other than an internal representation of her flat—piled high in a jumble sale of material that will never be used.

"I'd keep your own brain," Sara says. "Lily is all alone in hers. You get to be loved."

And Lily's fizzing pride dies like uncorked champagne at the end of the night.

As she puts the key in her pocket, she remembers about Philippa's. "When you moved Philippa's body, did you find her key?" she asks Sara.

"I hope you're not accusing me of anything?" Sara says, moving forward, hands on her hips.

Tom holds up his arms. "Nobody's accusing anyone. It's a valid question, and you brought it up the night she died."

"No one would have killed her just for the key, though," Holly says. "That's no justification."

"You think there *is* a valid justification for murder?" Sara says, glaring at Holly now.

Holly backs away. "Not at all, I just—"

"How about," Tom says, standing between Sara and Holly like a mediator in an unequal boxing match, "when Ronnie wakes up, we look in their room for the key. It'll be in a drawer, or a jewelry box, or somewhere. We don't know till we look."

"Makes sense," Sara says, the grudge in her voice obvious. She turns to Lily. "But are you sure you want that key, if Philippa could have been killed for hers?"

A shiver slides its finger up Lily's spine. The keys don't matter. She has to stay focused on who killed her mum. "You keep it then," she says, handing Sara the key.

Tom takes a deep breath. He'll give her grief for that later. Right now, she doesn't care. She pictures Philippa in her ice tomb and knows she doesn't want to be there. Lily realizes, then, that she's conjuring Philippa lying on her back, but she wouldn't be able to.

"When you moved Philippa," Lily says, "you made sure you didn't touch the knife, didn't you?"

Sara nods. "Of course. I've seen *Line of Duty*. Although..." she pauses.

"Although what?" Tom prompts, with a sigh that says, *What have you done now?*

"Gray reached out to steady it when we turned her over to place her on the ice."

"Face down?" Rachel says, shuddering.

"It was either that or pull the knife out," Sara says. "And that would be tampering with evidence."

"Bit late for that," Tom replies.

Lily opens the back door to see Gray leaning on the wall, smoking a cigarette as thin as he is. "Would you like one?" he asks.

She shakes her head. She gave up when she found out she was pregnant, and only had a week of bone-deep cravings before she found the smell of cigarette smoke made her feel sick. Same as red wine. From here, she can see Sara in the kitchen. If only pregnancy aversion kept her away from toxic people as well as substances.

"Are you going somewhere?" Gray asks, in surprise, as if she'd have no reason for being out of the house.

"To check on Philippa," Lily says. "Feels wrong, her being alone."

Gray nods. "I went earlier for the same reason. But it'll be difficult to get out there now. The snow's been coming on thick."

He's right. Despite the bright start to the day, the snow has resumed without her noticing.

"Don't worry. She's OK," Gray says. "I secured the icehouse. Made sure no animals could get in."

"Right," Lily says, blinking. "Well done." She hadn't even thought of that.

Gray sucks on his cigarette and blows out the smoke. The edge of his bandage shows over his cuff.

"Are you OK, though?" Lily asks. She gently touches his sleeve.

Gray backs away. "It's not what you think. I had an accident."

Lily nods, because that's what you do.

"No, really. Ask Sara. I was chopping wood, for the fire in her room, and slipped. That's all."

"You can tell me anything," Lily says. "I really do understand."

Gray looks into her eyes and comprehension passes between them. "I know you do." He looks as if he's considering it, maybe weighing up whether Lily is worth investing with his problems.

"If you'd rather not talk to me, I know Tom would be happy to listen."

"He is a good listener," Gray says, nodding slowly. He then drops his cigarette into the snow and watches as the spark dies. "The dead listen, too."

"I'm glad you're here," Lily says, "for Philippa's sake."

"I'm glad I am, too. She's my first proper dead person."

Unnerved, Lily watches as Gray walks slowly, sedately, across the kitchen garden and back into the house.

Chapter Twenty-Two

"I always feel sorry for leftovers," Holly says as she picks up a dinner plate from the buffet table. "It's like when you're an afterthought at a wedding because someone's dropped out."

Only if it's a cannibal's wedding, Lily thinks, and then feels terrible. How can she make jokes like this in her own head when someone's died?

"Only if it's a cannibal wedding," Tom says.

Everyone laughs, if a little guiltily, smiles hidden behind hands, and Lily feels glad that someone at least can speak their mind.

The buffet table *does* look a bit sorry for itself. The offcuts of cheese look imprisoned in their glass dome. The sausage rolls are the burned ones of the batch, and the grapes are well on their way to becoming raisins.

"Thanks for going to so much trouble, Mrs. Castle," Sara says, dripping saracasm over the lunch like chutney. She looks at the table with a pseudo-chef sneer, her nth since arriving at Endgame House what feels like weeks ago.

"You're entirely welcome, Miss," Mrs. Castle replies as she shoves heated-up mince pies on a plate. She counters the saracasm with relish. "Tuck in, by all means. And there I was thinking none of you would want much to eat, given the circumstances."

And it's true—nobody has much of an appetite, but they still dutifully fill their plates before retreating in cliques to their preferred corners of the house.

Lily sits with Tom in the living room. She halfheartedly picks at a turkey sandwich so dry in both bread and bird that she can't swallow. Tom is poking at the fire, breaking blackened wood into ash.

"I would've thought Ronnie would be awake by now," Lily says.

"I think Rachel gave him another two sedatives. That and the shock mean he needs to repair."

"Can he get better from this?" Lily asks. Her hope is not just for Ronnie.

Tom nods. "In time. With help from us, and a therapist. He might need some EMDR—that's eye movement desensitization and reprocessing—to try to process the trauma of finding her. He could easily get stuck in that moment and replay it again and again." He glances across at her but doesn't say the obvious.

"You don't need to say it. I'm stuck on finding Mum."

"I know I might be trespassing," he says. "But I could recommend someone who could help specifically with trauma. I've seen EMDR do great things. Might stop your nightmares."

Lily nods slowly. "When we get back, give me the number." Even saying that makes her anxiety rise. At least she's managed to keep Tom quiet for a while on that subject. She'll sort it herself, hopefully by finding Mum's killer.

Tom puts the poker back in the stand and leans into his chair. He smiles at her, and she longs to tell him what she's looking into. He might know something. He lived in Endgame House for a while after Mum died, until his parents passed, too. And while that was an accident, he must want to know about that time. She reckons he only got into psychology and psychotherapy in order to process his own sadness at one remove. We all deal with death in our own way.

And maybe helping her would be healing for him. "I need to tell you something, Tom," she says.

Tom turns to her, and then heavy footsteps are heard from the floor above.

"Ronnie's up," Lily says.

Ronnie is throwing objects across his room when Tom and Lily get up the first set of stairs. As Lily runs in, a book hits the door. "She can't be gone," he's saying, as if he's plugged straight back in to when he was last awake. He tears at his cheeks with his nails.

"Hey, sweetheart," Lily says, placing her arms round him.

He pushes her back into Tom, who steadies her and silently checks in with her by raising his eyebrows. She nods back. She's always wanted this level of communication. When you can't or don't want to speak, it's wonderful when someone can read you.

Ronnie grabs her by the shoulders. His eyes are crazy-paved with red. "I need to see Samuel."

"We can't at the moment, mate," Tom says, slowly moving Ronnie away from Lily. "Car trouble."

Ronnie holds Tom's head in his hands. "No one else can tell him. It's got to be me. You got it? Me."

"Of course, mate. You're his dad."

"That's right, I'm his dad." Ronnie's face contorts. "What am I going to do? She was the one who did everything. How's he going to cope without her?"

"You'll be there for each other," Tom says. "And we'll all be there for you both."

Ronnie puts his forehead against Tom's. "I'm going to need you, bruv," he says.

Lily and Tom spend the next few hours with Ronnie. Talking when he wants to, sitting quietly by his side when he doesn't. He won't leave the room, just sits on the bed, holding Philippa's shawl. He rubs the hem between his thumb and forefinger. Occasionally, he brings it to his face and sniffs.

Lily tries to look for Philippa's key, but it feels intrusive, too venal with Ronnie like this. She understands. She'd like to be in her own room now. Every part of her aches. Tiredness tugs at her eyes. She looks out of the window and sees the snow fall onto the grounds, and she thinks of being tucked up in bed. Head settling into a sinking pillow.

"When can I go and see her at the funeral parlor?" Ronnie asks after a long silence.

Lily and Tom share looks. "What do you mean?" says Tom.

Ronnie swallows. "I know I can't go immediately, that they need to—you know," he gags, and places his hand to his mouth. Lily feels an empathic peristaltic jolt. "Make her comfortable, as Gray said. But I'll be able to see her tomorrow, won't I?"

No one's told him that her body is in the icehouse. He's just assumed that her body was taken away while he slept. And it was. Just not in the way he imagines.

Lily can't let him think this. "I'm sorry, Ronnie," she says. "You've got the wrong impression. Philippa—"

Tom nudges Lily and she stops talking. "Can't be visited for a few days," he takes over. "Something to do with bank holidays and working days. You just concentrate on getting in a fit state to see her." He gives Lily a meaningful glance over Ronnie's bowed head, although she has no idea what it means.

Ronnie starts crying again. "I'm sorry," he says, wiping his nose. "I can't stop crying."

"You don't have to, mate," Tom says. "It's healthy."

"You should know, I suppose," Ronnie replies, trying to smile.

"Exactly," Tom says. "I'm a professional. And in my professional opinion, you need something to eat."

"Perhaps I should have more of Rachel's pills," Ronnie says. He looks at both Tom and Lily with such a pleading face.

"I don't know, Ronnie," Lily says, thinking about the way he uses alcohol.

"I know what you're thinking," Ronnie replies. "But this is different. With alcohol, I was self-medicating in order to function and get on with life. I want those pills to not get on with life. Not right now." He raises a hand as if reading her next objection. "And I don't want to check out either. I want things to stop for a bit. To stop hurting."

"We can all understand that, mate," Tom says. "Tell you what, you come down with us, have a bite to eat, take whatever you want from the pantry—or you could cook something. Sara would appreciate a chef at the helm."

Ronnie turns to Tom and grabs him by the shoulders. He's breathing quickly, grasping at breaths, as if staving off a panic attack. "I can't cook, not without Philippa."

When you lose someone that close, they drag part of you into death with them. Better to be alone.

Lily gets her way in the early evening. Having settled Ronnie into another sedated sleep, she takes herself to her room. She had intended to study the blueprint of the house that Isabelle gave her, but she's too tired to focus. She's sure her eyes are getting worse.

That's a side effect of pregnancy they don't tell you about: fluid retention in the eye or behind the eyeball can make the cornea change shape. Apparently, they'll go back to normal after the birth. Probably.

So many changes that she hadn't expected. Some good—her boobs resembling marble statues', for one. And her hair's extra thick because no strands fall out during pregnancy.

Of course, that means it'll all fall out, with extra for luck, after Bean is born. Grandma Violet used to claim that she'd lost a tooth for every one of her children—"They suck the calcium from your bones," she'd said at dinner once, making a Hannibal Lecter-eating-liver sound. "Leach all the good stuff out of you so they can grow. It's just fact. Marvelous little parasites, you lot are. And I wouldn't have it any other way."

Lily had also heard, with less basis in science, from her friend Natalie who she'd met at the one antenatal class she'd attended before stopping, that if you have a girl, they take your beauty for themselves.

"You take whatever you want, Beanie," she whispers to her bump. Bean seems to give a flippy fist bump back.

Knock, knock. "It's me, Miss Lily. I've brought you supper," Mrs. Castle says, her voice muffled from behind Lily's door.

Lily has become the pregnant cliché—moaning when standing up or sitting. Holding her back. She'd told everyone she was going to skip tea and have an early night, but her stomach is already rumbling. Bean wants more food, even if Lily doesn't. On opening the door, she sees Mrs. Castle holding a tray with cream crackers, cheese, ginger biscuits, salt and pepper, and a mug of murky peppermint tea. The pregnant person's supper.

"You know too, then," Lily says.

Mrs. Castle shrugs. "Obvious, isn't it?"

"To everyone?" Lily asks, thinking of the warning that both Isabelle and Liliana had given her.

Mrs. Castle shakes her head. Her curls somehow do not move. "The others are too self-absorbed to notice. Anyway, Liliana told me she suspected you were pregnant when you met up. Said you looked younger, felt queasy, and had the 'sheen.'" She barks a laugh. "I'll tell you what for nothing. Looking younger doesn't last. It's nature's last gift, or trick, before aging you a decade the minute they pop out."

"Thanks for that, Mrs. Castle. I look forward to it. Don't tell anyone else, will you?" Lily says. "I can't face all the questions about the house."

Mrs. Castle nods and hands her the tray.

Lily is about to turn when something occurs to her. "You said Liliana told you about me?"

Mrs. Castle nods. She tips her chin up as if defying Lily to ask anything personal.

"How did you know Liliana?" Lily asks. "I mean, I know you used to babysit for us when we were little, but did you work for her up until she died?"

"I looked after her and her house best I could. And I still do." Mrs. Castle looks down at her hands, rubs her ring finger as if it's arthritic from all the housework Liliana got her to do.

"I would've thought she'd have mentioned you," Lily says.

Mrs. Castle's laugh is full of rue, not mirth. "You'd think so, wouldn't you? Maybe she didn't feel she could."

"Why?" Lily asks.

"You're not the only member of the family to keep things to herself."

"I've just realized. I don't even know your name. I'm so sorry," Lily says.

"Liliana just called me Castle."

"Not the most informal nickname."

"Sometimes you take what you can get," Mrs. Castle says.

"So, you're not going to tell me your name?"

Mrs. Castle walks back to the door. "Eat your supper, Miss Lily," she says. The door closes slowly behind her.

When she's finished eating, Lily gets into bed. With the curtains open, she watches snowflakes settle on the sill. She counts these teeny cold alternatives to sheep, and drifts off to sleep.

Chapter Twenty-Three

December 28th
The Fourth Day of Christmas

It's 3:28 a.m. Lily is awake, and hungry. Again.

She walks down the corridor, not turning on any lights. Her feet know every turn of the house, just as they did when she went wandering at night as a child. When she lived here, the early hours were when Endgame House was hers. She'd pretend she was wearing a fine gown, swooping hooped skirts the width of doors down staircases. Occasionally, she'd sweep round a corner to find conference guests snogging, but most of the time, she heard them snoring from the bedrooms.

Tonight, though, trudging down the stairs in her big pajamas, on a hunt for carbohydrates, she hears other sounds coming from a bedroom. Sounds she hasn't heard in person for too many months. The kind of sounds that end in either shame, spooning, cystitis, goodbyes, or surprise pregnancy.

And they're coming from Sara's room.

Lily wishes she were the kind of person who could walk on and grin. Instead, she lingers on the stairs, trying to hear who Sara is with. It's hard to make out, as it were. The moans are Sara's, matched with someone else's low whispers. Lily looks down the corridor—the door to

Rachel and Holly's room is wide open. It wouldn't be Holly, would it? Lily feels a pang of jealousy and turns away. Best not examine why she feels that. Like sex itself, she's not going to like herself any more at the end of it.

Padding as quietly as she can, Lily goes down the stairs and into the kitchen. Moonlight reflects off the snow in the garden, letting in a slice of light that shows up the bread bin. Toast, that's what she needs. Lots of it.

Just as she's placing the bread in the toaster, she hears sounds coming from the pantry.

"Is that you, Mrs. Castle?" she asks. "It's only me, Lily. I'm grazing."

Something falls in the pantry, a tin maybe, onto the hard floor. Lily expects Mrs. Castle to come out, grumbling, instead she hears the back door open and someone slip out. Running to the window, Lily tries to get an angle that will let her see the figure, but they're just out of sight. She can hear them, though, dragging the door back, wood splintering.

Why would the person run away, unless they didn't want to be seen? Lily rushes into the pantry. The rotten door is open.

She stuffs her feet in a pair of wellies, grabs a torch from the wall, and wades out into the cold. Sleet bruises her skin as she shines the light over the grounds. She can't see anyone. Not even a fox. Only snow-pressed footsteps in the dark.

Back in the pantry, shivering, she checks to see if something's been taken, or something left. But how would she know? The jars and tins face forward like soldiers on parade. Pickled onions bob, piccalilli sits in silence. Whatever happened in here, they're saying nothing.

A pile of cinnamon whirls sits on a marble slab, covered with mesh, ready for breakfast. Lily takes one, nibbling it from one end to the middle—the easiest of mazes. She can hardly taste it, though. All she can think about is who ran away from her, and why.

※

"*The Yorkshire Dales are suffering the worst snowfall in years*," the radio announcer says to the guests gathered in the orangery the next morning for coffee. Lily thinks that modern society is just a snowstorm and a psychopath away from regressing to huddling round a wireless for all its information. "*With telephone and power lines down, it is feared that many older people are in danger, with no way of contacting help.*"

"What about younger people?" Sara says, picking a leaf off a rubber plant. "When are they going to start worrying about us?"

"At least we've still got power," Gray says.

"I know what you remind me of," Rachel says to him. "Mr. Rogers in a Tim Burton film."

Gray looks as if he has no idea what to do with that. "Um, thanks?"

"That's a massive compliment coming from Rachel," Holly says. Rachel nods slowly in solemn agreement.

"We've got gas central heating, and the stove is woodburning. And there's a backup generator if our power goes out," Mrs. Castle says. "Isabelle Stirling made sure it was serviced in case of this scenario."

"Ah, Isabelle," Sara says. "The golden girl. Mum talked about her in almost as glowing terms as Lily."

"Oh, just eat your brandy snaps, would you? You all make me sick," Mrs. Castle says, getting up from her wicker chair and striding out of the room.

All attention goes to the brandy snaps on a plate. The pockmarked biscuits are scrolled up like cinnamon sticks. "I bet the clues are in the middle," Holly says, grabbing one.

Sara makes sure she gets one before she says, "Rachel clearly chose you for your intelligence, Holly."

"Do you ever get sick of being an arsehole?" Rachel asks Sara.

"Let me think," Sara says, crushing the brandy snap in her fist. "No."

As Holly had predicted, each brandy snap contains a scrolled-up clue. Lily is the last to unfurl hers. Gray reads the poem out loud. Lily has never noticed how beautiful his voice is before, probably because he talks so quietly, as if he doesn't want his words to disturb the world. Reading his mum's sonnets, though, allows him to forget that. His voice is loam rich and grave deep as he reads of the dead:

An owl descends, the night's stone alibi.
It is the melancholy time between
Christmas and the New Year. The old days die,
Their ghosts still walk these halls, quiet, unseen
Yet felt. A slice of cold, cutting through skin,
A tinny whisper by your ear, a trace
Of lace that is not there. The veil is thin,
This time of year, take care. Let no one face
The specters, save that for Epiphany.

For now, enjoy the waiting room. Raise high
A glass to the annum's perineum.
Dance like Pan. Try a whirl on marble while
A buttery moon spreads its light on clouds.
These days are soon over. No ghosts allowed.

"Once again Mum delivers an uplifting little ditty," Sara says.

"I think it's her best sonnet yet," Gray replies. His voice is back to its dormouse-level creep, but he's speaking up at least. "She wants us to live while we can, in the in-between days."

"Thanks for the interpretation, brother," Sara says. "Does it extend to knowing where the key is?"

"The poem mentions marble and an owl. The terrace is made of marble, isn't it?" Holly touches Rachel's arm. "Didn't you say that there used to be dances on the terrace—'a whirl on marble.' And there's a stone owl on the wall," she says. "It could be under it?"

"Why don't you go and have a look?" Sara says, her eyes soft. "I'll follow you out."

Holly blushes, then very deliberately takes Rachel's hand. "You'll come with me, won't you?" she asks.

Rachel looks confused. "Of course. You don't need to ask."

Holly looks over her shoulder at Sara with a look of something like fear. Fear that Rachel will find out she was with Sara last night? Or is she afraid of something else?

"What was all that about?" Tom asks.

"You're supposed to be the one who knows about humans," Sara says, folding her arms. "You tell us."

"Why did you say you'd follow her?" Gray asks Sara.

"So she'd think she was right. That way I can go to the real hiding place."

"And that is…?" Lily replies.

"Wherever you and Tom lead us," Sara says. "If you go somewhere, I'm going, too. I'll be your shadow." Lily thinks of the figure that dashed from the pantry last night.

And in that moment knows where the next key is hidden.

"You'll have a long wait, then," Lily says, making her mind up what to do there and then. "Because I'm not playing today. It doesn't seem right. Poor Ronnie won't come down, he doesn't want us with him, and he still doesn't know—"

"That his wife is on ice?" Sara interrupts. She's the only one who laughs.

"That we're lying to him," Lily replies.

"Tom was the one who actively lied," Sara says. "Blame him. I'll take no responsibility." She's looking straight at Tom as if daring him to contradict her.

Tom, though, just places his head in his hands. "I didn't know what else to do." His shoulders start to shake.

Sara's lip flips into a sneer. She looks like she's about to pour more vinegar-soaked words on him.

"I'll give you a clue where the key is," Lily says. "Just so you'll leave us alone."

"That's more like it!" Sara says, coming over and patting Lily on the head. "Go on, then. Where is it?"

"It's not an anagram this time, at least the room isn't. It's right in front of you. Spelled out across two words."

Sara zips through the poem. Her eyes dart like a cat following a laser pointer. And then she stops. "Ha!" she says. "Not so clever this time, Mum."

When Sara and a shuffling Gray have left the orangery, Tom turns to Lily. "So where is it, then?"

Lily points to the middle of the twelfth line.

"Pantry! Can't believe I didn't spot that."

"I only saw it because I caught someone in the pantry earlier," Lily says. "Well, not *caught* exactly. I was getting a snack and heard a noise, but whoever it was ran away. Anyway, I put it together with 'buttery' and 'spreads,' and there were cinnamon whirls laid out on marble last night."

"So you could have heard Mrs. Castle, setting up the clue?"

"But why would she run away when I called out? She's more likely to tell me to piss off back to bed and mind my own business."

"True. But why would anyone here run away? They could have said they were hungry."

"That's what I've been going over ever since. What if there *is* someone else in the grounds, and they killed Philippa?"

Tom nods. And then he freezes.

"What is it?" Lily asks.

"What if they're in the house?" he says.

Chapter Twenty-Four

"At no point should we split up," Tom says as he and Lily start searching the house in case he's right and there's a stranger on the premises. "Even though this is going to take absolutely ages. I'm not having your death on my conscience."

"And I'd rather *you* didn't die full stop," Lily says.

"I'll do what I can."

They've already gone through all the first-floor rooms. Mrs. Castle had grumbled when they made her unlock her room and show them around. Lily had then tried to prize Tom from the pinball machine in the games room, but he just stood there, flicking the flippers, transfixed by the lights. It was only when she sneezed and distracted him that he lost his last ball and allowed himself to be led out.

Tom in turn had to drag Lily away as she listened outside the pantry to Sara getting increasingly frustrated with being unable to find the key. They'd also finished searching the second floor—Lily had seen the spa treatment rooms for the first time. They used to store the linen and pillows for the conference guest rooms on that floor. Tom reminded her that once they'd hidden from Ronnie under a pile of towels. Now, she smelled lavender and neroli and the ghosts of washing powder, but found no one hiding.

In the ballroom, Tom had grabbed her hand and shouted that he'd found them. Then realized he was seeing his own reflection in the mirrored wall. The old clock on the wall ticked them off.

They're now on the third floor. Most of its rooms are luxury hotel bedrooms. The suites looking out over the front lawn are by far the grandest, with canopied four posters, huge slipper baths, and extremely fancy coffee machines. They still have, however, the same aesthetic as even the smallest bedrooms, using a color palette of silver, burgundy, and pale blue. "It's like all the rooms are children from the same genetic stock," Tom says. "All different—bigger, smaller, chunkier, thinner—but similar, vying to impress and be the best. The chosen one."

"That wasn't what it was like for you and Ronnie, was it?" Lily asks. "I thought you always got on."

"We did!" Tom says. "We do. I was thinking more of Sara being jealous of you."

"Me? I'm only her *adopted* sister."

"And her cousin. She shares more DNA with you than she'd like."

"Maybe it's best to be an only child," Lily says. Her hand goes to her stomach before she can stop herself.

Tom smiles. "It's all right, you don't have to hide it. I know."

"Why didn't you say?" Lily asks.

"It's the kind of thing you wait for someone to reveal. It's sort of their right. Although I did hint. A lot."

"Did you?" Lily reels back through their conversations. He did ask if she had anything to tell him. If there was a reason they shouldn't drink… "Ah," she says. "So, did you see when I fainted?"

"Hard to miss when you're not flattening the fella."

"It's a girl."

Tom often smiles, but now his grin is so big he's mainly made of dimples. "In the middle of all this, and you're going to have a baby!" He grabs a cushion from the bed and stuffs it up his jumper.

Lily laughs. "Not right now. Four months or so."

"Spring. That's good," he says. "The hospital won't be too hot."

"Yup, the heating in the hospital will be my first concern when I'm about to give birth."

"Oi!" Tom says, removing the cushion and throwing it at her. "Leave the sarcasm to Sara." A thought seems to occur to him. He sits down on the bed and looks up at her. "What about the father? Was it IVF, a turkey-baster jobbie, or—"

"Turkey-baster jobbie? Really? Is that how you speak to your clients? Or to anyone? 'Cause I suggest that you don't."

"Well, I don't know, do I? I didn't think you were with anyone."

"I'm not."

"So…"

"It was a couple of nights that I thought might turn into us being a couple."

"But it didn't."

"It happens."

"Does he know about the baby?"

Lily thinks back to when she told Bean's dad. They were in a vegetarian restaurant in Brighton. She hadn't expected him to be pleased, exactly, but hadn't anticipated him getting up from his seat and leaving her with the bill, his yoga mat, and a little Bean to raise, then no bigger than a lentil. "Can you stop with the questions now?"

Tom puts his hands over his mouth. "Sorry. I'm a fool. Forget I mentioned him. Just know that I'm really happy for you." He searches her face. "If you are."

"I think I am," she says.

"Then that's good enough for me," Tom says.

"You won't say anything? It may make things complicated here."

Tom looks confused. Then says, "The contract! Yes, that would get up Sara's nose, wouldn't it?"

He looks so mischievous that Lily says, "It would. But that's no reason to tell her. It doesn't matter anyway as I don't want the house. It's just easier if no one knows."

Tom mimes zipping his mouth closed. "I'll keep mum," he says, and waits for Lily to groan at the pun.

There's only one place left to search on this floor. "You don't have to go in," Tom says when they're once more standing by Mariana's bedroom.

Lily opens the door, then hesitates. Once she steps in, she'll set off a trip wire of memories.

"Honestly. I can be in and out in a jiffy," Tom says. "Doesn't look like anyone's in there anyway."

Lily shakes her head and walks inside. The curtains are pulled back, allowing the shy light of winter into the room. She had expected a rise in panic, but instead she feels oddly calm. The wallpaper forest combined with the dark green carpet make the room itself feel like a clearing, a sacred space.

On Mum's bedside table is the snow globe, unfinished knitting, and a photo of Lily in a heart-shaped frame.

"Are you all right?" Tom asks from the doorway.

"Weirdly, yes," Lily says. And now she's ready to look up.

Steeling herself, as if fortifying herself with corset bones, she tips her head to look at the light fitting. It is still broken, pulled from the ceiling. The plaster is cracked like the icing of a dropped Christmas cake.

❄

"Well, if someone is hiding in the house, then all credit to them," Tom says as they return to the first floor and head for the kitchen. "They're the best at hide-and-seek ever."

"High praise coming from you," Lily replies.

Sara emerges from the pantry, her face dusted with flour. There are packets and jars and tins all over the kitchen table and work surfaces. Jars have been opened, tin lids peeled back to show their innards. "Just tell me where it is," Sara says. She looks exhausted.

Lily feels a pull of sympathy. "Look in the treacle tin."

"We've looked in *everything*." Sara turns to the counter and picks up the golden treacle. "It's empty apart from a tube of chocolate syrup."

"Oh, sorry," Lily says, realizing that she's read the whole sonnet wrong. "I saw 'tinny' and then 'care let,' which I rearranged into 'treacle.' I'm probably seeing anagrams where there aren't any." It makes her think of the ghost-hunting trip she went on with an old girlfriend. They'd camped out in an old fort in Kent while a bearded man called Ken communed with the dead and pointed out orbs, lucidly for the most part, until he was taken over by a seventeenth-century soldier who had been mentioned in the guidebook.

"Have you looked inside the tube?" Tom asks.

Sara sighs. "We couldn't open everything. Mrs. Castle has already threatened to kill me. But fine." She walks over to the sink with the tube of chocolate syrup and starts to squirt it down the plughole. It looks a lot like blood.

"Why waste it?" Lily asks, grabbing a bowl and placing it over the sink.

Sara rolls her eyes, but continues to squeeze the chocolate into the bowl. Her face holds its sardonic, weary mask until nearly all of the syrup is out. Then she squishes the tube harder. Her expression changes. She grabs a knife from the block and slits the tube. She reaches her hand in and pulls out a large key, dripping with chocolate syrup.

Chapter Twenty-Five

"Is something wrong?" Tom asks Lily after dinner. They've gone for a walk on the terrace, bundled up in coats and scarves. Even up here, near the warmth of the house, Lily can hardly lift her feet high enough to crunch down on the snow. "Only you've been really quiet since Sara got the key," he continues. "There's nothing wrong with the—" his eyes slide down to her tummy as he mouths, "baby, is there?"

Lily pulls Tom by the arm to one side. "I said don't say anything."

"I just want to know you're all right, that's all." He hangs his head. "Sorry."

"Doesn't matter. No one heard."

"You're not having second thoughts about giving Sara the key, are you? Or leading her to the next one? 'Cause I wouldn't blame you if you were. And it's OK to want the house, you know. You can tell me. I wouldn't blame you for that either, especially now with the ba—"

"Oh my God, Tom!" Lily shouts.

He raises his hands. "Sorry, sorry."

"It's reassuring, really, that you can't be discreet. There are so many secrets here, jostling like a pudding in a steamer. You blurting things out releases the pressure."

"I promise I'll shut up from now on."

And he does. Though it doesn't stop his meaningful looks when they get back inside. It's too much. Sometimes you have to get away from even your favorite people.

"I'm going to make hot chocolate," Lily says. "Do you want one?"

"I'll help," Tom says, rolling up his sleeves.

"I need a bit of space," Lily says, as gently as she can.

Tom's face falls. He nods lots, as if to cover it.

Guilt floods her. "I'm sorry," she says, giving him a quick hug. "I'm tired and it's all a bit much. Chocolate and an early night are what I need."

Tom is still nodding when he walks away. Lily wishes she didn't feel overwhelming relief at being on her own again. But that's her all over. Even in a house with a killer, she'd rather be alone.

There is another reason, other than Tom's unfathomable lack of discretion. Lily walks into the pantry that has been tidied, with all the jars lined up again on their shelves. She picks up the bowl of chocolate syrup and unpeels the plastic wrap she'd covered it with. Taking a sniff, Lily is thrown back into sense memory, just as she was earlier when Sara found the key in the syrup. She'd had to block it then, but now it is different.

She sits down at the kitchen table, closing her eyes.

Last time she smelled this syrup, she was also at this table. So many years ago. Uncle Edward was planning a solo show of *Hamlet* to be performed on the terrace at a Shakespeare conference, and he had wanted blood. "The secret to good fake blood," he'd said, "is to make it something you don't mind in your mouth." He'd then mixed corn syrup into the chocolate, added drops of water, red food coloring, and a touch of blue. He kept stirring and tasting and painting his skin with the mix. He always asked her what she thought, and nodded seriously at her suggestions.

At last, when they'd found the perfect consistency and color, Edward had offered Lily the spoon. "Do you want to try it?" he asked.

Lily nodded. It smelled tasty, and who wouldn't want fake blood pouring from their mouth?

She scooped a big spoonful of the mixture and dolloped it on her tongue.

Edward said, "Now go and scare your mother."

Lily giggled, and the fake blood oozed from her mouth.

Edward laughed. "Run, before it all leaks out."

Lily rushed out of the kitchen. She couldn't call for Mum as she'd spill the blood and spoil the surprise. She searched every floor, anxiety rising. Her throat wanted her to swallow, but she wouldn't.

If Mum wasn't inside, she must be in the grounds. Lily made a new plan. She'd run onto the terrace to call out, not caring anymore if she lost the blood—she just wanted her mum.

Just as she was running for the French doors, saliva pooling in her mouth, Mum walked up to her from behind. "Are you all right, love?" she asked.

Lily opened her mouth in surprise. The blood mix ran slowly down from her lips.

Mum screamed and grabbed her.

Edward ran out of the kitchen, a big smile on his face. "It's fake, sis, don't worry."

Mum glared at him.

"We made it together," Lily said.

Mum couldn't look at her. "Let's get you cleaned up," she said.

Lily couldn't understand why Mum didn't find it funny. She felt herself zipped into sadness as Mum wiped and scrubbed at Lily's face.

"Now put on some fresh clothes," Mum said. She still wasn't smiling. Lily couldn't work out what she'd done wrong.

"Are they ruined?" she asked, looking down at her T-shirt, now covered in thick blood.

"It'll come out of your clothes easily enough," Mum said. She looked as if she was about to cry.

Lily couldn't hug her, though, as she was covered in the blood. She'd run up and get changed, then hug Mum for ages. But what if she couldn't find her again?

"Where were you?" Lily asked. "I looked everywhere."

Mum glanced down the hall, and back again. "We must have missed each other," she said. She took a deep breath then, as if she was about to go underwater. And then her face softened. "Don't worry, I'll stay here until you get back. Then we can do some sewing together, calm us both down." Mum touched Lily's head lightly but with such tenderness. "I've got some new sequins."

Lily grinned and ran up the staircase, sadness unzipped. She stopped at the top and looked back down. Mum was still standing in exactly the same spot. But she looked scared. She had her hand at her throat. Tears fell down her face, as shiny as sequins.

Lily opens her eyes again.

Is this why the key was in the syrup, to remind Lily of the fake blood? It's the same make as the one Uncle Edward used. If so, is Aunt Liliana pointing to Lily's uncle as playing a part in Mariana's murder?

It can't be. Edward was wonderful. Everyone loved him. He was the one to make everyone laugh and smile. It's almost impossible to think of him as a killer. Almost.

Chapter Twenty-Six

December 29th
The Fifth Day of Christmas

As has become her habit, Lily looks in on Ronnie on her way down to breakfast. This time, though, instead of lying silently in bed, Ronnie is fully dressed, standing by the window. Lily joins him.

"Aunt Liliana would call it pathetic fallacy," Ronnie says. His voice is monotone, as flat as the pane of glass between him and the freezing fog that haunts the grounds.

Lily can't see the woods, or any trees at all. Everything is a mystery in white. "Is that how you feel?" she asks. "As if you're covered in mist?"

Ronnie nods. "Numb. Like there's nothing in front of me."

Lily nods. "I understand," she says. She tentatively places a hand on Ronnie's shoulder. He doesn't shrug it off, which is a start. "Do you feel up to coming down for breakfast?"

He hesitates. That's also a good sign. Then he nods. Even better.

"Take it easy," Lily says. "You can come back up any time you want."

"I'll come," he says. "And then I'll ask Mrs. Castle to drive me to see Philippa. I put on the suit she gave me. I thought she'd like to see it on." He shyly strokes the lapels of his lilac suit.

"Oh, Ronnie," Lily says. She has to tell him. It's not fair to lie to him like this.

"But I have to ask you something first," Ronnie says.

"Ask away," Lily says. She is glad of the brief reprieve and hates herself for it.

"And you have to answer me honestly." His Labrador eyes look so sad. "You promise?"

"I promise."

Ronnie takes a deep breath. "Why are you really here, if it's not for the house? Why are you so keen on solving the clues? 'Cause I may have hidden away up here, but I've been listening. And you are unraveling those anagrams like you used to sit at your mum's feet, getting knots out of wool." When it's Lily's turn to hesitate, he says, "Remember, you promised."

Lily thinks of Liliana's letter, to not trust *any* relatives, for their sake as much as hers, to keep her secrets while she found out those of the house.

But she's promised him. And it's time Lily started keeping her word and spilling her secrets. "Aunt Liliana told me that the clues would reveal things other than the keys."

"Like what?" He's staring at her intently.

Lily's turn for a deep breath now. "How my mum was murdered."

"What?" Ronnie says. His hand goes to his chest as if even now his heart is hurting for her.

"And other things that I haven't worked out yet. In fact, I haven't worked out anything."

Lily feels the tears of frustration welling. She's been here, what, five, six days now? And is she really any further on?

"You'll get there," Ronnie says. "Judging by the way you're finding the keys. Looks like Tom was right—you always were good at the Christmas Game."

"That'd be ironic," she says. "I find the keys and win someone the house, but not the secrets locked away inside."

"Aunt Lil always played the long game," Ronnie says. "Our last presents were only found if you looked at all the clues together."

"So I have to stay here till Twelfth Night?"

Ronnie shrugs. "Depends on how much you want to know the truth. And I may be able to help with that." He looks around to see if anyone is on the landing or the stairs. He closes the door to make sure. "Look, I've always found it hard to believe that your mum killed herself. It didn't make sense. She was so alive, always smiling."

"Smiling can cover many things."

"I know. But it never felt right. And then I saw something recently that made me doubt it more."

"What?"

In the hallway, footsteps cross the landing. Ronnie waits for them to pass, but a wariness has come over him like mist. "I'll dig it out and show you later."

"Thank you." Lily's guilt rises to the surface like rust. "And I need to tell you the whole truth."

The breakfast gong clangs.

"Tell me when everyone's running around the house looking for keys," Ronnie says. He puts his arms out and they hug until the gong goes again.

"I loved your mum, you know?" Ronnie says as they walk down the stairs. He points to Mariana's picture on the wall. "And I don't blame you for wanting to get as far away as possible."

"Is that how you feel now?" Lily asks.

Ronnie shakes his head. "You know, I thought I'd want nothing more to do with it. Philippa had plans for the house, not me. She was going to keep it as a hotel, and put me in the kitchen as executive chef. She thought I wanted that, and maybe I did. But now, I don't know. Maybe I should keep trying, for her sake."

"I think she'd like that," Lily replies.

The smell of kedgeree swims from the dining room, suggesting that the silver servers have been opened. Lily tries not to breathe in as she walks through the door.

"Lily! Have you seen the devil fog?" grins Tom, pointing out of the window. His smile drops as he sees Ronnie just behind her. "Sorry, mate. Didn't see you there."

"You don't have to be miserable around me," Ronnie replies.

"Exactly," Sara says from her chair, her spoon already filled with spiced rice and fish. "Life goes on."

And that's all it takes for Ronnie to run back upstairs.

"Well done, Sara," Tom says.

"Just telling it like it is," Sara replies.

"As you're so keen on the truth," Lily says. "I was wondering if you were able to tell me anything about my mum's death."

"I wouldn't have thought you'd want to dwell on that," Sara says, "given that you caused it by being such a terrible daughter." Fake sympathy swamps her face.

Holly and Gray gasp at the same time, Rachel shakes her head, Tom tuts, and Lily pictures herself slamming Sara's face into the kedgeree—of that face surfacing with a mustache of fish flakes.

"I've been led to believe that's not the case," Lily says, swallowing her anger with her orange juice.

"By whom?" Sara asks.

"I'm not going to tell you."

"All I know is what Dad said about your mum," Tom says. "It was at her funeral. He said, 'Sisters always have an issue with their sisters,' and looked at Aunt Liliana who was standing by your mum's coffin. He then said, 'If it wasn't for Liliana, your aunt would still be alive.' I asked him what he meant, but he wouldn't say. I found it all horrible, thinking of Mariana in there, but it seemed weird at the time so I remembered it."

"Are you saying that Mum did something to make her sister kill herself?" Sara asks. "Because I know she was vindictive, but not in that way, surely." She doesn't, however, seem sure.

Gray clears his throat. "Your mum was lovely," he says, looking at Lily. "And Mum loved her more than anything. That's why she loved you."

Sara glares at Lily.

"You see," Tom says, "even adopted sisters have issues with each other."

※

Later, Lily is in the orangery, on weather watch. The snow seems to have stopped, and the sun is shining bright and low over the grounds of Endgame. If it can get up enough wattage, maybe the sunshine can melt enough snow to let them move more easily outside and, most importantly, allow cars to pass through the country roads. They can then move the fallen tree, drive to a police station, and stop lying to Ronnie.

She tries to go up to him a few times, but Sara always follows, suspecting Lily of having found the next clue and not telling anyone. Lily can't shake her. And she won't impose Sara on Ronnie.

Sara's morning, and half of her afternoon, is spent in anticipation of the next sonnet. Every time Mrs. Castle glooms in with new food or drink, she picks though it like a magpie looking for shiny things. It's not until the stretched-out afternoon that Gray cries out, "Here!"

Everyone rushes in from wherever they're sitting.

Gray is standing in the hallway, pointing to the Christmas tree. Very carefully, he lifts a huge red bauble from the tree. "There's something inside." He holds it up to the light. It looks like a translucent pomegranate. Gray shakes it gently as if to jiggle its pips. A rolled-up piece of paper tips from one side of the bauble to the other.

"What if it's for another day?" Sara asks. "You might forfeit the chance of the house."

"They weren't here yesterday," Gray says, "I'm sure of it."

"What, you go around clocking everything that changes?" Sara asks, her voice rising with incredulity. "In a house this size?"

Gray scratches his neck and shrugs. "Can't help it, my mind just does it."

"There are some strange brains in this family," Sara says, shaking her head. She looks over to Lily. "But they're useful. Come on then, give it over." She holds out her hand and Gray places the bauble gently on her palm.

Sara examines the decoration, then unscrews the crown-like top. She tips out the paper and reads it out loud.

Really, we should be marking Haloa,
A winter festival where vines were pruned
Wines were tasted, time was taken slower.
Women gathered together in festooned
Streets, gave phallic gifts, elders whispering
To maidens, tacit secrets they should know.
They feasted on gentle foods, left off 'rings
Of first fruits to Demeter in the snow.

Bring this tradition down from history:
For inside every model woman grows
A true Eleusinian mystery.
Don't worry. I won't give you a dildo,
This old woman whispers to a maiden:
Unveil all the gifts you have been given.

When she finishes reading, she throws the sonnet and the decoration on the floor. The bauble smashes, sending pomegranate shards across the floor. Gray stoops to pick up the pieces.

"Is that really necessary, Sara?" Rachel says. Impatience crackles in her voice. Holly is standing in the doorway. Neither of them has opened up a bauble.

"Haloa? How are we supposed to know what *that* is? Mum's punishing me all over again for not wanting to read her precious books," Sara says.

"What if she's talking to you?" Holly asks. "You could be the maiden, and she's the woman whispering her secrets, telling you to use your gifts."

Sara's laugh is harsh and abrupt. "Mum didn't think I had any gifts." She turns to Tom. "You did Greek. What's this all about?"

Tom reads through it again. "You're right. If you know a bit of Greek, then today's location is implicit in the clue. You could say it's 'tacit.'"

Lily laughs.

"Even Lily gets it," Sara replies. Her face is going red, whether from shame or anger is hard to tell. Maybe they're the same feeling, standing back to back.

"Just tell us, would you?" Rachel replies. "We don't need talking through all the things we don't get."

"Anyone know the prestige language spoken in ancient Greece?" Tom asks.

"Er, ancient Greek?" Holly says.

"Otherwise known as 'attic,'" Tom replies.

"Thank you, Tom." Sara bends to pick up the clue, then runs up the staircase.

"I'm hoping it's in a dildo," Rachel says, following Sara slowly up the stairs. "And prim Sara has to open it. That'd be entertaining."

"Not sure she's that prim," Lily says, rehearing the noises Sara was making the night before.

"Oh, really!" Tom says, rubbing his hands. "If you have gossip, it's only right you share it. Though I can't imagine Sara indulging in more than a gloved frig. Sin, sexually at least, and Sara seem very far apart."

Lily tries not to laugh but can't stop herself. "That's an image I really didn't want," she says.

Lily stands on one leg and knocks on Ronnie's door with her foot. "I've cobbled together a lunch tray for you," she says. "The others are chasing keys, so I thought we could talk while you ate."

When there's no answer, she places the tray outside his room. "It's out here. I won't intrude. Come and find me when you're ready." She presses her hand to the door. "Love you," she says.

At the top of the house, Sara, Gray, Rachel, and Holly are making floorboards groan as they search the attic. The air feels fresher in here since Lily was in a few days ago. The skylight is open. A stream of dusk-lilac light is showing up the far end. There is warmth in the sun, even now. Maybe the snow will melt after all.

A memory comes back, ghostly, the figures almost in place before her.

Lily sitting with Isabelle in the attic, under the open skylight. One winter's day, encouraged by Aunt Liliana, they'd written *LILYANDISABELLE* on paper and cut out each letter, then rearranged them to make anagrams.

Isabelle had found rude words of four or five letters, but Lily managed to fit all the letters in their names into "Naiad Belle Silly."

"You should be Naiad, that's pretty," Isabelle had said. "And I'll be Belle."

"Then who's silly?" Lily asked.

"We both are," Isabelle said, and they'd settled down under the skylight to read, sucking rhubarb and custard sweets till their tongues dried out.

That memory had been underneath all the others in this house. Coming up to the attic again has whipped off the dust sheet and allowed her to see it for the first time in years. And the others must be going through something similar.

Gray strokes the mane of the rocking horse that used to be in the nursery.

Tom is making a Lego house next to a toppled Jenga tower.

Rachel is going through a box of photos and papers, passing them to Holly and explaining who everyone is in the old pictures.

Sara, though, is still on track, referring back to the sonnet, brow furrowed. "I really hope we're not looking for a dildo," she says.

Rachel sniggers.

"Fuck sake, Rachel," Sara says, turning her back on Rachel. "Tom, you need to help me."

"I really don't," Tom replies, getting out a Playmobil set. "I already told you to look up here. I reckon you owe me."

"We could be in here for years," Sara says, gesturing toward the wall of boxes.

"Fine by me," Tom replies, not looking up.

"We all know I'm going to win," Sara says, "so you might as well help me."

Anger, simmering in Lily for too long, bubbles to the surface. She imagines Sara throwing everything out of the house, trouncing the memories of Lily and Tom and Ronnie. There's Ronnie, lying in bed, mourning his love, and Sara, not giving a shit about anything, making it clear that "life goes on." And it should go on. But this house would have a much better life if Ronnie were the chef in its restaurant and it was run by Rachel and Holly.

Lily knows she hasn't helped. In the last few days, she's led Sara to a key, even given her another. And if Sara took the key from Philippa, killed her for it perhaps, then she has a fair chance of having the right key to win the house.

Time for Lily to tip the balance in the house's favor and win the key for Ronnie.

She takes out the sonnet again and, while Sara is busy throwing things out of a trunk, she reads. Tom sees her, and smiles. He zips his lips shut again.

Lily starts rearranging the letters of words that stand out: "maiden" is in there twice, and that's an anagram of "die man," and…no, that's a dead end.

She looks around the attic, taking in the old lampstands and bureaus; tables etched with initials; and the old dressmaker's dummy that Mum had used to teach her to make clothes.

And what is a mannequin other than a "model woman"?

Slowly, Lily gets up.

Seeing Lily go toward the dummy, Tom calls out, "Sara, come here!" Sara snaps her head up and follows Tom into the corner of the attic. He buries his head in an old dress-up box. "I reckon the key's in here somewhere."

Sara has her serious face on as she pulls out scarves and hats and old clothes they'd used to put on plays.

Lily, meanwhile, turns round the dummy. A zip runs down the spine like a brace. That never used to be there. She learned how to attach zips by using this dummy, but there was never one actually on it.

Trying not to make too much noise, Lily pulls down the zip. Tucked inside, attached to the underside of the mannequin's skin, is the fifth key.

✳

Lily is still smiling when she goes back down the stairs. Sara has disappeared in a grump, Rachel can't stop laughing, Gray has asked to be left
alone in the attic, mending an old playpen, and Tom's gone to help Mrs.
Castle get dinner ready.

Stopping outside Ronnie's door again, Lily sees that his lunch tray
hasn't been touched. The tea is cold in its pot, the scrambled egg more
of a jellified lump, the toast floppy on the plate. Only the apple looks
untouched by time.

She knocks on the door. "Ronnie? Can I come in?"

No answer.

"I know I said I wouldn't intrude, but I want to know you're OK."

The lack of reply isn't unusual; he's often not answered when she's
checked on him. This time, though, the silence is different. She'd never
thought about whether a room feels inhabited or not, but now the room
feels empty.

Fear pricks her skin. She opens the door before thinking about it.

Ronnie is on the floor. His head is a mess of red.

Lily's heart resounds in her ears but not as loudly as her scream. She
runs over, wants to touch him, soothe him. But she knows it's to soothe
herself, not him. This isn't fake blood. Ronnie is dead.

Chapter Twenty-Seven

December 30th
The Sixth Day of Christmas

It's gone midnight by the time Lily leaves the others to their arguments and alibis and goes back upstairs. But only to the second floor.

Ronnie is still lying on the carpet. She has refused to let anyone touch him. She's wearing her dressmaker's gloves to try not to disturb anything. Now, in the quiet, she sits cross-legged a few meters away from him. Even though his eyes are open, staring at nothing, and his limbs have stiffened in his suit, the way his fingers lie curled in his palm makes her think that, somehow, he is asleep.

Philippa never got to see him in the suit. And he never got to say goodbye to her while wearing it. Mortality at Christmas is the cruelest. Since Mum died, she's used to how trauma doesn't pay attention to the calendar. Death comes at Christmas as much, if not more, as any other time of the year. But for someone to take life during the supposed festive season requires particular cruelty. She thinks of little Samuel, Ronnie and Philippa's son. Only four and he's an orphan. Is it good or bad that he won't have many memories of them? Either way, he'll carry this with him forever. Christmas will always haunt him.

She understands why Gray has gone to the tiny chapel to pray. He says he can't comprehend any of this. That he needs answers. Lily, though, would rather whisper her words to Ronnie than God. If God can hear her, then so can Ronnie, and God gets enough conversation. Let Ronnie get her spoken love.

"I asked you to tell me about Philippa," Lily says. She's lying on the floor, on the other side of the bed, as if they were having a sleepover. This way, she can look up at the ceiling rose, whorled like a fingerprint, and pretend that Ronnie's just listening to her monologue, as she listened to his only days before. "So now I'm going to tell you what I love about you. And for once you can't laugh it off, or go and cook, or distract me in some other way."

She pauses, as if expecting him to interject with a joke or a fart. She then carries on, a smile warming up her voice. "I love the way you always have your buttons done up wrong. Even on your chef's whites, one side is longer than the other. I love how everything is the best, for you. The best sunset you've ever seen, the best walk you've ever had, until the next one. I bet, if heaven exists, you're saying it's the best afterlife ever." Lily has to stop for a moment, in case a sob breaks out.

"I love your laugh and how it can make a whole room join in with you. I love your patented chili-based hangover cures, how you collect stones from every beach you've been to, your love for absolutely everyone you've ever met. I love how you love football, and are absolutely useless at it but don't care a bit. I love the way you put bright pink laces in your Doc Martens. I love your soft heart and sharp mind.

"Your impression of a ferret is unsurpassed, including your attempt to climb up your own trousers. I love that you have an inexplicable fondness for blancmange. And your food really is delicious. I'll never forget the time you cooked me a raspberry soufflé that you brought in on your head like a wobbly toque. I wish you'd had the chance to run this place. I would've even come back to eat here." She realizes as she says it that this is true. The house is working its way into her heart.

"And I'll tell you another thing. You'd have made a brilliant uncle. I'm so sorry I didn't tell you this morning. I should have. About everything.

I should have spoken up and I didn't, and that will always stay with me. But I'll tell my little girl all about you. So will Tom. We'll make you so present it's like you're still alive."

A sigh comes from Ronnie.

Lily sits up. What if she was wrong? What if he was unconscious and has just come round? It's possible, right?

She scrambles up so she can see him. A slow hiss escapes his lips, but his chest is not moving. It's just air leaving his lungs for good. She wishes she believed that the soul leaves the body in a last exhale. Even so—and knowing Ronnie would laugh at her—she moves over to the window. They had stood here this morning and looked out into the murk. If she'd known what would happen, she'd have followed Ronnie upstairs and not let him out of her sight. She opens the window wide. If there is such a thing as ghosts, then he shouldn't be trapped in this house.

Footsteps come up the stairs, turn the corner to walk along the landing, and slow to a stop outside the room. Lily holds her breath. The door opens.

Gray steps in. He's about to turn on the light, then sees Lily. "You've come to be with him, too," he says, "I'll leave you to it."

He's about to go, when Lily says, "Could you take over the vigil? At dawn? And don't let anyone take him away."

Gray nods, as if sleepovers with the dead are perfectly normal. And for some, they are. Friends and relatives take turns to watch over the departed. She wonders who will watch over her.

When Charlie, one of Lily's pagan friends, had died at the age of forty-five, his wife and young daughter spent all night with his body. They had washed and dressed him, sang and kept him company. The next day, at the woodland burial site, Lily and the other mourners had thrown compost, buttons, letters, coins, and flowers into his grave, and said goodbye.

Lily had thrown in Charlie's favorite flower, a rose, and then stepped through an archway covered in evergreen fir. Once through the arch, everyone danced and sang, because they'd entered a new relationship with Charlie. One that would never die.

While Lily is here on a vigil because whoever killed Ronnie might want to move him, she also wants to welcome a new relationship with him. That way, she'll always hear his voice in her head.

Lily makes herself as comfortable as possible on the floor. Pregnancy keeps her awake enough as it is, she might as well make use of it.

The night passes slowly, as interminable as a Monopoly game. The fog has cleared, and now the sky is without cloud. The winter stars stand out like white dots on dominoes.

Every now and then, she glances over at Ronnie. In the moonlight he looks gilded with silver, as if he could take his place among the statues in the garden. She tries to remember what he said to her that morning. Whether he had given anything away that might be of use. What had he seen that made him think that she was right about Mum being murdered? A conversation with someone that he overheard? No, he said that he'd dig it out and show her later; that must mean it's physical. Was it something in the house?

Or in this room. She looks around, aware that if she disturbs anything, then she is guilty of tampering with a crime scene. But her cousin was killed for a reason. And he might have hidden the reason nearby.

She opens drawers, looks inside his suitcase, under the bed. She doesn't know what she's looking for. Whatever Ronnie had wanted to show her could be anywhere. At least she might find the key, that'd be something to show for the pain she's feeling. Going through all of Philippa and Ronnie's small things, their personal effects—the lipstick and the shaver charger, the tampons and the Eiffel Tower key ring from when they went to Paris on honeymoon—carry such enormous weight. She has to stop several times to cry.

She has almost given up and is just looking in the clothes hanging in the wardrobe. In the inside pocket of a jacket, Lily finds an envelope. Written on it, in Liliana's swirly script, is Ronnie's name. And inside that is another letter, addressed to Lily. From her mother.

Chapter Twenty-Eight

As soon as the sky shows a stripe of orange light the next morning, Gray appears in the doorway. Lily feels a last-minute pang, wondering if he will keep his word.

"I'll keep watch," Gray says. He already has the solemn bearing of an undertaker.

Taking one last look at Ronnie, and tucking the letters into her own pocket, she leaves the room and goes across to Tom's. She knocks three times. "It's almost light. And it hasn't snowed all night," she says, loud enough to barge through even Tom's deep sleep.

Tom opens the door, hair all over the place. He ruffles it and it stands up some more. "What time is it?" he asks, words distorted by a yawn.

"Just after eight," Lily replies. "We're going to move that oak tree."

"But how?" he asks. "Without Ronnie to help lift it..." he tails off.

He looks over to his brother's room where Gray stands guard.

"I know it's hard," Lily says. "But we have to get out. Staying here is too dangerous."

Tom nods. As they walk to the hallway, Gray approaches. He holds out his hand to Tom. "My sincere condolences," he says. "I am sorry for your loss." He then bows his head as they pass by.

"Well, that was weird," Tom says when they're dressed up and trudging through the snow outside.

It's still cold—when Lily exhales, her breath forms full stops in the air. Gray clouds form a committee overhead, scheduling when to snow.

They need to leave *now*.

Lily walks faster, trying not to slip. "I think he's just doing what he's being trained to do."

"But Ronnie's his cousin," Tom says. "Not a client. He's acting as if he has no feelings. Like you, but with worse dress sense."

Lily has the sensation of a stake stuck through her solar plexus. "I've got a lot of emotions, Tom," she says calmly, when she can control the feelings fighting to get out. "You know that."

"I'm not saying you don't, you just keep them locked up. Either Gray's the same, or, and this is probable, he's like his sister, and Ronnie's death doesn't matter to him. Or surprise him."

"You don't think he could have killed Ronnie?" But Lily's mind takes her back to what Gray said the night Philippa died. That she was his first dead body. Now Ronnie is his second.

"You never really know a person, but I'm not sure about leaving him alone with the body. He was the one who took Philippa away, remember."

"With Sara."

"True. And Rachel didn't stop them." Tom pauses, then shivers. "Well, he's in the right profession. His eyes remind me of the silver obols placed on the eyelids of the dead."

They've reached the car. The tree doesn't look as huge by daylight, although they are still going to need a chainsaw to cut it. "I'll back the car up," Tom says. "Then we can see what we're dealing with."

Tom gets into the car and places the key in the ignition. Nothing happens. He winds down the window. "The battery must have gone flat," he says.

"Shouldn't have done," Lily says, "you drove it a long way on Christmas Eve, and it started fine the other night."

Tom shrugs. "Maybe it got frozzed by the cold. I'd give up if I were out in this." Getting back out of the car, he opens the trunk and takes out the jump leads. "You bring your Mini down here, if you can, then I can jump-start mine."

"You'd better check you can open the hood first," Lily says, pointing to how close Tom's car is to the tree.

"Easy," Tom says, leaning into the car and flicking a switch. The hood clicks open. He lifts it up. "Ta-da!" And then his face crumples.

"What?" Lily says.

Tom's face mirrors the ashen sky above. "Open your hood."

Lily frowns, but tramps over to her car and its carapace of snow to do as he asks. The hood sighs as it opens.

"See anything?" Tom calls over.

Lily doesn't know what she should be looking for. Then she notices that something's missing. "The battery's gone," she shouts.

Tom slams his hood. "Mine too. And I bet the others have had theirs taken as well. We have to go back."

Lily thinks of Ronnie and Philippa. This could be her only chance to get help. And to get away from a house that could end up killing her mother, her daughter, and herself. She places her hand in her coat pocket, feeling the letter from her mum. "We have to go on foot," she says.

"No, Lily," Tom says.

"We'll gather supplies, it'll be fine," Lily replies. "We'll take the map. Can't be that far to the nearest village. Someone there will have a mobile. Then the police will find a way through. They'll have to. It's a double murder."

"It's what, ten miles to the village? On icy roads, most of which are treacherous, downright impassable to pedestrians as well as cars, it could take ten hours to get there. Longer if we go over the fields and hills. We'll only have good light for half that time. If one of us loses our footing, or gets tired and has to rest—which is likely given you are pregnant and look like you haven't slept in weeks—well, we might not get back up again. It's freezing. And we don't have mobile phones. One or both of us could die of exposure. Do you want to put yourself, me, or your little passenger in danger?"

"If we stay in the house, we're in danger."

"I don't know what to say, Lily," Tom says, his hands dropping to his sides. "I've lost my aunt and my brother. I don't want to lose you, too." His eyes glisten with tears. "I'm scared."

Lily takes his gloved hand in hers. "Me too."

"And there's one more reason to stay," Tom says.

"What?" Lily asks.

"I've been thinking about all this. I want us to win the house, in Ronnie's name. We set up a cooperative with Rachel and Holly, do whatever we can to not let Endgame fall into Sara's hands. Or Gray's."

"I can't believe Gray could have killed them."

"In theory *anyone* here could have killed Philippa at night, or Ronnie in the day. But something else is going on. And I can't help thinking Sara is behind it. Tell me you disagree."

"I can't," she says.

Tom looks at the house, the sky darkening around it as the snow starts falling again. Then turns back to Lily. "You're hiding something, I know you are. You've got to tell me."

Lily sees the same softness in his eyes as Ronnie's. Talking about Mum's murder could have gotten Ronnie killed. Her instinct is shouting at her that it did. And she's not going to ignore her instincts anymore. She's going to keep Tom safe, even if it means keeping him in the dark. At least he'll be alive.

"I don't know anything," Lily says, dropping his hand so she can take his arm as they walk back to the house. A study in strength. "Let's find out what's going on together."

Chapter Twenty-Nine

Gray birds fly against a purple-lined sky. Lily and Holly walk behind Tom, Rachel, Sara, and Mrs. Castle as they carry Ronnie down to the icehouse. A dawn internment next to his wife.

Each time one of them stumbles, losing their grip on Ronnie's arm or leg, Lily's heart contracts. She vows again to tell her daughter about her uncle Ronnie.

When he is placed next to Philippa, their hands touching, Lily's tears spill and won't stop.

No one talks at breakfast. The only sounds are the crunch of toast, the slurp of tea, and the slop-crunch of cereal. Lily can only manage a piece of dry bread. Rachel and Holly sit huddled at one end of the table, not looking at anyone. Tom stares down at his plate, looking as lost as the car batteries missing—they've found—from all of their cars. Even Sara's.

Rachel starts crying, silently; Holly leans over and nuzzles Rachel's ear with her nose.

Lily has to look away—it's too intimate, too painful—and catches Sara staring at her. Sara inclines her head to one side and pulls a pastry apart, not blinking once. Earlier, she expressed resentment that Gray was still outside, standing by the icehouse. She can't get over Gray not being by her side. Lily wonders if Sara can get over anything.

Mrs. Castle enters the dining room with a fresh pot of coffee. She places it on the table, then looks at them all. "I haven't heard a word uttered in an hour," she says. "And it's driving me crazy. This situation is bad enough as it is without silence setting in. The house doesn't like it. And neither do I. Go and look for the clues, would you?"

"The sonnets are available, then?" Sara asks.

"Listen," Mrs. Castle says, waving a long, pointy finger, "I'm not allowed to tell you about them or where they are. But I'm telling you to look. So, what do you think?" She leans forward, her face an inch from Sara's.

Sara rears back. Lily feels her lips twitch. Every home needs a Castle.

Tom's face hardens into resolution. He stands up and leaves the room. Sara isn't far behind.

Rachel and Holly don't move. "I don't want to play anymore," Rachel says.

"I know what you mean," Lily replies.

"Have they gone?" Rachel asks, looking toward the door.

Holly leaps up and goes to check the hallway. "Can't see anyone."

Rachel reaches down beneath the table and pulls out a box. "I thought you might want to look at this. I brought it down from the attic. It was right by the mannequin, the box opened, as if we were supposed to look inside."

"I saw you sharing the photos with Holly," Lily says.

Rachel nods. "After what you said about your mum, well, I thought you'd want to look at some of the documents." Rachel hands over the box, and her shoulders drop, as if she's handing over responsibility, too.

"Thank you," Lily says. The box feels lighter than its contents.

"Don't tell Sara I gave it to you," Rachel says. "I'm worried it would put us all in danger."

"I wouldn't," Lily replies, a little hurt that Rachel would even suggest it.

"We know," Holly says, "otherwise we wouldn't have given it to you. We just want you to be safe."

Rachel strokes the side of Holly's face with the back of her hand. Holly looks at her with such passion that Lily can't believe it was her with Sara the other night. She's been wrong before in thinking that someone wouldn't be deceitful. But Holly doesn't seem the sort. Maybe they're poly. Whatever their situation, the world needs more of their kind of love.

"You'd better go and get key hunting," Rachel says to Lily. "We're rooting for you to win."

"But I don't—"

"Want the house, yes, we know," Rachel says. "You keep saying."

"But maybe the house wants you," says Holly.

The floor above them creaks, but whether that's the house agreeing, objecting, or someone walking on the floorboards is hard to tell.

After taking the box up to her room, Lily bumps into an out-of-breath Tom in the corridor. He's holding up a colorful paper chain, draped over his arms like a party-time Jacob Marley. "Found it. Well, Gray did." He points to a new decoration hanging on the banister. "I ran as fast as I could but he got there first and then gave it to me. Can you believe it? There are others hanging from the next floor, so Sara's not far behind."

"Come into my room," he says. "That way they won't be able to see your brain at work."

Tom's room is at the side of the house. He plays with the tinsel on his Christmas tree, wrapping it around his wrist. He looks out of the balcony window overlooking the orchard. "I reckon," he says, "that if I got a fishing net, a really long one, then I could scrobble an apple from here."

Lily unloops each of the fourteen paper chains, keeping them in order. On the back of each is a line of the poem. As she reads, the red, blue, and green shiny pieces of gummed paper glint under the Christmas tree lights.

Downstairs, today. That cuts out a number
Of rooms: don't say I don't treat you. Pay me
Back: be fabulous. Do not slumber
In mediocrity. Be stars, mages,
Wizards, soldiers, kings, queens, singers, coders…
Ask yourself: What would Bowie do?

At the halfway point, you're getting colder.
Don't be alarmed, or misconstrue,
You'll find your way home, one day, but playing
This game is as difficult as digging
Iron-hard dirt for your sister's grave. In
Fact, although you're nearer now the finish
Line, the house always wins, it'll not die:
Throw yourself instead into your best life.

"Downstairs," Lily says. She's trying not to think about—or picture—the iron-hard grave of her mum. Grieving over that will have to wait.

"You sure?" Tom asks, so surprised at the speed of her announcement that he stumbles on his way to the door, still tied up in tinsel.

"It says so in the first line." Lily is already out the door, headed for the stairs.

"And then what?"

"And then we play some games," Lily replies.

"It's definitely in here?" Tom asks, looking around the games room.

"'Mages' is an anagram of 'games,'" Lily says quickly. "And then there's 'wizards' as in pinball, 'kings, queens' as in chess, 'singers' the karaoke machine, 'coders,' well, that's games again."

"Fine," says Tom. "Superbrain does it again. So, where's the key?"

Gray walks in, holding strips of paper chain. His face is red on one side, as if he's fallen. Or been hit.

"Are you OK, Gray?" Lily asks.

Gray's hand goes to his face, hiding it from view. "There's nothing wrong," he says.

"Very convincing," Tom says, going over to him. "You can tell us, you know. Did Sara hit you?"

Gray looks afraid, his eyes darting to the door. "I can't."

"I understand," Tom says in a gentle voice. "But we can look after you. You just need to stick with us."

Gray looks at Lily with a plea in his eyes. Then he shakes his head. "I've got to find the key."

He breaks his gaze from Lily's and looks through the clues. He's mouthing them. Lily sees his eyes go to the games cupboard. He dashes over, opens it up, and takes out a box of dice. "'Die,'" Lily says.

Gray nods, then continues his search. It's fascinating. He thinks like Lily. And like his mum. Lily feels her family weave closer together.

"This isn't a spectator sport," Tom says to Lily. "You're the brains, tell me where to look!"

"Start with the chess set, I'll look at the pinball machine," Lily says.

With half an eye on Gray as he rifles through a mini casino game—*"the house always wins,"* she thinks—Lily looks underneath the pinball machine. No sign of a key, just cracks in the wall that the machine hides. There's always something sinister behind a game.

"Nothing here," Tom says. "I'll try the karaoke machine."

Lily goes over the poem, knowing that there's something she's missing.

"Got it!" Gray says. He's standing in the corner of the room, holding the dartboard. The key is strapped to its back.

Chapter Thirty

"I think we should all stick together this evening," Tom says as he walks Lily up to her room. "At least stay with me. That way I'll know you're safe. I'll sleep on the floor, you can have the whole bed, I'll hook apples for us in the morning."

"Thanks, but I'll be OK," Lily says.

"Just looking out for you."

"You will make someone a lovely husband one day," Lily says.

"Don't know about that."

"You're sweet, kind, loyal, clever, funny…" Lily says.

"You're forgetting extremely attractive," Tom says, waggling his eyebrows. "And I do it with such apparent ease. Aging sexily isn't for everyone, you know."

"Someone special will see that."

"You'll find someone, too," Tom says to Lily. "Someone who stays, and I can actually meet."

"Maybe. For now, though, I'm jiggered. Just want to go to bed."

"Watch out, your Yorkshire's showing," Tom says. "Your accent's getting stronger too, like a tea bag left in to brew."

Lily laughs. It's true. "The past is always there, hidden."

"Like a picture behind an advent calendar door."

They're both quiet for a moment. Lily thinks of everything that has opened up in her since being here, and wonders what's still to come. Whatever Tom's thinking, it's making him look so sad. "Talking of doors," Lily says, as brightly as she can, "you should lock yours, too."

Tom smiles again, seems to shiver off the past. "But I'm staying outside your door till you've locked it, OK?"

"Good night, Mr. Tom," she says, as she used to when they were little. His smile is so sweet, wide, and shy that she leans over and kisses his cheek.

Walking into her bedroom, locking her door behind her, Lily listens to Tom walking away, whistling "We Wish You a Merry Christmas." As she unlaces the maternity corset, she lets out a sigh that's not just about being released.

Lily has ached to look at the card from her mum again all day, and placed it in the box Rachel gave her when she hid it in her room. But only in bed does she let herself read it. Liliana's letter to Ronnie asks him to give the card to Lily on the last day of the game, "To prove it to her for good."

The picture on the card is Endgame House at Christmas, etched by Aunt Veronica. The family is on the lawn, singing Christmas carols. Inside, in her mother's writing, she reads:

> Happy Christmas, my beautiful daughter. I love you. I may have given birth to you, but you give me life. You gift me joy every day, and I can't wait for more of our adventures. I'll be here for you forever. Dare to be as fabulous as you really are. But most of all, just be you. Keep singing, and dark days will pass, and summer will always come.

Not the words of a woman about to kill herself.

The words also echo Liliana's poem today. What was it? "*Be fabulous. Do not slumber in mediocrity.*" Trust Aunt Lil to add the mediocrity. Sometimes, Lily thinks Sara has a point. If Liliana had accepted her, then would Sara be the person she is today? If she hadn't expected Sara to be a Bowie, a mage, or a star, or to wield words or a paintbrush, and had simply asked her to be herself, would Lily even suspect Sara of having the capacity to kill?

If Mum had lived, then Lily knows she'd be able to speak up now. She wouldn't be strung with cowardice; she wouldn't have to lace up her corsets so no one could see her real shape. That's what she has to give Little Bean. The space to be her own shape.

She thinks about her mother singing Kooks and Christmas carols to get her to sleep and, very quietly, so just Bean and the mice in the walls can hear, hums "In the Bleak Midwinter."

Chapter Thirty-One

December 31st—New Year's Eve
The Seventh Day of Christmas

New Year's Eve. People treat it like it's a due date. So much pressure placed on the day, celebrations are planned, and then usually the calendar turns and nothing happens. You start the next day a bit fatter than the one before. Most first-time mothers go over their due date, so Lily will have to wait for champagne. It should be on tap in delivery suites, next to the gas and air.

Lily is awake early, reading through all the papers in the box that Rachel gave her, placing them next to the blueprint of the house from Isabelle. All of this must mean something; she just doesn't know what.

The last item in the box makes her hands start to shake. A coroner's report, of her mum's death. In it, Sir Archibald Fleming states that Mariana had attempted to hang herself in her bedroom. Then, when that failed due to an "insecure attachment of rope to ceiling," she'd gone into the maze and slit her wrists.

It's all written here, black and white like the keys on her mum's piano. Liliana must have gotten it wrong. In the room next door, Mum really had tried to kill herself while Lily slept. And then, as Mariana always saw things through, she'd tried again in the maze, and succeeded. But then, why would there be fake blood on her coat? And why didn't the police take it in for evidence? And, if she was going to kill herself in her room, why then go to the maze?

She takes out her mum's card again, reads through the words that are full of hope. But what else would you say to your child? Lily touches the bump that seems to be growing every day. It's solid, more solid somehow than the rest of her. *Stay in as long as possible, Little Bean*, she thinks. *It's hard out here.*

As Lily is putting the papers away, she sees a checkbook stub. It's so small, this relic of an analog era. It's also evidence of a check for £45,000, made out to Sir Archibald Fleming. The coroner. And it's signed by Uncle Edward.

Lily stands in front of her bathroom mirror, wearing the dress she'd based on an upside-down champagne flute. Lily had stitched on three thousand yellow seed-bead bubbles by hand. She hopes that their sparkle will distract from the sadness she can see in her own face. If, as it looks like, Edward bribed the coroner, and probably murdered Mum, then Tom must never know. It'd kill him.

When she opens her door, she finds a card on the floor. On the front is an invitation to a New Year's Eve party, on the back is today's sonnet.

> *Key clue today! Stop right now and listen:*
> *One of you will find this too hard to bear*
> *And hide away inside their room, missing*
> *An amazing chance to be my soul heir.*
> *It sounds corny, but it is essential*
> *That you get round it. You can't go any*
> *Other way. Your walls are existential.*
> *Separate as threads in a spinning Jenny;*
> *You must weave yourself together. This world*

Is cruel but you must be in it. Immerse
Yourself. Find your route and follow. These pearls
May be clichés, strung out to shine in verse,
But I mean them. You must find room to win.
The seeds were sown long ago. Now begin.

Lily's breath feels stuck in her corset, her heart pushed up between her collarbones. She'd known one of the keys would be in the maze. And today's the day. New Year, the ceremonial passing under the arch from one dead year into a relationship with the next one. It does sound "corny," yes, Liliana.

Lily's anger bubbles like shaken champagne. Liliana's message to her couldn't be clearer. Get over yourself and inside the maze. The place where Mum died. Lily again feels for Sara, and Liliana's students. Her aunt's cruelty could come in the guise of pep talks, and she still lectures from her grave.

Now, Lily is trapped in a maze of Liliana's making. Either she breaks down the walls she's put up and joins the search in the maze, or she does as Liliana predicted and cowers in her room.

This is why she doesn't want to be known, or seen.

Footsteps are coming up the stairs. Tom appears, waving a gilt-edged invitation. "You've got yours, then."

"Liliana made sure I got it," Lily says. "I don't think anyone needs my help to know where this key is."

Tom walks tentatively toward her, hunched as if wondering how Lily will react. "I'm sorry, I didn't realize Aunt Lil would be so, well..."

"So much of a bitch?" Sara says, walking up behind Tom.

Tom spins round. "I wouldn't call her that."

"You're too nice," Sara says. "Doesn't do you any good in the end. Look at Lily's mum. Oh, you can't. She's dead."

Lily can feel Sara's sadness, worn like a lining under her rage. And she gets it. Some people turn anger inwards, and some outwards. Tom and Lily are innies, Sara an outie. And Liliana made her that way.

"Your mum is dead, too," Lily says, feeding her voice with compassion like a Christmas cake with whisky. "And I get why you're angry with her, and me, and everyone." A sudden memory comes of Sara smashing the perfect house of cards that Gray had taken a day to build. His tears falling like spades down his cheeks. "And why you'd want to take a wrecking ball to Endgame House and start again."

"You know nothing about me," Sara spits. Her eyes are rage spiked. This is why Lily should never speak up. "Or Mother, and what she was capable of. If I were you, I'd keep it that way."

"What do you mean?" Tom asks.

"You know exactly what I mean," Sara says, coming up close to Tom and pointing her finger centimeters from his face. Tom backs up into the wall. Sara puts her hand in her pocket and Lily leaps forward, thinking Sara has a knife. Instead, Sara pulls out her copy of the invitation. "This shows how much Mum thought of me. Nothing. A whole sonnet devoted to her precious niece and sometime daughter. She doesn't even bother with anagrams on this one. 'Amazing.' Right in the middle, as if playing games was for the rest of us and the real text is for her little Lily. I looked through the previous clues. They're all either about finding out secrets or finding yourself. All of it is to *her*."

She turns to Lily. Her eyes are full of tears that won't go anywhere.

"I'm sorry," Lily says. And she is, because Sara is right.

Sara's chin shakes, her lips shiver. She looks into Lily's eyes and the intensity burns. There is too much information. Lily looks away.

"And there you go," Sara says, pointing at Lily. "Mum was right again. You are a coward, and you'll never be the heir of her soul, or anything else. At least she was brave. She acted, for good and bad."

As Sara walks away, Lily's voices of self-hate surge. Bean flips like a fortune fish as if she can hear those voices, too. Now Lily can't direct it inwards. But where does she put all that hurt, those spikes? Maybe Sara's right: Tom and Lily, and Mariana before them, are too nice. And it doesn't lead to winning. She should accept that. Not even try.

"You should go down to the maze," Lily says to Tom as he reaches out to comfort her. "I'm going to do exactly as Aunt Liliana predicted, and stay in my room."

※

Lily watches from her window all morning as her cousins search the maze. She sees Tom's bobble hat appearing and disappearing, Sara's red coat, Holly's yellow hood, Rachel searching the outside hedge of the maze, Gray standing at the entrance, smoking.

Curses rise to her open window. The deep snow is making it impossible to search for the key. Lily imagines their gloved hands searching under hedges, then getting covered in snow so they look like an extra pair of white mittens. Taking off the gloves, only for their hands to turn red and stiff, snow-burned and useless.

She keeps deciding to join them, gets as far as her door, then stops. Endgame may be growing on her like ivy, but the maze is still too much. All she can do is be a spectator while her cousins search in the place where Mum's last breath hung in the winter air.

Rachel and Holly give up first. They emerge from the maze hand in hand at lunchtime. Lily walks down the stairs to join them. The decorations have changed downstairs. Banners shouting "Happy New Year" hang from beams. Balloons bob against the ceiling, bellies stretched to the point of discomfort.

Mrs. Castle brings out Welsh rarebit for the three of them. "Happy New Year's Eve," she says, her tone as celebratory as a rock through a window.

Holly is still shivering. "I can't see how anyone's going to find the key," she says. "There are so many hedges, and it could be inside any of them."

"I thought you didn't want to play anymore?" Lily asks.

Rachel and Holly exchange a smile. "We wanted to find the key," Rachel says, "and give it to you. Make up for all the presents I haven't sent you. Not that the plan worked. Still," Rachel raises her fork, "at least it's sparked my appetite. I haven't felt like eating in days."

Lily pushes her plate toward her. "Have mine."

"Thanks. You couldn't see anything in the sonnet that suggested a hiding place?" Rachel asks Lily.

Lily shakes her head.

"Typical," Rachel says. "The location is really obvious, just not where the most important part actually is. Liliana certainly knows how to fuck with us."

For the rest of the day, Lily is back at her window, watching. From outside, she must look like a ghost. The White Lady herself. But she has even less power than a specter.

It's dusk by the time Sara and Gray come out of the maze. Lily waits for Tom to exit, too. But he doesn't. Two hours later, and still no sign. Darkness drapes over the labyrinth.

Worry spreading through her, Lily hurries downstairs. "Have you seen Tom?" she asks Holly and Rachel, who are getting pissed on champagne in the drawing room.

"Not since the maze," Holly says. "But he was determined to find the key."

Sara and Gray are playing cards in the orangery. "We left him out there," Sara says when Lily asks. Gray doesn't look up at Lily. He stares at his run of hearts as if they might tell his fortune.

"Don't you think we should check up on him?" Lily says. "He's been out there alone for hours."

"Go ahead," Sara says, and returns to her winning hand. "Good luck to him if he's found the key. I didn't fancy dying out there trying to find it."

Lily bundles up once more and goes out into the snow. It soaks through her skirt. It's so cold it feels like her dress is freezing immediately, as if she's walking in a chandelier.

"You can do this," she says out loud to herself, trying to recall all the geeing-up words Aunt Liliana had written. But how is it fabulous to just go in a maze? It's pathetic, the way she can't.

Lily reaches the entrance to the maze. "Tom!" she shouts into the dark hedge corridors.

No response.

"Tom!"

Nothing, only a mocking echo of her voice across the snow.

She thinks of how she called for Ronnie and he never replied.

At the entrance to the maze, she sees a branch lying on the ground. The floodlights pick out berry-red blood on the bark. Her heart beats faster. Not Tom. Please, not Tom.

Stomping through the snow, she rounds the outer edge of the maze and finds Tom lying on his front. Blood sticks his hair to his head. Lily bends, reaches for his wrist. She can feel her own heartbeat, but not his.

She adjusts her fingers on his wrist. Holds her breath.

A pulse. Faint, erratic, but present.

Little Bean vibrates inside her. Tom's alive. Just.

Lily kneels next to him. "Tom," she says, gently. "Can you hear me?"

His eyelids quiver.

"Tom, love. You need to wake up."

Tom groans. A trickle of blood comes out of his mouth. His eyes open. "Lily," he says. He tries to sit up, but falls back on his side.

"Take it easy," Lily says.

"My head," he says, too slowly. "Feels like. It's been. In a washing machine." He slumps back, exhausted.

Lily, though, feels a giddy rush—he's trying to make jokes. "It'd be cleaner if it had. There's blood all over. I thought there'd been a murder in the snow."

"Not this time." Tom slowly peels himself off the snow to sit upright. His head lolls back and forth, his eyes aren't focusing.

"Do you know what happened?" Lily asks.

Tom shakes his head and winces. He lifts his hand to his wound and then looks at his palm, covered in blood. "I came out of the maze to look for Gray—to cadge his tobacco—but he wasn't there. I heard someone behind me and…" He tails off. "That's all I remember."

"Someone tried to kill you," Lily says. "The same way they did Ronnie."

"But why?" Tom asks.

"I don't know," Lily replies. "We'll work that out later. First we need to get you inside."

With Lily's help, Tom gets to his feet. He sways, and Lily holds on to him tighter.

"If they manage to murder me next time, you'll get revenge, won't you?" he asks as they walk slowly toward the house. His words fall quicker now. Coming in flurries. "Imagine the headline: CORSETIERE AVENGES MAN. WINS. SWIMS OFF INTO THE SUNSET."

"Bit of a mouthful," Lily says. "And isn't it 'sails off into the sunset'?"

"Yeah, but you can't afford a boat," Tom says.

"Again, I'm going to have to ask you not to die," Lily says.

"I've managed not to expire today, so that's something to be grateful for. Grateful to you, too—you prevented another little Christmas murder."

From inside the house, they hear shouting, "Ten, nine, eight, seven, six, five, four, three, two, one!"

"Happy New Year," Lily says.

Singing comes from indoors, and she's taken back to New Year here when she was a child. Staying up till midnight, asleep on Mum's lap by the last chime of Big Ben. At Endgame House, old acquaintances would always be brought to mind. For the sake of *auld lang syne*.

Chapter Thirty-Two

January 1st—New Year's Day
The Eighth Day of Christmas

Lily's eyes snap open. She tries to draw in a breath but can't. A hand is at her throat, squeezing. She tries to prize away the gloved fingers, but they are too strong. The figure looms over her. They're hooded, and it's too dark to see their face.

Kicking, rolling, Lily tries to get free, but the figure stays still. Unnaturally so. The hand tightens round Lily's neck. She thinks of Mum, the marks around her neck; she thinks of her Bean, unable to breathe if Lily can't.

Lily pushes her hands up into the figure's face. It feels like there's nothing there. Or like silk that has just passed through her fingers.

Darkness is coming, narrowing Lily's vision. She hears her own last breath.

And then her throat is released.

Lily rolls off the bed, onto the floor, taking deep breaths. Cradling her tummy.

There's a scuffle in the room, two figures now, fighting. Her books are knocked from the shelves. Scrabbling for the light, she pulls at the lead and the lamp falls to the floor. By the time she manages to switch it on, both figures have disappeared.

She looks out into the hallway, but no one is there either. She'd love to put it down to the worst of dreams, but the soreness of her throat, and the red marks around her neck, let her know she can't.

Someone, though, had protected her.

Tom comes to his door quickly when she knocks a few minutes later. He unlocks the bolt and opens up. He blinks in the hallway light, yawning as he tries to stick his arms through the sleeves of his dressing gown and keeps missing. The blood has partly dried on his head into a nasty, wet scab.

She tells him what happened, and he wakes up as if she's chucked ice in his face. "You were right. Soon as it's light and we've eaten, we're leaving by foot, taking Rachel and Holly with us, and Gray, if he can tear himself away from his sister's butcher's apron strings. Safety in numbers, that's what we need."

"You think it was Sara who attacked me?"

"Who else? I heard the way she spoke to you yesterday. Saw the way she looked at you."

"She hates me," Lily says.

"She hates herself more," Tom replies. "But you're her scapegoat. Her coming here must be bringing all of her stuff to the surface as much as ours. And I'm not having you be the sacrificial lamb to her psychosis."

"The thing I want to know," Lily says, "is who saved me."

"That's a good point," Tom says, eyes widening. "You didn't recognize them?"

"All I could see was dark shadows." She doesn't tell him about the strange sensation of touching her attacker's face. Nor does she tell him that there's one person she really hopes was looking out for her. Her mum.

✳

"I can't serve you 'breakfast,'" Mrs. Castle says, indicating with her eyes and glaring verbal quote marks that she means the clues, "until Misses Rachel and Holly get down here. Those are my instructions for today."

"Not even some toast?" Tom says, with one of his puppy grins. "I'm wounded, I need sustenance."

Mrs. Castle turns away, but Lily can still see her slight smile. "Especially not toast."

Sara is sitting opposite Lily, tapping her fingers. Her ear is cocked toward the door, waiting for Rachel and Holly to walk down the staircase.

"Is no one going to ask me how I am?" Tom asks. "Or maybe how Lily is, given how she was nearly made into an Endgame ghost, too?"

"What do you mean?" Gray asks. He looks from Lily to Tom. Either he is a very good actor, taking after his uncle Edward, or he has no idea about Lily being attacked.

Lily tries to kick Tom under the table to get him to shut up, but her legs can't quite reach.

"Someone tried to strangle Lily last night," Tom says.

"Did they manage?" Sara asks, as dry as leftover turkey. "It's hard to tell."

"Someone was watching over me, luckily," Lily replies. "Otherwise, they would have done." She pulls her silk scarf to one side, showing the hand marks around her neck.

"Well, aren't you lucky to have a guardian angel," Sara replies. She looks at Tom. "Who's yours?"

"Lily, obviously. She found me, stopped it from being murder. In the snow, as cold as it was? If I'd been left there, I would've died. So, Lily is my angel."

"And wouldn't she look lovely on top of your tree," Sara replies. She stands then, and stalks into the hallway where she bangs the gong. "Get up, you two!" she shouts up the stairs. "We may not be able to find the key inside the maze. But we need to find the next one." She waits for a few seconds. Then she shouts again: "WAKE UP, RACHEL!"

Her voice is impressive, glancing off wood and glass and walls to echo round the house.

But there's no sound coming from upstairs.

Lily feels like she's dropped a stitch. What if they've been attacked? What if the killer had tried to murder her and Tom, but went for Rachel and Holly instead?

Fear scissors through her as she gets up and goes up the stairs, then the next flight.

Tom is running up the stairs now, too. Sara's still standing at the bottom. "Tell the lazy arses that they're wasting my time."

Lily doesn't even knock on their door, just barges in. She is so expecting to see them lying on their bed or the floor, pupils fixed, that she almost sees them.

But they're not there.

There is nothing of theirs in the room, no suitcase, the wardrobe empty. The only thing left is a note on the bed.

Dear Lily,

We had to go. I know that Tom was attacked, and I can't let that happen to Holly. Beatrice needs us and we have to put her first. We've taken all we need to go on foot. We'll be OK. And if we're not, then at least this was our doing, not someone else's. Good luck. We'll hold off from raising the alarm until the fifth. Hopefully, you'll have won the house. You deserve it more than anyone. Your mum would want you to stay. And Liliana.

Be brave. Be smart. And be careful.

Hope to see you after all this. We can make that new start.

Rachel xx

Tom reads the note after Lily. "See? Told you we should go." He starts pacing. "We should have gone straight to them and left together."

"Do you think that one of them stopped me from being strangled?"

she asks. She tries to think back to the shape of her angel, but none of it is clear.

"Maybe," Tom says.

"And you think Sara is doing all this, right?" Lily says.

Tom nods.

"And she wants the house."

Another nod.

"Well, I'm not going to let her have it."

Chapter Thirty-Three

When Tom and Lily come down, Mrs. Castle follows them into the dining room, holding aloft a toast rack. Instead of toast, though, four thick pieces of card are placed in the slots.

Sara snatches a card and starts reading. Gray, once again, reads it out loud.

> *I wonder what it is to be dead. A*
> *Silence like that after a recital's*
> *Dying note, but with no applause? Better,*
> *Watch the living like French films, subtitle*
> *Free, or sitting on the prisoner side*
> *Of glass that's soundproofed and opaque, able*
> *To speak but never heard or seen? Will I*
> *Become an Endgame ghost, tipping tables,*
> *Freezing breath, moaning like the wind, scaring*
> *Horses till they whicker? No. If the lights*
> *Flicker, it is not me. If an earring*
> *Of mine appears, or my shadow in sight—*
> *Coincidence, that's all. I'd only haunt*
> *Those that wronged me. And who could harm their aunt?*

"Now what's she wittering on about?" Sara says. "No one wronged Mum. She made sure of it. And the idea of her haunting us?" She shakes her head as if to disperse thoughts of her mother. "Doesn't matter. The key's the only important thing." She crosses her arms and nods at Lily. "We're waiting."

Lily tries to ignore her, as much as she can when Sara's stare sticks to her like Sellotape. Gray stands and slips out of the room. "I've told him to stop smoking," Sara says. "But he doesn't do right by himself."

Lily reads through the poem once more. This clue isn't so easy. Lots of references to music, but the house doesn't have a music room. Besides, music is mentioned in several of the sonnets, which makes sense as both Liliana and Mum loved it so much. Mum was the one who was good at it, though. She could make any instrument, and everyone around her, sing. Lily wished she had that confidence.

So where could the key be? "The horses" could point to the old stables; "glass," does that suggest a looking glass or panes? And what about "tipping tables"? That could refer to the morning room, where Grandma Violet said seances used to be held. It could be that—there are many mentions of ghosts, and of Liliana haunting them. Lily remembers the dark shadow who saved her last night.

"I found it," Gray says from the doorway. "It was in a plant pot in the orangery." Lily hadn't even noticed him come back in. He holds the key between his two hands as if it were a golden ticket. Which it might just be.

Lily leaves Sara to bicker with Gray—"Why didn't you tell me?" and "'Whicker' as in wicker chairs?"

That's another key lost.

Tom follows her out and up the stairs. "Are you all right?" he asks.

"Other than the obvious, I'm fine. Why?"

"Just that it's not like you not to get it. The clue, I mean."

"You think I'm losing my touch?" Lily says.

"I didn't mean *that*," Tom says, looking horrified. "Sorry, I'm not expressing myself properly." His hand goes to his head, picking at his scab. "I'm just worried about you."

"You're right," Lily replies, "I'm not seeing them as clues anymore. I keep trying to work out what they mean, and then I lose my grip on what I'm doing."

"You just need some rest," Tom says when they reach her room.

Lily nods. But she's got other things to do. She feels the equal pull of her bed and the box of papers Rachel gave her. And then she thinks of the letter Rachel left. The papers win.

"I'll get some sleep," she says.

"I'll make sure you're not disturbed," Tom says. "I'll sit outside your door if I have to."

"That won't be necessary," Lily laughs.

Inside her room, door locked, and a table pushed against it to stop anyone coming in with a key—as they must have done last night—Lily once again lays out everything in the box across her room.

She goes through each page, ignoring her hunger pangs, knowing the dark is once again pushing against the house. The view from the window brings a potential dress in one image: midnight silk, all scattered with sequin stars.

She can't see anything else useful in the papers. Until she finds a newspaper cutting from the car crash that killed Edward and Veronica. It was recorded as an accident—faulty brakes, worn thin. This isn't news to Lily. She remembers the day Liliana came home from work and told her, Sara, and Gray that their uncle and aunt had died. Liliana looked broken. All her siblings gone in the space of a year. Edward was known for forgetting to get the car serviced, or insurance updated, and the police thought it was a tragic mistake. Aunt Liliana hadn't stopped crying for a week. Grandma Violet had never recovered. Cancer claimed her not long after, but she had already given up.

Lily hadn't seen the color picture that accompanied the article. It's not the kind of thing you show children: Edward's vintage car smashed into the wall. The bodies had been taken away, but evidence of their deaths remained. Bloodstains on the dashboard, steering wheel, and cracked windscreen. Lily stares at the picture for a long time, wondering what she's seeing.

In the close-up of the shot, there's a yellow ribbon with red dots in the footwell, just like the ones round the crackers and the presents.

But she has no idea what it means.

Chapter Thirty-Four

January 2nd
The Ninth Day of Christmas

> *Like incense smoke in space, even keen prayer*
> *Cannot travel through a vacuum. You all*
> *Lie, like amoral Lino, I s o swear:*
> *Slippy, shifting, cracked; everyone here crawls*
> *Between Truth and sin-filled falsehoods, the gray*
> *Areas where Vanity sits at its*
> *Altar and Greed denies its guilt. You Lie*
> *Preachers smile and say, "He who casts…": sit*
> *On that stone and wait for my judgment. He*
> *Who killed will be revealed, the darkest veil*
> *Lifted from a desiccated bride. She*
> *Has one shot to prove she at no point failed*
> *In life or death. Be like her. Breathe in Truth.*
> *Your home relies upon the right accused.*

"I don't think we need to follow Lily this time," Sara says once her brother has read the sonnet, which had been concealed in the curves of croissants. "Last time Gray found the key before she even knew what was going on."

Gray blushes. "It was just a guess," he says. "Lucky shot."

"Yeah, right," Sara says. "Come on, then, what's your latest guess?"

Gray looks straight at Lily as he says, "The chapel."

Sara skim-reads the poem, nodding. "Incense, prayer, altar. That follows."

"And abstract nouns," Lily agrees. "Truth, greed, vanity, sin—all religious concepts."

"As you are an agnostic," Sara says to Lily, "I think it's best you stay here. Wouldn't want the smell of hypocrisy in a sanctified space."

As Sara leads Gray out of the breakfast room, he turns back to Lily. She wishes she knew the meaning of the strong look he's giving her.

"Aren't we going, too?" Tom asks.

"Not there," Lily replies.

"You're not going to listen to her, are you?" Tom says. "She's gaslighting you. If anyone is a hypocrite, she is."

"I think Gray's giving us time to find the real location."

"Why would he do that?"

"I don't know. It was the way he looked at me. A hunch."

"But he's never rebelled against Sara," Tom says. "He never has, and he never will."

"You're a therapist and you don't believe that people can change?"

"They can change," Tom says, looking away. "But they don't get better."

"This house is getting to you," Lily says, standing up. "Let's go and cheer you up."

"You know where the key is!" Tom says, his face suddenly all smiles again.

"Follow me," she replies.

Liliana's room is an altar to books and Bowie. Bookshelves ladder the walls. Her dressing table is gothic and ornate, strung with Victorian mourning beads. Family photographs stand next to those of Ziggy, Jareth, and the Thin White Duke. On the bedstand next to the bed, there's a jar of silver coins—five-, ten-, twenty-, and fifty-pence pieces— all shined up.

"What was it that gave the location away?" Tom asks as he carefully goes through the costume jewelry in a tall chest of drawers.

"When I saw 'Truth,' I thought of Liliana's perfume," Lily says, walking over to the photographs. "So, when I noticed the weird layout of 'amoral lino, I s o,' I removed the errant 's' and wiggled the letters around in my head."

Tom bites his tongue as he thinks. "Liliana's room!" he says, punching the air.

"If you look in the dressing table drawers, I'll think you'll find the key," Lily says.

"Why?" Tom asks, going over anyway.

"Another name for it is—"

"Vanity!" Tom opens the top drawer and tenderly traces his fingers over the remains of Liliana's makeup. His respect is touching.

Lily picks up a photograph of her aunt with her mum. They're on the terrace at Endgame, watching conference guests play rounders.

"And we have a key!" Tom says.

But Lily can't look over. Her gaze is stuck on the photo. On Mum's bright hair, tied back in a ponytail. By a yellow ribbon with red dots.

Chapter Thirty-Five

"Well done," Sara says when Tom and Lily come downstairs. "Guess you were lucky this time."

"Nope," Tom says, holding the key in the same way Gray did yesterday. Lily nudges him to stop—that will only antagonize Sara.

"Congratulations," Gray says. There it is again, he's looking into Lily's eyes, trying to communicate something. "I guess I love the chapel so much it was wishful thinking."

"Whatever it was, it cost us the key," Sara snaps.

"There'll be others," Gray says. And the way he says it suggests he's not talking about the keys.

Lily spends the rest of the day trying to talk to Gray alone. She follows him out into the kitchen garden when he goes for a smoke, and then Sara is right behind her. She stands next to him as they serve themselves lunch, but Sara pushes between them. It isn't until Sara has to go to the toilet that Gray sidles up to Lily.

"I'd like to talk," he whispers. "I need your help."

"What can I do?" she whispers back.

"I don't know how to start." Gray's shoulders begin to shake. She hears him struggle to control his breath. "It's gone far beyond what was supposed to happen."

"And what was that?"

Sara's quick footsteps tick off the tiles in the hall.

"I'll tell you when Sara's gone to bed," Gray says. "We'll meet outside. Look out your window." Then he slides, back to being a shadow
against the wall.

The rest of the day passes slowly. She and Tom play charades and I spy
and their old The Game of Life board. They change the rules: no more
pink pegs next to the blue, with two of each kind behind to show you
win. Lily's car has a blue peg in the front for herself, and one in the back
for Bean. "And which peg goes next to you?" Tom asks, holding up both
pink and blue ones.

"Whichever one I love," Lily replies.

Sara goes to bed at nine, and Lily makes yawning noises shortly after.
In her bedroom, she doesn't get into her pajamas; instead she puts on as
many layers as possible, then pulls over her dressing gown that skims her
ankles. If she's caught, she'll just say she needed something to eat. The
potential for this to be a trap keeps rising up, again and again. She wishes
she could tell Tom, but what if he gets in more trouble? He's already been
injured. She has to risk it. Gray looks like he wants to betray Sara, to
make a decision between black and white. She has to trust him.

Every fox or badger crossing the snow makes her heart beat faster,
thinking it's Gray. And then he's there. He looks up and points toward
the east of the grounds. Then slinks back into the dark.

Lily pads out of her room and goes downstairs. Borrowing Tom's
boots, she hurries out of the French doors. On the terrace, Gray's foot-
prints are fast disappearing under a fresh flurry of snow.

A Gray-shaped shadow appears on the lawn, beckoning to her. He
runs off and she follows, across the field, through the long grasses of

the wild garden that poke their noses through the snow. He's heading toward the chapel. His sanctuary. She quickens her pace but still feels too slow. The snow is getting thicker. She can hardly see or feel her feet. The chapel, the house, all bearings are obliterated, wiped out in the whiteout. Nothing exists.

She should never have come out. Tom doesn't even know she's gone. This could all be a trap, Gray leading her to death.

Precious seconds are ticking. She stumbles on, hoping she can trust Gray and her sense of direction. At last, the wind pulls back the curtain of snow to reveal the chapel. Made of cream stone, it stands out against the slate sky. The door is already open. Light spills out onto snow.

"Gray?" she calls out as she enters. Her voice becomes big in this small space. She walks down the aisle, surrounded by pews. Her mum had told her that she could get married here, and Lily had said she'd never get married. At the time, she couldn't see why she could marry a man and not a woman. That was stupid. *Some things change for the better, Tom*, she thinks.

Half-burned votives flicker on the family altar. The censer is still warm, leeching out the last of its frankincense smoke. Next to it, an empty urn stands in tipped-out cremains. Gray has made sure Liliana is home. But there's no other sign of him.

Maybe he's left. Inspired by Rachel and Holly, he took his things and walked away. Well done, Gray. A rebel at last.

Lily turns to walk back, then sees a foot sticking out of the far side of one of the pews. And a stripy sock. It's Gray. *Tom was OK*, she says to herself as she goes to him. Maybe Gray's injured.

When she gets to him, though, he's not OK. And he won't be again. *In splendoribus sanctorum*. He lies on stones etched with the names of Endgame's dead. A stream of blood flows from his head. His beautiful eyes stare out but don't see her, and his mouth is wrenched open, jaw broken. Filled with pieces of shiny silver.

Killed in his own place of safety. Punished for wanting to tell the truth. At the end, Anglican in deed, sin, if it exists, hopefully, forgiven.

She kneels next to him. "I'm so sorry," she says. She takes his hand

and, as she unfurls his curled fingers, finds a piece of twine with a key attached. She looks closer. It's the one she gave him, in the car. He was going to give it back to her. Lily gently takes the key and closes Gray's hand.

The chapel door slams.

Lily stands, unsteady on her feet. She wants to stay with him, guard Gray as he did Philippa and Ronnie, but whoever did this to him must be close.

Outside, she sees a shadow, a figure wearing black, seem to fly across the snow. Heading back toward the house.

As she wades after them, the snow falls as if in slow motion. The whole sky grieves for Gray, wearing gray in his honor.

Lily's lungs burn. She'd cut down her gym visits in the first twelve weeks of pregnancy, and, now that she's carrying a baby bath inside her, it's showing. The figure stops, and looks back. Then turns toward the maze.

They know she can't go in there. They know *her*. She's too cold to know if that hurts more or less. This isn't a stranger, or if they are, they've been listening to everything.

At the entrance to the maze, she stops. Hands on hips, she tries to catch her breath. She can hear the figure stamping through the snow. If she stays here, they'll have to come back past her as the entrance is also the exit. Or they could scale one of the hedges and escape over the side. She knows the maze better than anyone; she has to go in.

But she can't. She's paralyzed. Again. If she remains frozen, Gray's killer will get away. And she'll be the coward Sara believes her to be.

Lily leans down, takes a scoop of snow in her hand and presses it to her face. The burn kicks off her adrenaline again, and she walks into the maze. As quietly as she can, she moves in after the figure. She has no idea what she'll do when she gets them. She just needs to know who it is, to confirm that it's Sara. The hedges rise into the sky around her. But she won't go back.

Even in Tom's boots, her feet know their way around the maze. As Lily rounds a corner, memories blizzard around her. The walls closing in when she found Mum. Twigs scratching at her as she ran out.

She moves faster, trying to outpace the memories. Turning a sudden left, she stops. Shallow breathing. A hedge away.

Lily walks forward three steps, then turns to face the stranger. The figure in black extends their arms, hood up, face concealed behind mesh. For a moment, she thinks it's a ghost, or Death. Then the figure slams their hands into her chest. Forced back against the hedge, she stumbles. Tripping over a hidden root, she lands on the ground, pulling at the branches with snow-caked hands.

The figure stands over her. Then stamps on Lily's foot, placing all their weight on it. And then jumps on it again.

Lily screams. Her ankle is red hot in the snow. The black figure runs down the green aisle. Lily leans back on a pillow of snow.

She has failed. Again. How can she be a good mother when she put herself and her child in danger, when she tries to help but makes everything worse? If it weren't for her, Gray would still be alive. And maybe Ronnie. And Philippa knew something, too. She has no chance of getting the house from Sara. Or even of staying alive to the end of the game.

Snow is falling fast, covering Lily in a weighted blanket. And she could give in. Hypothermia is supposed to be one of the best ways to die. You're so cold you get warm as your blood retreats to your central organs. At some point you drift into a snowy doze, and don't wake up. Sleep reaches for her, and she wants it so much.

Then Bean flutters inside her.

Lily crawls forward, reaching for a root or anything to help pull herself up. Her hand closes on something hard. She grabs it, but it comes away. She lifts her gloved hand out of the snow.

In the center of her palm is a key. There's still a chance.

Grabbing on to the hedge, Lily drags herself to standing. Fistfuls of green leaves fall to the snow-laid ground. Her ankle screams at her, so she bends and packs more snow into the boot. Stop the swelling, shush the searing pain.

Once outside the maze, a weight lifts as the memories slink back to within its walls. She picks up the branch used to attack Tom, and puts it under her armpit. Once a weapon, now a crutch.

She slowly makes her way up the back lawn. As she passes the rose garden, she has a strong urge to lie on the snow-cushioned bench and sleep like a rosehip till spring.

"Lily!" Tom shouts. His footsteps stomp on the terrace as he runs to the wall. And there he is. He runs down the steps, almost slipping into a snowbank. Within moments he's next to her, slinging his arm around her, taking her weight.

"What happened?" he asks.

Lily sees a flash of Gray's body lying on the memorial flagstones. She wants to tell Tom, but she should tell Sara first, if she doesn't already know. "I ran after a figure into the maze," Lily says. "The one who tried to attack me. I caught up with them, then they stamped on my ankle and I lost them."

"Oh, Lily," Tom says. There's a catch in his throat. "I'm so sorry."

"At least I went in," Lily says.

"Wait, you're right. You went in?"

Lily nods. She tries on a smile.

"That's a-maze-ing!"

Lily groans at the pun but its silliness and familiarity warm her.

With Tom holding her, they gradually make it up to the terrace. Sara hurries out through the French doors. She hugs herself against the cold. "Have you seen Gray?" she asks, scanning the grounds.

"You really are self-obsessed," Tom says. "Can't you see something's happened to Lily?"

Sara focuses on Lily, briefly. She frowns. "What's wrong with you?"

"As if you don't know," Tom mutters.

"What was that?" Sara snaps.

"Lily's been attacked. Again. And I can't see me or Gray doing that to anyone."

Sara's hands go to her hips. "You're not accusing me of murder, are you? Because that's libel."

"Slander," Lily says before she can stop herself. It's as if the corset laces on her mouth are unraveling.

Sara turns to her. "What are you talking about?"

"Doesn't matter," Lily says. "Sara, I'm so sorry, but I've got—"

"She means that it's libel if written down," Tom says, "slander if spoken. So, I slandered you. Although, if you took it to court, you'd have to prove you're not a murderer."

Sara steps forward, nose to nose with Tom.

"Can we please stop all this and go in?" Lily asks. "There's something I need to tell Sara."

Sara's cry reverberates around the house. From the drawing room, the grandmother clock chimes as if joining her in keening. "Not Gray," she says. "It can't be." She keeps shaking her head as if that will make the horror stop. But nothing can.

Tom looks almost as shocked as Sara. "There's got to be someone else on the grounds," he says. "Mrs. Castle was in the kitchen and I was here with Sara, so it can't be her. Besides, she'd never do that to Gray."

Sara marches into the hall and throws on her coat. "I don't believe it," she says. "You must have imagined it. I'll show you." She runs toward the kitchen, with Tom following. Lily limps along behind, holding on to walls.

Sara opens the door into the kitchen garden, and another slice of cold air cuts through the house.

"I'll go with you," Tom says, trying to put his arm round Sara.

"No!" Sara shouts, pushing him away.

Lily puts a hand on Sara's arm. "But if there's someone out there, none of us should be alone."

"Stay away from me and Gray, both of you. And don't follow me." She stumbles out and Tom rocks on the threshold.

"What should I do?" he asks, eyes wide. He looks like a little boy.

"We respect what she wants," Lily says. "And we're here for her when she gets back."

"Are you sure?" Tom asks, looking out after Sara.

"I'm not sure about anything anymore," Lily replies.

✳

"I've been thinking," Tom says, when he and Lily have changed into dry clothes. They've brought mugs of tea into the orangery. It's the best place to keep watch for Sara's return. "Let's say an outsider is behind all this. We need to find out who it is."

Lily nods. She'd been thinking the same thing. "But who would have a motive? If it's about the house, and it must be, then the only eligible people are—or were—here. Or are you thinking that the cats have enlisted Mrs. Castle to kill us all so that they end up with the house?"

"I was thinking more of someone human. A *particular* human," Tom says. He's avoiding Lily's eyes, staring into the gaze of the wood burner instead.

"Who?"

"What if your mum had been married to your dad, without us knowing?"

"I don't have a dad," Lily says, keeping her voice level.

"I'm sorry, Lily, but, technically, biologically, you do have another parent. What if they have a claim?"

"Isabelle would have known about that, wouldn't she?" Lily asks. She can hear the anxiety flashing in her voice.

Tom nods, slowly. "Yeah, you're probably right. I've also thought of another reason why it's an outsider. And you're not going to like this one either." He looks at her corseted belly. "Whoever is the killer, they clearly don't know about your little hitchhiker. Otherwise, you'd both be dead by now."

Lily's hand flies to her stomach. "I've been attacked twice."

"But the first time you were saved, the second time they stamped on your leg—hardly fatal."

Lily nods. It's true. Why kill Gray and not her?

"That could even support the thought that it's your dad. He wants Endgame, but doesn't want to kill you." Tom's eyes light up here as his brain leaps. "Maybe he even saved you, from his accomplice."

"So now there are *two* killers?" Lily raises her eyebrows to skeptic heights.

"Yeah," Tom says. "Maybe I'm getting carried away. I just want answers."

"Me too. It's why I came here in the first place."

Tom isn't listening, however. "What if the motive isn't financial? What if it's revenge?"

"For what?"

"God, I don't know," Tom says, standing up and pacing. "I'm trying to think my way out of a panic attack. You're the one who's good at puzzles. And Gray. But you're the only…" He leaves the rest of the sentence unsaid, but it's there in the air. Lily is the only one left.

A feeling of loneliness soaks through to her skin, digs into her bones. She turns to Tom. "I need to show you something," she says.

Upstairs, in her bedroom, Lily tells Tom the real reason she's here. She shows him Liliana's letter, explains about the coat, and shyly tells him how she now believes that her mum didn't kill herself.

Tom exhales. "Whoa," he says. He rubs his forehead as if that will help the new knowledge sink in. "I don't know how to feel for you. Pleased that you're rid of the burden of responsibility you've carried, or enraged on your behalf that she was taken from you."

"I don't know how I feel yet either."

They sit cross-legged on the rug, like when they played Top Trumps as kids. Only this time, they're trading pictures of red-dotted, yellow ribbons. She keeps the one of the car crash hidden away. He doesn't need to see a close-up of where his parents died.

"What am I looking at?" he asks.

"That's Mum's ribbon," Lily says, pointing to the photo she found in the box of her mum wearing it in her hair. "For some reason, Liliana wanted me to pay attention to it. It was around the crackers, wrapped up the presents that the clues were in."

"So?" Tom asks.

Lily pauses, wondering how to phrase the next part, before saying, "And the same type of ribbon was found in the car that your mum and dad died in."

Tom goes pale. His hands clench round his kneecaps. He looks up at her. "I don't know what any of it means," he says.

"Neither do I." She's about to show him the coroner's report, then stops. She is potentially telling him that his dad killed her mum. And that would change their relationship forever. If it hasn't already.

Chapter Thirty-Six

January 3rd
The Tenth Day of Christmas

Sara isn't at breakfast the next morning, but Mrs. Castle is.

"We need to talk," Mrs. Castle says when Tom and Lily enter the room. They're about to sit opposite her when she gestures to Tom. "Not you, son. Off you pop." She tosses him a piece of toast, which he catches with some bafflement before leaving.

"Why can't Tom stay?" Lily asks. "He shouldn't be on his own with what's going on."

"Less he knows, the less danger he'll be in." Mrs. Castle scrutinizes Lily's face. "You haven't told him owt?"

"Only about why Aunt Lil asked me to come. The stuff about Mum."

Mrs. Castle sighs and helps herself to a bap and tears it open, letting out the steam. She dollops on a spoonful of loganberry jam. "That was not a good move, Lily."

"I thought you were supposed to be impartial."

"I was employed to keep my counsel, serve you food and sonnets, and stay out of the way. I'm under strict instructions not to interfere. But we are stuck in this house with no sign of the snow letting us out. Three people dead. You and Tom are lucky to be alive. And the one person who looked likely to be a killer is currently in the chapel, mourning her brother. So I'm not so worried about sticking to my contract."

"You could leave," Lily says. "Like Rachel and Holly."

"Hmm," Mrs. Castle says, taking a big bite of bap.

"What is it? You sound suspicious."

"We've only got that note to say that they've left. Is it definitely Rachel's handwriting?"

Lily thinks back to when they were little and Rachel's scrawled signature. She doesn't think she's received so much as a Christmas card since. "I don't know. Sounded like her."

"What if it isn't? What if they are still on the grounds?"

"You don't think they're dead?" Lily asks, holding her heart as she pictures all the places that bodies could be kept on a snowy estate. They still haven't searched the outhouses in the back fields, the stables, the smokehouse, the old cottages, or—

"I hope they're not, and I hope I'm wrong, but there's another option. What if one of them is the killer?"

Lily shakes her head. "No way."

"Or they both could be working together with Sara. They killed Gray, but she didn't know. They've gone rogue."

"Can't see Rachel being capable of that. And Holly? Absolutely not."

"And you're such a good judge of character, are you?"

Lily thinks back to some of her friendships and relationships. She says nothing. Maybe she just doesn't want to think of Holly like that.

"Didn't think so," Mrs. Castle says. "Best plan, I think, is for you to tell me everything you've found out so far. Any suspects for Mariana's murder I should know about? Or clues?"

"What kind of clues?" Lily asks.

"Alleged prints on a…I don't know, a glass? What else do you find in mysteries?"

"Why would I tell you all that?" Lily says.

Mrs. Castle grabs Lily's hand and squeezes it. "So I can help you, daftie."

Lily would love to sit down with this woman who seems to know how life works, who has a history with her family that she'd love to unravel, for her to guide Lily and tell her what to do with all the information that's mulling in her head, like those other strong women tried to, to show Lily how to be a mum.

But that would be incredibly selfish. Enough people have died. "You said yourself that the less people know about it, the better for them. Keeping you in the dark will keep you safe."

"I'm not rhubarb," Mrs. Castle replies. "I'll not be forced into darkness, thank you very much, missie." She takes another bite of berried bap and looks at Lily, weighing her up. "Why do you think I took the job, really? Because, I tell you, it wasn't for the money."

"Peace and quiet in the countryside? The company of such pleasant people?"

"Your aunt had a sarcastic tongue, just like you and Sara."

"You still haven't said much about you and her," Lily says. "Please, I'd like to know."

Mrs. Castle looks like her drawbridge might be lowered for the first time. Then it slams shut. "You'll have to figure that out yourself, like everything else."

"And I'll say the same to you," Lily says. "Telling people secrets is dangerous. Look what's happened here. You should leave now and take your chances in the snow. All I want to do is keep you safe."

"Back at you, love," Mrs. Castle says. She finishes the last bit of her bap in one bite. "But if I die first, make sure you eat this jam, won't you? If I say so myself, it's delicious."

The next sonnet doesn't appear till just before dinner. Mrs. Castle had charged Tom with making everyone predinner old-fashioneds, and he had found the clues wrapped around sugar cubes.

> *Let's call a truce, what do you say? Will no*
> *One agree? Put our quarrels to one side—*

It's Christmas after all. Go with the flow,
And other sayings, it's all cut and dried
And in the past. Isn't it? Mix my gin
And tonic on the rocks and call it quits
While I muddle up your old-fashioneds in
Cut glass mixers that would not cut your wrists.
This house is sick, its roots twist. Cold compress
On its roof won't help, it's gone past that point.
Maybe it can be saved. Withdraw. Confess
What you have been told. You could all conjoin,
You know, melt into just one winning team,
Pool key resources, or is that a dream?

Sara sits in the corner of the orangery where Gray liked to roll his cigarettes. She swirls a sphere of ice in her glass. Her face looks like it's sunken in on itself. Her sonnet is on the table, unread.

Lily walks over, still halting slightly, although her ankle has improved. "I'm so sorry, Sara," she says.

"So you said yesterday," Sara replies.

"I wish I'd gotten to know him more, before…" Lily trails off. She knows there's nothing she can say that will help. "I'm here, if you want to talk."

"I told you. Stay away."

Lily walks over to the sofa, where Tom is trying to light the end of a twist of orange peel. "You're supposed to let it smolder and burn to release the orange molecules in the skin," he says. "Then you smell it, and the drink tastes different."

"You don't need to tell me about the potency of smell," Lily says. "Pregnancy turns it into a superpower. Although I don't know how I'd use it to further humankind." She looks over toward Sara. "I can't even comfort her."

"I tried earlier," Tom says. "She wouldn't even look at me." He leans forward and lowers his voice. "Is it really hypocritical and awful that I'm itching to work out the clue with you?"

"Maybe a little insensitive," Lily says. "But understandable."

"I like to see you playing detective. Taking on crime at Christmas. You remind me more of Grandma Violet all the time."

"Why thank you." Lily takes a bow.

"Now I've fed your ego," Tom says, "can we go and find the key? Please?"

"Fine," Lily says. She picks through the poem. "But I can't find an anagram that will help. This one isn't going to be easy."

"All I know," Tom says, "is that there are lots of cutting involved."

"Cutting wrists," Lily says. "We know what that's referring to." She sees Tom looking worried and quickly says, "Don't worry, I'm fine. It's saying that Mum didn't. It's all good, I promise."

"I'm going to sit here drinking while you use your other superpower." Tom picks up his old-fashioned and rattles the remains of the ice against the beveled glass. "Ice melts quickly when drowned in booze."

"Say that again," Lily says, picking up her pen and leaning it on the poem.

"Ice melts—"

Lily draws a circle round the final couplet of the poem. "Ice 'melts,' it 'pools.'" She taps the pen further up the page. "You 'cut' ice, ice can be 'dried,' and ice 'flows.' And what are spirits served on?"

"'On the rocks,'" Tom says. His celebratory grin fades. "But that means I know where we're going."

Lily circles the line that says, "This house is sick." "The icehouse," she says.

"And we're the winning team," Tom says.

Chapter Thirty-Seven

It's snowing again when they get outside. And velvet dark. Snowflakes bite into Lily's skin like ice mosquitoes. Tom and Lily train their torches on the icehouse in front of them. It's still a tomb for two. Sara has insisted that Gray stay in the chapel, for now, at least. She keeps the incense flowing and candles glowing. "Just as he liked it," she says.

"We should go in," Tom says, swallowing. "It's too cold to stay out here."

"Colder in there," Lily replies. Tom doesn't disagree.

Even so, they approach the icehouse. The door has frozen again, and it takes Tom several kicks to get it unstuck. They leave it firmly open, wedged by several large rocks to stop anyone from locking them in.

"We should put incense in here, too," Tom says. "To honor them, like Gray."

Lily knows, though, that he wants to cover the smell of decay that, despite the ice, hangs in the air as on a butcher's hook.

Lily walks over to Ronnie's body. She wants to cover him up in a blanket, keep him warm. She always wanted to look after him, and it seems that doesn't stop in death. It's why she thinks marriage vows are strange. Why until death do you part? Doesn't love carry on *after* death? She holds her mum in her heart, why not someone she loves enough to cleave to forever?

"It feels wrong to look for the key," Tom says. He's staring down at his brother. His tears drop onto the ice. "He'd be gutted that we haven't had a proper wake for him."

"He'd say that if he wasn't drinking, everyone else should be. He'd want you to dream up macabre, punny names for cocktails for him to make, using this ice."

"It's true," Tom says, wiping his eyes. "He'd be making mortinis for everyone. And morgue-aritas."

Lily laughs, putting her hand over her mouth. "Those are terrible, Tom. Ronnie would have loved them."

"He loved *you* very much, Lily," Tom says. "And so do I."

"Then let's find the key for him."

With a peripheral search of the icehouse completed and no key found—including looking at the outer walls and roof—Lily starts to worry that they'll have to move Ronnie and Philippa outside to get to the ice. She can tell Tom is, too. He's lying on the cold floor, peering into the ice blocks. "I can't see anything," he says. He chews his lip, glances at the bodies, then away.

Lily then notices that the ice pick has moved. When they left Ronnie lying on the ice, the pick had been hanging on the wall. Now it's placed against the far side of the ice blocks, away from Ronnie and Philippa.

"We should try the blocks at the end," she says. "The ones nearest the ice pick."

Tom grabs the ice pick and begins.

Over an hour later, they emerge from the icehouse with red faces and an ice-cold key. Mrs. Castle is standing deep in the snow with two thermoses on a tray and tartan wraps over her arm. She hands Tom and Lily one of each. "Don't tell me waiting for us out here was in the rules as well, Mrs. C," Tom says. "Because if it was, Aunt Lil was taking things too far."

"It wasn't," Mrs. Castle says. "I thought you might have frozen in there." She then turns and stomps back across the fields toward the house.

"That's practically a marriage proposal from Mrs. Castle," Tom says as they follow her into the dark.

✳

After a dinner of soup, made with vegetables and barley, and fresh baked bread with seaweed butter, Tom and Lily go up to bed. This time, it's Lily who suggests they sleep in the same room. "Do you think we should ask Sara, too?" Lily asks, really hoping he says no. "She's in a bad way; I've never seen her like this. She almost seemed nice earlier."

Tom's laugh reverberates round her bedroom. "Absolutely not. There is no way I'm going to sleep with her nearby. I'd be killed midsnore. But don't worry, I absolve you of the responsibility of looking after her."

Excusing herself, Lily goes into her little bathroom while Tom fetches things to sleep on and in. Corset unlaced and on the floor, she turns sideways to the mirror. She strokes the swell of her belly in a way she never has before. It's bigger than when she left London. "That'll be all the Yorkshire air," she says to Bean.

Through the door, she can hear Tom lugging his mattress across the floor. He walks back, and she hears a key turn in the lock. They'll be safe tonight.

She pulls on her flannel pajamas and looks around for something to cover her tummy. And then stops. This is Tom. If she doesn't let *him* see her as she truly is, she'll never let anyone.

Lily opens the bathroom door and steps into her bedroom. Tom is nestling into his makeshift bed on the floor. He glances up at her and grins. "Good to see you not hiding my niece away." He waves at Lily's belly. "Hello in there, little one!" His face grows serious. "You'll still have to be careful, though. If Sara is the killer, then she can't know about the baby. She was saying earlier that it was suspicious that you haven't drunk *at all*, but I fended her off by saying you are on mega-antibiotics for your terrible cystitis."

Lily groans. "Oh, Tom."

"What I think you mean to say is, 'Thank you, Tom, for your discretion and valor.'"

"I do mean that, you're right," Lily says as she clambers over Tom's bed and gets into her own. "And thank you for always thinking of me. I'm not sure I deserve it." As she wriggles deeper under the cold sheets, her feet find something warm at the bottom. Reaching down, Lily pulls up a hot water bottle in her old fleecy penguin cover.

"Mrs. C is being a sweetie again, then," Tom says. "She can't fool us with that stern schtick anymore."

Lily places the hot water bottle against her aching back and lies down in her own nest of arranged pillows.

"Grief is weird," Tom says, his sleepy voice slurring. "I was just thinking how brilliant it is that I'll be an uncle again, and then I plummeted, thinking that Ronnie won't meet her. And he's such a good one, too. Better than me." He puts his face into the pillow. She can't hear his sobs, but she can see his shoulders shake.

"I'm so sorry, Tom."

Lily moves to get out of bed, but Tom says, his voice still wobbly, "Stay there, cuz. You need to rest. We just need to hold on for another few days. Isabelle will be here on Twelfth Night, or maybe Rachel and Holly will have contacted the police."

"And then we can leave this place forever," Lily says.

"Unless we win it," Tom says. He sits up now. The moonlight creeping through the gap in the curtains lights up his open face. "Imagine what we could do with all this space."

"This cursed space." Lily feels her mood descend again. Tom's right. Grief is weird, making you giddy one minute and plummeting the next. She keeps seeing Gray on the chapel floor. He had been about to tell her something. Something that had him killed, with the silver coins of the betrayer left in his mouth.

"Whatever it is, someone really wants to get their hands on it. And I don't want them to get it." Tom's voice has ice in it now.

"You don't think it could really be my dad, do you? The murderer?" Lily asks. She hears her voice—it sounds so young. So scared.

"I should never have said that," Tom replies. "I was just speculating, conjecturing. But that's not fair on you. Sometimes my mouth flaps before my synapses adjudicate. I'm sorry."

"Apology accepted." But the thought of her dad being out there, waiting for her, even being the figure who saved her, remains. Like a piano note fading but never going away.

"I'm glad you're here, Lily," Tom says. "Despite all the horror."

"So am I, surprisingly," Lily replies. And it's true. It's been a while since she has consciously wished she were somewhere else. She doesn't want to know what that says about her. "It'd be nothing without you, though."

"Naturally," Tom replies through a yawn. "And you've made my worst Christmas the best it could possibly be."

Lily switches off her bedside light. The restful quiet of two people who can be silent with each other settles over them like an extra duvet. Darkness tucks them up tight. Outside, an owl *twits*; its partner answers with a *twoo*. Maybe she and Tom can make it through till Twelfth Night after all.

Chapter Thirty-Eight

January 4th
The Eleventh Day of Christmas

"YOU WERE RIGHT, MISS LILY," Sara reads aloud from the letter left on the kitchen table. "*I don't need to stay in danger. I'll take my chances in the snow. You take care of yourself and that Tom. Get yourself more firewood from the store for your last day. May your epiphany be a good one. Lenora Castle.*" Sara throws the note into the bin. "Well, that's charming. Guess she didn't like me, then?"

"Not really," Lily replies, even pipping Tom to the post. Is this what it's like to say what you think? She takes the letter out of the bin. "You missed a bit, Sara."

Tom leans over and reads out loud: "*PS: Your next clue will be found where things go round and round. See, I can poem, too. LAC.*" Tom places his hand on his chest and sighs. "I think I love Mrs. Castle."

"'Round and round'?" Sara says. "What, like a record player?"

"Even you're getting good at this," Tom says, clapping Sara on the back.

The old record player is in the drawing room. Sara searches by the speakers and turntable, while Tom and Lily take out records from the cabinet underneath. They go through each disc, looking in the sleeve and any booklet. Tom takes out the last record on his row, and gasps. He hands the LP over to Lily.

Lily starts to tremble. On the front is a picture of Mum. She's wearing her green coat, with an extra fluffy hood, and standing under the snow-heavy weeping willow on the lawn of Endgame. At the top, in a yellow box, it says:

CHRISTMAS CAROLS, VOICE AND CELLO
BY MARIANA ARMITAGE, INCLUDING
"IN THE BLEAK MIDWINTER" IN F MAJOR.

"Did you know she'd released that?" Tom asks Lily, his eyes soft.

Lily shakes her head. "I knew she was a professional musician, but I never really wanted details because…"

"Because it hurt too much," Tom finishes for her.

Lily nods.

"We should put it on," Tom says, taking the record out of its sleeve. Three pieces of paper fall out.

"Looks like my mum wanted you to find yours," Sara says. "That's nice." There's not a hint of saracasm in her voice.

Tom's forehead creases and he puts his arms out. Sara crumples into them.

Part of Lily wants to join them. All orphans now. All lacking a mum. But Sara's face is so serene, Lily feels that she's intruding. She steps back and looks at the sonnet.

> *Early in the year, possibilities*
> *Spring before new shoots appear, ambitions*
> *Grow through the dark and snow, fertility*
> *Helped by beds of thyme ahead and driven*
> *By conviction: this year will be different.*
> *And it could be. Instead of the pledges*
> *To lose this or gain that, rock your current*

Shape. Lie on the soft white, stretch wings and fledge,
Soar on the floor, the sky Artexed with clouds,
Arc up and down, round and round. Inhale air
Nut brittle sharp-sweet, crack a smile, allow
Yourself to be more you, but be aware:
Snow angels fade as the sun gets stronger
And dreams diminish as nights get shorter.

Lots of references to the outdoors—"shoots," things that "grow," "thyme," "beds," "nut brittle" air, making "snow angels"—but then there are hints that it's inside—"bed," "floor," "plaster." She looks again at a phrase that sticks out: "beds of thyme." Seems a strange way of putting it. Could be straightforward, there's thyme in the kitchen garden. But it also suggests bedtime. So, it could be a bedroom, and "fertility" could mean it's where one of them was conceived or born or fed, which would go with "rock" and "fledge," which suggests the—

"You do know you're talking out loud," Sara says. There's a smile on her face.

Lily feels the sickening creep of shame. "Was I?"

"It's impressive," Tom says. "Really. So, you know where we're going, then?"

Lily looks with reluctance at the record cover again. Her mum, singing the song she always sang to Lily. Recorded forever. She longs to listen to it, but not in front of anyone. They might not understand, but this is something she needs to do alone. She puts it back on the shelf. "The nursery," she says.

"Now I don't want to get all psychoanalytic on you," Tom says as Lily walks with him and Sara down the corridor, "but we're going back into the nursery. Where we all played as kids. And we all know what kind of regression could happen there."

"You're working up to a pun on 'Jung' and 'young,' aren't you?" Lily says.

Tom grins. "You know me so well!"

Sara laughs along with him. Again, no saracasm. Lily shivers. It makes her uneasy, seeing Sara like this. Like a snake whose teeth have been removed but still smiles.

"Look," Sara says, running through the nursery door. "Mum's old rocking horse!" Someone has brought it down from the attic. She strokes the horse's mane, as Gray did before.

"There's the painted sky," Tom says, pointing up to the ceiling. "And the soft white rug—great for snow angels, terrible for bringing up children. Shows up everything. Looks like we're in the right place again, Lily." He goes over to a box full of cuddly toys and pulls out an original Dipsy by his dipstick. "I used to love this thing," he says, shaking his head.

Lily has also found one of her favorites. She takes her Jessie from *Toy Story* doll down from her place next to Buzz and Woody. Lily had been obsessed with Jessie. Had worn her cowgirl costume to every one of her friend's birthday parties, fancy dress or not. Every day deserves a fancy dress.

Still holding Dipsy, Tom walks over to join her. He points to Woody and, just from looking at his face, Lily can tell he's going to make another pun. "And you can stop right there," Lily says. "There are children present." She points to her tummy.

"And another over there," Tom says, looking over to Sara. She's on the wooden horse, rocking backward and forward. Her smile is beatific, and the most unnerving thing Lily has ever seen.

"What do we do?" Lily whispers to Tom. "We've got to help her."

"Getting her out of the nursery would be a start, and then the house. The longer she stays here, the worse it could be."

"Then we should get on with the game?"

"Quite right. Time for adult things. Where first?"

Lily refers back to the clue, then scans the room. "As we're looking for something that goes round and round, I reckon—"

"Don't tell me," Tom says, rushing to a cupboard and pulling out boxes. All games they used to play, some bought for them, some as old as the Armitages who moved into Endgame in 1955. There are *Star Wars* Monopoly, Twister, Battleship, Tinkertoys…and a railway set.

"This goes round and round till the battery gives out," Tom says, tearing off the lid. But no key inside.

Lily opens drawer after drawer filled with old baby clothes and toys. She picks up a crochet baby blanket that Grandma Violet said had been made by *her* grandmother and holds it to her chest. It's coming back to London with her.

Under it is exactly what she's been looking for.

Tom appears at her shoulder. "Your old music box," he says as Lily opens it. Immediately the ballerina in the center of the box starts twirling. "Round and round."

Sara steps off the horse, leaving it to rock by itself. "How did you know it was this?" she asks.

"Can you tell what it's playing?" Lily asks.

Sara puts her hand on Tom's shoulder as she leans in to listen. "I recognize it," she says, softly.

"It's the 'Dance of the Sugar Plum Fairy,' from—"

"*The Nutcracker Suite!*" Tom shouts. He takes the poem back from Lily. "'Nut brittle sharp-sweet, crack a'—it's all there." He takes Sara by the hand, and they dance across the room. Sara laughs, her eyes shine. She looks at Tom as if a sundial never casts a shadow across his face. Gray's death has made her shell crack.

"Your mum took you, me, and Gray to see the ballet, do you remember?" Lily asks gently, as Tom whirls Sara to a stop.

Sara stays in Tom's arms, her eyes unfocused. "We had ice cream during the interval," she says.

"We did. You had strawberry, I had chocolate, and Gray had vanilla."

Sara strokes Tom's cheek with her finger. "Tom likes coffee ice cream. And sometimes pistachio. But only on special occasions."

Tom steps away from Sara. "I'm really sorry, Sara, but I think we need to get you downstairs and wrapped up in front of the fire. You're not feeling well."

Sara stumbles forward, her brow creased, her arms open. "Why are you backing away, Tommy? We're supposed to stay here forever."

"She thinks I'm Gray," Tom whispers, edging closer to Lily. "It's a common projection in these circumstances. She needs to believe Gray is alive, so places him on a living person."

"I killed them for you," she says, moving slowly toward Tom but with eyes that still don't focus.

"She's trapped in the past. Trauma-bound. She must have killed the others, and justified her actions by saying it was all for Gray. Then, when Gray was trying to help you, she snapped. If it wasn't so scary, it'd be sad."

Lily nods, but something is bothering her. It tickles. Prickles. She runs through her recent conversations with Tom. There's not one line where she tells him about Gray coming to her and helping. A slow, icy dread takes hold of her heart. She can't run, but her mind can. Sprinting through the times that Sara and Tom or Tom and Gray gave each other alibis. Or how she's been helping Tom get the keys every day. Or how tenderly an unwary Sara touched Tom, and how fiercely, and publicly, they've been fighting. And then she remembers what she heard coming from Sara's bedroom.

She could hide. Play the game. Get away.

Or have her say. "How did you know that Gray wanted to talk to me?" Lily asks.

"You told me," Tom says, smiling at her with his wide, open eyes. "Last night, at our sleepover."

"Right," she says. "Sorry, I've forgotten."

"There's a lot going on," Tom says, patting her on the back. Lily flinches, and hopes she managed to hide it.

Sara is staring at Tom. "You slept in her room?"

"On the floor," Tom says, brightly. His eyes, though, are fixed on Lily.

"You told me you wanted to be alone last night." Sara's eyes are full of hurt. It was Tom she was having sex with. And Tom she killed for.

Tom stage-whispers to Lily, "I told her not to stay overnight with Gray in the chapel. That she needed rest."

"Poor thing," Lily says. And means it. "We should do as you say, get her warm and safe downstairs. Then look again at leaving for help."

Tom nods. "Deal," he says. But his eyes flick toward Sara, and hers flick to his. He nods.

Lily walks as slowly as she can bear toward the nursery door.

"We're not leaving," Sara says.

Lily doesn't look back. *Keep walking*, she says to herself.

The sound of a gun being cocked as Sara says, "And neither are you."

Lily turns around. Sara is pointing a gun at Lily's head.

"No, Sara," Tom says, his hands up as if he's not a threat. "Give the gun to me."

"Only if you tell her about us," she says, eyes pleading with Tom.

"I think Lily already knows," Tom replies. His eyes have hardened. "Come on, Lily. You've gotten so good at figuring things out, just not good enough to prevent people dying."

"That's right, Lily," Sara says, standing again next to Tom. "Unwrap the puzzle."

Lily tries to think, piece it all together. But her mind is a maze full of dead ends. "I haven't worked it out yet," Lily says. "But I think you and Tom planned this together. And that you even killed Liliana. That, between you, you've whittled down the heirs until only you two remain, and you'll blame it all on Gray."

"Not Gray," Sara says. "Never Gray."

"Well, we'll have to see about that, darling," Tom says. "It might be easier. After all, he did cut down the tree and mess with the cars, and hit me with the branch to keep Lily off the track. His fingerprints will be everywhere. Including on the weapon that killed him."

Sara just shakes her head. "You shouldn't have hurt him, Tom."

"He was going to tell Lily everything," Tom says. "He told you as much."

Sara's eyes are wild. "We'll say Lily came at us with the gun, so we wrestled it off her and shot her by accident. Then we'll plant all the evidence."

Tom considers this. "Accidents do run in the family. And we *do* need to get rid of potential witnesses," he says. "Same reason we got rid of Philippa and Ronnie. They saw too much, knew too much. Philippa saw us kiss and got suspicious."

Sara points the gun back at Lily. Her hand quivers.

"I'll do it," Tom says. "As a show of my love to you, Sara, and to prevent your shaking hand missing Lily, and shooting into our attic."

As Sara hands the gun to Tom, a familiar smug smile settles on her face.

And then falls as Tom turns the gun on Sara. And shoots.

Chapter Thirty-Nine

Tom presses the gun into Lily's back, marching her along the corridor. He kicks open the door to her bedroom and, keeping the gun trained on her, ushers her in. He takes the key out of the keyhole and pockets it.

"What now?" Lily asks.

Tom grabs her desk chair and places it in the middle of the room, away from anything she could grab. "Sit down and face me. Keep your hands in your lap."

Lily places her hands on her legs, her thumbs pressed against her tummy for reassurance, for both her and Bean. Bean flips, as if to reassure Lily, too.

"Presumably you're going to keep me here till tomorrow, then get me to find the last key and kill me."

"I *really* don't want to kill you," Tom says.

"But I'd have solved all the clues," Lily replies.

Tom comes a few paces toward her. He places the gun in his coat pocket. "We get along, don't we?"

"I thought we did."

"I wasn't joking before—we could run the place together. And if we get our stories straight, the police will place it all on Sara and Gray. The batteries from the cars are in Sara's wardrobe, along with the carving knife she used to kill Philippa. Gray's fingerprints are on the chainsaw he used to cut down the tree *and* the branch. I also made him pick up the weapon I used to kill Ronnie and then him. We could say he threatened us with it, and Sara felt she had to kill him to make him stop."

"Gray doesn't deserve any of that," Lily says.

Tom shrugs. "Gray's dead."

"Because you killed him."

Tom sighs. "You're an intelligent girl. There wasn't anything else I could do."

Lily's fingers form into a claw at the word "girl." She bets that when she replays their conversations—as she hopes she'll get to do one day—he'll always be full of these kinds of micromanipulation. Mrs. Castle was right; she is a terrible judge of character.

"He was going to tell you everything," Tom continues. "Sara didn't have him under control anymore."

"She'd lost her usefulness."

"I knew I was going to have to kill her when she attacked you. She was acting on emotion."

"So you came in here to stop her from attacking me."

"Wasn't me," Tom replies. "Must have been Gray. He had a soft spot for you. In his head. At least he has now." He laughs. Lily can't believe that she ever loved how it sounded. Now it feels like a scraper on an iced windscreen. "His eyes really did gray over, you know, when he died. I'm not religious, but I watched him leave. Another ghost for Endgame."

"Didn't you love Sara at all?"

"Maybe. I don't know. She had no discretion, you saw her, kept pawing at me in the nursery. She was a weak link. She'd never have stood up to police questioning."

"And I will?" Lily asks.

"You are the most contained, locked-in person I've ever met. You teem with emotion but don't show it. Under investigation, you'd be cool, restrained, and clipped. You'd be an English murder queen." Tom kneels down in front of her in a display of openness, trust, and worship. His hand, though, is still on the gun.

"And what do I get for going along with it?"

"Half a house?" Tom says, laughing. "The chance to get out of London and back where you belong? To let your little girl have a place to run around and play in? Or is that not enough?"

"I want to know one more thing," Lily says. "Did you kill Liliana?"

Tom shakes his head sadly. "That was all Sara. She got Aunt Lil into a state by telling her what we were going to do to her family, then she took away her inhaler. Her own mother—I mean, that's colder than the icehouse. Simple. Effective. Hard to prove anything other than an accident. We didn't have to bribe any coroner. Oh, yes, I saw what you were hiding from me the night I stayed in your room."

"I know Sara hated how Liliana treated her, but why would she want her dead?"

"She wanted the house, or more importantly, she didn't want anyone else getting it. She thought she could prevent the Christmas Game by killing Aunt Lil. Turns out she was wrong. Aunt Lil had put things into place already, but I'm glad she did, because thanks to you, I've recently come to suspect that—"

"Liliana killed your parents. The 'accidental' slicing of brakes. Mum's yellow ribbon left in your mum and dad's car."

"Told you that you were brilliant," Tom replies.

"You know why she killed them then, if you saw the coroner's report?"

"Dad killed Mariana. But then I've always kinda known that."

"What?" Lily says. She feels as cold as if she were in the icehouse.

"I found Dad making fake blood on that Christmas Eve. He said he was going to do a magic show, but then he woke me up when he came into the adjoining room at 2:00 a.m., Boxing Day morning. When he'd gone to sleep, I went into our bathroom. I found fake blood running down the sink, and a bloody razor on the side of the bath. The next morning, they were gone and I found out about Aunt Mariana. You're not the only genius in the family. Maybe with all that talent, I'll win the Christmas Game tomorrow."

"*We'll* win, you mean," Lily says.

Alexandra Benedict

"Exactly," Tom says. He stands up and removes a piece of fluff from his knees. "Now, you are going to get some sleep. I need that brain of yours firing for the last clue. I'll lock you in, of course, keep you safe. Might even sleep outside your room to be sure." He leans forward and kisses her on the cheek, while the gun points at her belly.

There's no way he's going to let her, or her Bean, live.

The door closes behind him, and the key turns.

Chapter Forty

January 5th—Twelfth Night/Epiphany
The Twelfth Day of Christmas

"No time for a lie-in," Tom says, bursting through her bedroom door.

"It's still dark," Lily says, pulling the duvet up to her neck.

"Can't you hear the drummers drumming? It's the last day. We've got till four this afternoon to find the secret room."

"Yay," Lily says.

"I've told you before, Lily," Tom says, coming so close to her she can smell yesterday's booze metabolizing through his pores. "Leave the sarcasm. It doesn't suit you. You're better than that."

"How are we going to get the last sonnet without Mrs. Castle to spoon-feed us?" Lily asks.

"Bless the old coot, Mrs. Castle thought of that. I went to get fire-wood from the store as she said, and on top of the basket of kindling was a cake."

"A Twelfth Night cake," Lily says. "We always used to have one." A sense memory comes back to her of spiced cake, dusted with icing sugar. One Christmas, Tom had found the traditional dried bean inside his piece of cake and so was crowned King of the Revels for the night. Sara had found the dried pea in hers that made her Queen. They had paraded around the house as if they'd owned it.

"Yeah, I remembered that things were hidden inside the cake," Tom says. "So I smashed it, and there were the sonnets. Only two of them, though, as if she knew."

Tom pulls the sonnets from his pocket. He makes sure she sees that the other pocket contains the gun. "I'll read it to you," Tom says, "I saw how much you liked Gray's recitals. Shame he's not here."

> Dance, let's, you and I, when we're dead and gone,
> A room that echoes with past laughter, dance
> Our ghosts across the floor till we're done in,
> Again. The living will give us room, glance
> Our way and shiver, never knowing why.
> Death won't be a dirge for us, we will sing
> Our favorite songs and never say goodbye.
>
> Our bones will rest, phalanges entwining
> Within our tomb, while our specters foxtrot
> And watch old movies on repeat. They'll think
> The telly's on the blink, the old clock stopped,
> Taps ever dripping in a mist-filled sink,
> 'Cause they're faulty, not us, being naughty,
> And we thought we had fun with our bodies…

It feels wrong to hear those words said by Tom. He has no awareness of rhythm, no dynamics, no beauty. And that last line, said with his waggling eyebrows, makes her want to run and be sick.

"Romantic, huh?" Tom says.

"Who do you think Liliana was talking to in this one?" Lily asks. "Because it doesn't feel like me."

"Aunt Lil didn't have a boyfriend, did she? I was barely alive when Uncle Robert died so I've never seen her with anyone," Tom says.

"It might be to my mum. It says they were both done in. Suggests their ghosts will dance here forever."

"What does it matter?" Tom says, impatience cracking through. "Where do we look for the key?"

Lily once again—and for the last time—turns her brain to the sonnet. She smiles at "Dance, let's." Liliana couldn't resist a last Bowie reference. "It mentions the 'living,'" she says, "and 'room' in one line, so it could be there. But this feels so different, a love poem to two people dancing forever together. I think this clue could be the simplest of them all," Lily says. "Where else would you dance at the Twelfth Night Ball?"

The clue makes Lily sees the ballroom anew. She can almost see the ghosts twirling, reflected in the mirrored walls. There's Lily's five-year-old self, standing on Mum's feet. There's Rachel with her back to them all, reading. And there's Liliana and Mum pirouetting together when they were young. Maybe they danced here with their loves. Maybe the poem is from Liliana to her late husband, Robert. Telling him she'll join him in a dance after her death. Or maybe it's to someone else entirely.

"We don't have time for you to look at yourself in the mirror," Tom says. "Do your thing."

"My what?"

"Your magic eye thing, where the clues fall into line before you."

Lily gives a cursory look at the clue. "I think even you can work this one out."

Tom flushes. He bites his lip. He's the little boy again, the one who can't bear to be seen as stupid. He takes the gun from his pocket. "You'll tell me where to look," he says.

Lily wants to say that if he shoots her, he'll never be able to find the key, or the secret room. But that would just anger him, and she'll never know the truth if she's dead.

"Look in the clock. The clue says it's stopped, so maybe the key is arresting the mechanism." Lily points to the "old clock" hanging on the wall. She imagines a ball where it chimes at midnight, and a stunning woman in a dress half rags, half riches runs away. She'd like to make that dress. She'd like to meet the woman.

Keeping the gun trained on her, Tom steps slowly backward until he's by the antique oval clock. In the silence, its lack of ticking is obvious.

Tom stares into the face of the clock. "The key's here," he says. "You were wrong; it had replaced one of the hands. Not so clever now, eh?"

Lily doesn't reply.

"Tell you what," Tom says, coming over to her, his open grin stitched back in place. "Let's celebrate getting the final key by having a dance."

"Here?" Lily asks.

"Where else?" Tom echoes her from earlier. He reaches for her, to pull her into his arms as he did Sara.

Lily turns away, wrapping her arms around herself.

Tom's face turns. His jaw clenches and his eyes bore into her.

"There's no time," Lily says, quickly. "I need to work out where the secret room is. We've only got till four, then Isabelle will get the house and give it to the cats."

Tom flexes his fist. Points the gun at her head. "Then you'd better get to work," he says.

Chapter Forty-One

Locked in her room again, Lily lies on the bed, her hand on her stomach. She's supposed to be figuring out the location of the hidden room. But she only told him that to get him to leave. What's the point in trying? She'll die whatever happens. Either she'll locate the room and then Tom will kill her, or she'll refuse and *then* he'll kill her. Tom would then paint himself as a hero to the police, and Isabelle would probably sign the house over to him.

All Lily has achieved at Endgame is get people killed and help a killer. She should never have trusted anyone. She should have stayed in the maze that never lets her go and waited for a snow shroud.

Outside, the frosted wind moans as it rushes past Lily's room. The curtains are open, showing windows covered with snowflakes that look like hardanger lace.

And then she gets that same tickle, the feeling of a memory settling on her.

Something to do with lace. The campfire conversation not long before Mum died. She closes her eyes to replay the scene, and the words weave back to her. "Some people seem as fragile as lace," Mum had said, staring at Uncle Edward and Aunt Veronica, "but if it's made of hardanger, it'll lead them through whatever they need to do."

Veronica had then walked over and bent down to whisper in Mum's ear. It's loud enough, though, for Lily to hear. Never underestimate children. "Liliana is opposing our plans for the hotel and persuading the board," Veronica had said. "We'd like you to vote against her."

Mum had shaken her head. Veronica then looked at Lily, and bent closer to Mum. Lily couldn't hear what she said, but it made Mum grab hold of Lily and hold her tight.

Veronica's face when she walked away was one of hard anger.

Her and Edward's hard anger had killed Mum. As a result, Liliana's hard anger led her to kill her own brother and sister-in-law, which ultimately led to her death. Tom and Sara's hard anger had seen them through murder.

Lily's hard anger, however, would keep her and Little Bean alive, and stop Tom getting his hands on this house.

Sweeping her legs off the bed, Lily gets up and arranges all the sonnet clues next to each other on the floor. There's a thread that runs through them—Liliana would have made sure of that—she just has to find it, and pull.

Scrabbling in her bag, she gets out the letter Liliana had written to her. She reads it again, and stops at a line that tickles: "*They will be there, in every clue: the beginning and end of all that has haunted our family for so many years.*" That's repeated in one of the sonnets, she's sure of it. Skimming through the poems, she finds it—the couplet of the Boxing Day sonnet: "*At great volume, you'll cry/The beginning and end mark of the line.*"

Does this mean the beginning and end of the bloodline? Is she thinking of Lily's baby, of Bean? But what then would be the beginning? Or what if it means line as in verse?

Adrenaline coursing, Lily writes down the first and last letter, the "mark" of the initial line of each sonnet.

Spelled out in an acrostic, one of Grandma Violet's favorite games, is the answer to one of Endgame's cold cases:

Elephants are said to remember, I'm
Do you feel safe? Safe as hot brandied cocoa?
We used to sing together, remember?
An owl descends, the night's stone alibi.
Really, we should be marking Haloa,
Downstairs, today. My home is a castle!
Key clue today! Stop now and listen:
I wonder what it is to be dead. A
Like incense smoke in space, even keen prayer
Let's call a truce, what do you say? Will no
Early in the year, possibilities
Dance, let's, you and I, when we're dead and gone,

EDWARD KILLED MARIAENA ROSE

Lily had known it, but she still finds herself breathing out in relief. He murdered Mariana for the house and then Liliana killed him. But why that spelling of Mariana? It wasn't on her birth certificate. And Liliana doesn't make mistakes, not with words anyway.

Lily knows by now that errors can be deliberate. She looks at the whole line where the error sits: "My home is a castle." And then she gets it. As always, she's drawing Lily's attention to anomalies. And this one tells her something that makes her smile. Aunt Liliana's home was Mrs. Castle. That's what Liliana meant by one of the clues not being a message to Lily. The last sonnet was for Mrs. Castle, requesting a dance to David Bowie when they're both dead. Modern love.

Lily can't stop a sob this time. She stifles it, though, when she hears the key again in the lock.

"Have you solved it yet?" Tom asks, scanning the floor with all the copies of the sonnets.

"Only confirming that your dad killed my mum. It says it here, the first and last mark of the lines."

Tom nods. "So really, what I've done is complete a game that started decades ago. The longest game of Monopoly not on record. And I win."

"Only if we find the secret room," Lily says.

Tom marches out the door and comes back with a sledgehammer covered with dried blood. Lily shrinks back. "That's what you used to kill Ronnie and Gray."

"What does it matter?" Tom says. "If you can't find the room the brainy way, then I'll have to use old-fashioned methods." He swings the sledgehammer back and slams it into her wardrobe. The wood gives in, splintering and cracking.

The house creaks around them as if in fear. "Don't," Lily says. "I'll find it, I promise."

"I knew you wanted this place for yourself. You're as selfish as the rest of us." Tom blows her a kiss and leaves, locking her in once more.

Bean skips in her tummy as Lily frantically goes over the sonnets. There are so many motifs running through them: music, death, singing, Bowie.

Lily stops at Bowie, as everyone always should. "What Would Bowie Do?" indeed.

But what does that mean? David Bowie was an incandescent chameleon. Magnetic. He didn't need to present any one version of himself to the world. What has Bowie got to do with Lily, here, now?

What is she not seeing? Lily pulls Christina off the bed and onto her lap. She rubs the hem of the ragdoll's skirt between her fingers for comfort, feeling the seams that connect the old pieces of clothes together.

That's it.

Bowie used to cut up articles, books, thoughts, anything, and randomly jumbled them to make his lyrics. Borrowing from Burroughs, he scissored words and sewed them into new interpretations.

So that's what Lily will do.

She grabs the scissors from her desk and starts slicing up the spare sets of sonnets into pieces. "Let's dance," she says.

Chapter Forty-Two

Lily tries to ignore the sounds of Tom taking the sledgehammer to the walls, but it gets under her skin like a splinter from the banister. She can feel the house resisting; she doesn't know how, but she can.

"Concentrate," she says as she scatters the cut pieces in front of her. The words merge, cross-pollinating, making new connections. "'Awkward relationships,' Bowie had called it." Lily is talking out loud consciously now, hearing her voice echo round the room. Whenever Bean hears her voice, she flutters. Imagine what Bean will do if Lily really sings.

"Sing." That word comes up again and again. "*Keep singing,*" her mum says in her card. "*Maybe you will have the fortitude to sing out,*" Liliana says in the letter. But what should she sing? Doodling the Endgame maze has always helped her think, so she takes a pen and sets her hand free to draw.

She thinks of the aria that Mum sang, but there's nothing in the sonnets to support it. She knows that she's looking for a song. Just a simple song. She's trying to connect the pieces. Turn them into constellations.

And then she sees it.

The words lie scattered like stars on the dark carpet.

"iron," "earth," "stone," "Winter," "Bleak," "water," "long ago."

A descant of clues playing like a song. The song her mum sang. "In the Bleak Midwinter."

And, in that moment, she knows she wants the house. But how will she win? She only has one of the twelve possible keys.

Keys. Twelve of them.

There are twelve possible keys in the major scale.

"In the Bleak Midwinter" in F Major.

Again, that tickle of déjà vu runs under her skin. She goes back through Liliana's letter. And it's repeated here, another mistake showing the way forward. "*Cast those corsets of* ***f. Major*** *clues are hidden among the minor.*"

F Major. The key of the song. Otherwise known as the tonic, from the "gin and tonic" in the sonnet, or the root mentioned in the same one. Also known as the thing she wants most: home.

It all centers around the key of F Major. And maybe that's the key everyone's been looking for all along.

So, she has the key but no door.

THWACK

The house shudders around her. She has to press on. She still needs the location of the secret room. *Think.*

She doodles the maze again, then remembers another part of the letter: Liliana told her to transpose those doodles onto the real world. At the time, Lily had dismissed it as another snark from Liliana about Lily's designs, the kind of belittling that Sara knew well. But maybe it meant something else. The picture that she draws all the time, has always doodled to marshal her thoughts, is the maze. The maze that has been at the center of her life. The maze that appears on every tablecloth, coaster, place mat, plate, cup, saucer, thimble, even, in the house. The answer could have been right there, in her peripheral vision, all throughout her life and since she arrived. The maze.

Liliana has been pointing to it all along, giving Lily everything she needs to win. But how will that help her find the hidden room?

And then she remembers.

Lily snaps open the folder and takes out the blueprint of Endgame.

The house and the maze are the same size. She closes her eyes. Placing a pen on the blueprint, at the front door, she takes herself through the maze in her mind's eye and lets her pen follow. It twists and turns, and ends up in the hidden room where Lily hid, and Mariana died.

Leaving her pen on the page, Lily opens her eyes. The secret room of the maze maps onto the games room of the house. Of course it does. It was always going to end in a game.

If she is going to get to the secret room before Tom destroys the house, she'll have to get out. Her door, though, is locked, and Tom has the key. *Think harder.*

In her letter, Liliana said she wanted to give Lily a way out.

And keys give protection and freedom. Lily goes through the pockets of her coat and takes out the key she found in the maze, and the one Gray had returned to her.

She places the first one in the keyhole. It fits. And then she tries her old key, the one that she wore round her neck as a child. And that fits, too. She bets all of the keys fit. That could be how the figures entered her room. Liliana wouldn't have known she'd need more than a symbolic way out, but it doesn't matter. Lily opens her door, and has her freedom.

Lily rushes out onto the landing. On the floor below, Tom is smashing through doors toward the back of Endgame. Lily reaches out and strokes the walls of the house. She's sure it flexes to meet her hand.

The wind cries round the house as if to cause a distraction, covering her as she descends the stairs, avoiding every creaky tread. She must win this last game of hide-and-seek.

Reaching the games room, she looks around, feeling the ghosts of herself, Tom, and Gray from only a few days ago pressing against the present. She sneezes, just as she did last time she was in here. Where would a secret room be hiding? She then remembers the cracks in the wall by the pinball machine.

Lily pulls at the legs of the machine, but it barely moves. She tries pushing it to one side, and that's easier, but her hand slips and presses the on button.

The pinball machine flashes and beeps into life. And that's the only sound she hears. The steady cull of the sledgehammer has stopped. And now there are footsteps running down the stairs.

Lily pushes as hard as she can, knowing that she shouldn't be doing this in her "condition," but what else can she do? The pinball machine turns just enough for her to place a finger along a seam that runs down the wall.

Something clicks. And a door opens.

Lily blinks as she steps into a warm room filled with musical instruments. There's an Irish harp, a drum kit, a worn cello, a harpsichord… and on the walls are pictures of Lily and her mum. So many photos. In one, they're singing together, under the willow tree. This is the music room her mum always wanted, hidden away from conference goers and anyone else. A silent room of music.

A hand grabs her shoulder from behind. Tom pushes her as he rushes past, searching for the title deeds. Lily loses her footing and crashes into a timpani drum. The sound reverberates round the room and Lily then knows what to do.

She takes a deep breath, swallows, and, with her hand on her stomach, opens her mouth with the right key—the tonic, the home—of "In the Bleak Midwinter."

Tom turns to her, eyes wide.

And then a door opens within the far wall of the music room. One secret room giving birth to another.

Isabelle Stirling ducks under the door frame and steps into the room, holding a folder. "And we have a winner," she says. "Lily Armitage, I declare you the owner of Endgame House."

Tom reaches for his gun. He holds it out, inches away from Lily's head.

A gray cat steps out from behind Isabelle, weaving round her ankles. Lily thinks she must be hallucinating, already dead.

Tom stares at the cat, "What the—" and doesn't see at first the figure in black rushing past Isabelle toward him, knocking him and the gun to the ground.

The figure bends and picks up Tom's gun.

Mrs. Castle pulls down her hood so Tom can see her face. And then shoots him.

Chapter Forty-Three

"You're to sit here, Miss Lily," Mrs. Castle says, gesturing to the armchair by the fire. Lily sinks down into the leather, listening to it creak and settle around her. Mrs. Castle places one of the tartan wraps over Lily's lap. "The landline's working so I've called the police. Kettle's on. I'll have rustled up something sweet by the time it's boiled." She then pats Lily on the shoulder and bustles out of the drawing room.

Lily stares after her. Mrs. Castle shot Tom. And now she's making tea.

Isabelle stands by the fireplace, just as she did that first day here. "It's a lot to take in," she says. "Be gentle with yourself. I've had a long time to process things."

"You knew everything?" Lily asks.

"Pretty much. Liliana only trusted me and Castle. She tried to go to the police about what really happened to your mum, but they wouldn't listen. 'Not enough evidence. Not in the public interest.'" From the kitchen comes the sound of a kettle whistling and TV murmurs. "Middlemen grew unreliable, so she relied on us," Isabelle says, and sits down in the other armchair, skin glowing in the firelight. She bends down to stroke the big gray cat now rubbing its head on her ankles and pours him onto her lap. Its eyes are rheumy and unseeing.

"It's Winston!" Lily says. Winston raises his head at the sound of Lily's voice and purrs. She gets up and crosses over to Isabelle's chair. "Hi, big fella." Winston sits up tall and butts his head into Lily's hand.

"He's been living with me," Isabelle says when Lily sits back down. "Had quite the Christmas break at Endgame, haven't you, Winston?"

"Wait, you've been here all the way through? Both of you?"

"You must have a lot of questions," Isabelle says. Winston purrs beneath her strokes.

"So many," Lily says. Questions that fall around her, building up, one on top of the other like snowflakes. "And I've no idea where to start."

"Then let me. After I saw you in your room, I left and placed all of the mobile phones in the Stirling vault, as Liliana unfortunately requested, then—"

"Why unfortunately?" Lily asks.

"Because, in trying to prevent people from cheating, and rivaling you, she took away the very thing that could have kept you safe." She looks over at Lily and seems to blush. "And the others, of course. If you'd been able to call the police when Philippa was killed, then Ronnie and Gray would still be alive."

"And Samuel would have a parent."

"Yes," Isabelle says. "Liliana would hate what's happened to him. She loved him so much."

"Who wouldn't? Sorry, carry on. I interrupted you."

"It's all those questions falling like snowflakes," Isabelle says. Her golden eyes set on Lily's. "Anyway, so I deposited the phones—including mine as I stupidly followed your aunt's rules, too—then I came back. A taxi dropped me off at the far end of the estate, and I walked through the woods and back fields, waited in the smokehouse till you'd all gone to bed, then Lenora let me in."

Mrs. Castle walks in carrying a cake stand stacked with sandwiches and cake. It's as if they were back in this room on Christmas Eve and the twelve days of Christmas never happened. She prods Lily's shoulder again. "Eat parkin," she says. "I'll be back with the teapot."

Isabelle watches her go this time, and Lily watches Isabelle. Her hair looks like it's seen several tins of dry shampoo but no water in a week, and there are plum-pudding-colored shadows under her eyes. "Lenora's been brilliant," Isabelle says. She turns back to Lily. "Did you work out who she is?"

"She's Aunt Liliana's home."

Isabelle smiles sadly and nods. "They were lovers before Robert died and then—when he passed—they were only apart when one of you lot was around. Which was a lot to start with. When you all went off to university, Lenora moved to Grantchester."

"Liliana was her home, too."

"She still is," Mrs. Castle says as she brings in the tea. She pours them each a cup, then reaches into her apron pocket and pulls out a gold ring. A wedding band. She places it on her ring finger. "Felt wrong, not having it on. Liliana's idea, of course, not mine. Never mine. Said it would avoid awkward questions. But I think she just wanted to avoid it." Mrs. Castle's eyes shine, but they do not spill.

Liliana had carried too many secrets; some of them should have been shared long before now.

"Anyway," Isabelle says. "Liliana's instructions were that Winston and I were to stay in the music room, and the hidden bedroom within it, to keep an eye on everyone, make sure they were following the rules, etcetera. Lenora would bring us food and drink, and change his litter, thank God. She ended up having to stay in there when she pretended to leave. Quite a squeeze. At least Winston got to have a roam around the games room when everyone was in bed."

"That's why I always sneezed in there," Lily says, already feeling the itchy scratch at the back of her throat and in her ears.

"I kind of hoped you'd work it out just from that," Isabelle says.

"I'm not *that* good," Lily replies.

"Oh, but you are."

"Get on with it, Izzy," Mrs. Castle says. "I've got to make dinner."

"You're off the clock," Isabelle says. "Go and relax. Decide what you're going to tell the police."

"I'll tell the truth," Mrs. Castle says, sitting down on a chair and rubbing her neck. Winston jumps down from Isabelle's lap and heads toward Mrs. Castle's voice. "There have been enough lies."

"As the police are on their way, I'd better do as Lenora says and hurry," Isabelle says. "I had CCTV to watch on the perimeter, until they all went down, and some internal cameras, but not many. Mrs. Castle was my main eyes and ears."

Mrs. Castle raises her cup in acknowledgment and then takes a gulp of barely milked tea while Winston settles on her feet. "Liliana thought she'd planned for every eventuality," she says. "But she didn't predict that her own daughter would kill her, and plan the death of others. She had too much of an ego for that." Mrs. Castle smiles and looks into the fire as if her memories are kept alive in the grate. The smile fades. "And she would never have suspected Tom. Even though, when you see him for what he is, he's the very portrait of a murderer."

"Didn't you try and stop them?" Lily asks Isabelle.

Isabelle lowers her head so Lily can't see her eyes. "I didn't know who was responsible to start with. Lenora came to the music room after Philippa was found, and we talked it through. I couldn't find any footage that would tell us who it was. And obviously I was as snowed in as all of you. But I kept watch. I roamed the halls at night, keeping an eye on you."

Lily sits upright, crumbs falling from her lap. "You spoke to me. I thought it was ghosts."

Isabelle nods. "I often kept vigil in Liliana or Mariana's room, which is how you heard me through the walls."

"That's not all she did," Mrs. Castle says as she hauls Winston onto her lap.

And then Lily realizes. "You were the one who saved me," she says.

Isabelle nods. "I had to."

"But that means you bent the rule about not interfering."

"As you said on Christmas Eve, it depends if the rule is fair. And if the person you've loved since you were a child is being strangled…"

Lily feels her pulse beating in her neck. She tells herself that Isabelle just means platonic love. Sisterly, cis-ter*ish* love.

"I was worried that Rachel or Holly would be killed, so Mrs. Castle persuaded them to go to the old groundskeeper's cottage at the far edges of the estate and leave a note saying they'd left. That way they'd be safe."

"So, they're still on the grounds?" Lily asks. She rubs at her head.

"I'll go and get them," Mrs. Castle says. "Tell them the coast is clear. They must be desperate to get back to Beatrice." She then walks out, but not before winking at Lily and flicking her eyebrows toward Isabelle. Now Lily is the one blushing.

"Before they get here," Isabelle says, "I've got one more note from Liliana to give you."

"Not another clue?" Lily says. "Because my brain is pudding."

"See for yourself," Isabelle says, taking an envelope from her pocket.

Lily takes a deep breath and opens the envelope. The smell of Truth comes out, and Lily feels her tears begin to build.

Dearest Lily, the letter inside says, *if you're reading this, then I am dead and you are the owner of Endgame. Congratulations, darling, I knew you could do it.*

I should have told you all this before. I nearly did, so many times. But I didn't have your courage. Only now can I spell it out. I killed Edward and Veronica, after finding out that Edward killed Mariana. I had suspicions, as I knew your mum would never leave you or me. And the night before she died, she'd told me that Edward and Veronica had demanded she collude with them in excluding me, or hand over the house to him. They threatened your life, and told Mariana that it wouldn't be fake blood next time. She told them she wouldn't. Next morning, she was dead. I tracked down the coroner and, on being presented with a check and a guarantee that I wouldn't tell the police, he told me what really happened. Edward tried to hang Mariana from her own ceiling to look like suicide, but his noose wasn't good enough. Mariana managed to get down and ran away as far as the maze, but Edward followed and strangled her. He then slit her wrists to make it look like she'd tried again, but she was already dead so hardly bled. Edward placed the fake blood on her sleeves, then bribed the coroner. I confronted Edward and he admitted it to me, laughing. And so that's why I killed him and his wife. And I am still glad I did.

But because of that, I shut away all the wonderful things of my life, too, and never shared them with you. Like how Mariana had the music room made so that she could get away from the conference guests. And that little extra hidden room was for you, to sing along with her from your cot.

"That's why I saw her appearing suddenly," Lily says, breaking her gaze from the page to look at Isabelle. "And Philippa saw someone emerging from the walls."

"Which also explains the rumors of the White Lady," Isabelle adds. "At least, I hope so. I'm never quite sure anyone's alone in this place."

Lily keeps on reading.

Like how everything you did delighted her, and that she loved you, and would never, ever have left you. I should have told you that every day; instead I let you believe a lie. And that is unforgivable.

Do whatever you like with the house. All I ask is that you turn toward yourself, not away like I did, that you look after my home, and find your own.

With all my love,
Liliana Armitage-Castle

Lily puts the letter down and lets her tears fall. The grandmother clock rings out four times. The Christmas Game is over.

❄

Lily and Isabelle walk out of the house, together. The air is crisp and cleansing. Snow has fallen again. Enough to Wite-Out the grounds and the roof of the house. You'd never know what has happened in these grounds if you didn't scratch off the surface. The secrets of this house are about to be exposed, and that is good. Maybe then both it and Lily can be exorcised.

Because Lily isn't hiding anymore. She has sung and she has spoken.

Sirens call from beyond the valley. The police can get through at last. The days ahead will be difficult, but not as hard as the last twelve. Nothing could be as bad as those. That's as good a place as any to start a new life.

"What do you think you'll do with the house?" Isabelle asks.

"I don't know," Lily replies. "That's not a question I thought I'd be facing."

"If you want to leave and never come back, I wouldn't blame you for a moment. I could arrange for it to be sold. Several developers are already interested. And it's a lot of money."

Lily glances back at the house. She thinks of Mum, and all the wonderful memories of her that are kept in the house like a music box. Of Ronnie and Gray, both brilliant in their own way. And then there's Liliana, cruel and loving, sitting in the open door between right and wrong, getting Lily to close it. And Tom and Sara, and Edward and Veronica, killing to possess a house that amounts to dust in the end.

Endgame House seems to be holding its breath, smoke from the chimney frozen in the air as it waits for her answer. She feels like it still presses down on her shoulders, but it's now reassuring. Thinking of it broken up into posh people's apartments makes her feel unaccountably sad. And the thought of the house bulldozed to the ground feels even worse. For a moment, she thinks she sees a figure up in her own window. Mrs. Castle, maybe. But she was downstairs when they left the house. From here she can't see a face, but she gets the impression it's Mum. And then a cloud passes over the sun and the figure disappears.

Lily continues walking. "I think I'll keep it," she says. Ghosts need somewhere to walk, even if they are in her own head. "There must be some good to come out of this house."

"That's a lot of space for one person," Isabelle says. She's looking away, extending her head toward the flower bed as if inspecting the snow-tipped rosehips.

Lily's heart sewing-machines at the implication behind Isabelle's words. No, Isabelle wouldn't mean that.

"There'll be at least two people," she says. "Me and the baby."

Isabelle grins. "I was wondering when you'd tell me. I was hoping you'd let me in on the secret on Christmas Eve. But now seems better."

"I would have, if I'd known you were always around, watching over me like the best stalker in the world."

Isabelle's laugh sends a bird flying from the trees, wings clapping in agreement.

"And I'll need a lot of room to make clothes," Lily says. "I could make my own range from here. Endgame Couture."

"Perfect," Isabelle says.

"Or I could teach, have a college for couture. Or run retreats for people with trauma. Or a place for Samuel and orphans like him, and me. I don't know. I'll probably do all of it over time, stitch it all together into one life and one house containing it all. Lift the curse for good. I'm going to ask Mrs. Castle to run it all with me, fifty-fifty." The possibilities connect, as if going through an overlocker, pulling in all her raw seams.

"Liliana would love all that." Isabelle pauses. "So would your mum."

Lily nods. So many feelings run through her. All the strands of her life are joining into one strong skein.

As they pass the sundial, she feels the urge to ask Isabelle something. It feels wildly inappropriate, embarrassing if she's got the wrong idea, and most of her is screaming at her to be silent. *There is not time enough.* "Have you got a date for Valentine's Day?" she asks, heart reaching out through words.

Isabelle stops walking, her fine eyebrows heading for her hairline. "Are you asking me out, Lily Armitage?"

Lily once again feels the urge to retreat, to swallow back the words.

To hide behind a code, layers of meaning beneath fear. She takes a breath, and steps through from fear into excitement. "Yes, Belle," she says. Isabelle gasps, but Lily keeps on talking. "I was thinking an intimate dinner somewhere in the middle of a crowded city. Nowhere near the country."

"On one condition, Naiad," Isabelle says.

Lily grins. Her heart stitches together. "More rules?"

"Only one—you make me a dress to wear on our date. Of your own design. The first in your collection. Don't make the corset too tight, though."

"Deal," Lily says. "As long as you don't mind me not wearing a corset."

Isabelle's eyebrows now leap under her fringe. "Never thought I'd hear that."

"Time I showed the shape of me."

"You already have," Isabelle says.

Lily looks back again at Endgame House. Its curtains are open. Maybe she won't put any up at all. Let daylight stream in, showing up the stains and tears an old house carries in its heart. Let moonlight show up the ghosts that live inside.

They walk in time with each other's footsteps. Isabelle takes her hand. It's warm and soft and feels like home.

Snow is falling, snow on snow. In the bleak midwinter, now and long ago.

The Game within
The Christmas Murder Game:
Answers

Game 1: Twelve Days of Anagrams

A partridge in a pear tree—"rearranged a petite pair," p. 97

Two turtle doves—"trusted, love. Owt," p. 141

Three French hens—"chef sneer, her nth," p. 155

Four colly birds—"orbs, lucidly for," p. 172

Five gold rings—"'devil fog?' grins," p. 179; and, as I couldn't resist, "gloved frig. Sin," p. 183

Six geese a-laying—"ease. Aging sexily," p. 200

Seven swans a-swimming—"Avenges Man. Wins. Swims," p. 210

Eight maids a-milking—"image: midnight silk, a," p. 218

Nine ladies dancing—"Anglican in deed, sin," p. 225

Ten lords a-leaping—"Alleged prints on a," p. 234

Eleven pipers piping—"replies, even pipping," p. 243

Twelve drummers drumming—"TV murmurs. 'Middlemen grew,'" p. 267

Game 2: Title Deeds

A Christmas Party (Georgette Heyer), p. 99

Murder for Christmas (Francis Duncan), p. 111

The Adventure of the Christmas Pudding (Agatha Christie), p. 133

Footsteps in the Dark (Georgette Heyer), p. 163

A Mystery in White (J. Jefferson Farjeon), p. 177

Death Comes at Christmas (Gladys Mitchell), p. 187

Tied Up in Tinsel (Ngaio Marsh), p. 198

Another Little Christmas Murder (Lorna Nicholl Morgan), p. 210

Murder in the Snow (Gladys Mitchell), p. 209 and 213

Crime at Christmas (C. H. B. Kitchin), p. 237

An English Murder (Cyril Hare), p. 252

Portrait of a Murderer (Anne Meredith), p. 270

Acknowledgments

I've hidden the many wonderful people I want to thank in this acknowledgments word search. They've all helped me and/or this book through a very difficult time and I'm very grateful. The names to look for are below—see if you can find them all. I also couldn't resist inviting you to play one more game.

Lurking in the word search is a song, one mentioned in *The Christmas Murder Game*. It is Lily's favorite song to sing at karaoke, and mine too. Good luck, and Merry Christmas!

AgathaChristie

Bonnier

DameMargaretRutherford

EleanorStammeijer

JonAppleton

KellySmith

LouandSteve

MichelleandSam

PamRussell

SamandNigel

StephBroadribb

AngelaChrismasShadbolt

CiaraCorrigan

DavidandCarolina

Guy

KarenMinto

LouiseVoss

MumandDad

PriandColin

SheilaandTony

StephenDumughn

Verity

TinaandDave

BenWillis

ColinScott

DiandAntonio

JennaPetts

KatherineArmstrong

LinandJohn

MaureenandLeo

NickStearn

RozDavies

SofiaMaia

SusiHolliday

```
E O T G O W P C A J D K H V N W X M P R M L D D Y K
H Y M U Q X H D I T E A E R D N H R Q I L O A R P A
U V Y T O J I G A A E N R L P U E D C R I U V O Z T
N E O F W D Y I M V R L N B L J E H G W N A I F U H
E I T S I R H C A H T A G A I Y E C N N A N D R B E
L J C V E H I D I S S R C E P L S L P D N D A E B R
A E F K B U D K F K D C M O L E R M H W D S N H B I
H D G E S N Z Y O O L M L E R M T K I I J T D T I N
N U C I A T Z I S T A O A J A R Q T E T O E C U R E
T L Y A N I E I R T V N N C C P I Q S I H V A R D A
N R N L Z D P A S T D L H W R D I G F N N E R T A R
O I U O W W N R R S L L E S S U R M A P W A O E O M
T Y F U W W O A A N T N M R L Q V B L N A Y L R R S
L W V I L N N M M K A R E N M I N T O S R N I A B T
G J A S A M B X W A N I L O C D N A I R P O N G H R
A N G E L A C H R I S M A S S H A D B O L T A R P O
X M L V Q E R Y E V S E I V A D Z O R F M D B A E N
Z E C O M S T E P H E N D U M U G H N U O N E M T G
K M U S K P Q S I H I R U F N K L H M U Y A N E S X
Y J B S V H D V D N V H I S D Q G A G P T A W M R G
J A K Z J F W V F A N Z U T F U N Q B K L L I A X Q
J O N A P P L E T O N O W V Y D I R V K O I L D G I
T T O C S N I L O C T C B W D R T O L G F E L P I U
D I A N D A N T O N I O E A G B S V B Y A H I Z T E
K N E M A U R E E N A N D L E O K U C J X S S O U S
S U S I H O L L I D A Y W X L K S D G B I P F T R L
```

About the Author

Alexandra Benedict is an award-winning writer of novels, short stories, and scripts. As A. K. Benedict, she published the critically acclaimed *The Beauty of Murder, The Evidence of Ghosts,* and *The Stone House.* Alexandra has also composed music for film, TV, and radio, most recently for productions on BBC Sounds and Audible. She taught and ran the highly successful Crime Thrillers MA at City University, and now mentors, coaches, and edits writers. She lives by the sea with writer Guy Adams; their daughter, Verity; and dog, Dame Margaret Rutherford.